The Young Apollo

AND OTHER STORIES

Also by Louis Auchincloss

The Young Apollo

AND OTHER STORIES

Louis Auchincloss

Houghton Mifflin Company

BOSTON   NEW YORK

2006

For information about permission to reproduce selections from
this book, write to Permissions, Houghton Mifflin Company,
215 Park Avenue South, New York, New York 10003.

Visit our Web site: www.houghtonmifflinbooks.com.

Library of Congress Cataloging-in-Publication Data

Auchincloss, Louis.
   The young Apollo and other stories / Louis Auchincloss.
      p. cm.
   ISBN-13: 978-0-618-55115-6
   ISBN-10: 0-618-55115-8
   1. New York (N.Y.) — Social life and customs — Fiction.
   2. Upper class — Fiction.   3. Rich people — Fiction.
   I. Title.
   PS3501.U25Y68 2005
   813'.54 — dc22   2005019899

Book design by Anne Chalmers
Typefaces: Janson Text, Fournier, Rococo Ornaments

Printed in the United States of America

MP 10 9 8 7 6 5 4 3 2 1

To my granddaughter,

ADELE BURDEN AUCHINCLOSS

Contents

The Young Apollo

AND OTHER STORIES

The Young Apollo

I HAVE DECIDED to put my thoughts about Lionel Manning together in this memorandum. I have to make up my mind, and soon, whether or not I shall accede to Senator Manning's request that I compose a short life of his son, Lionel, or "Lion" as we elders used to call him. It is now five years since Lion died of heart failure, aged thirty-one, in 1913, just before the outbreak of the long and terrible war that has cast the stain of doubt over the ideals we thought our boys were fighting for, as seemingly exemplified in the golden image of my young friend. I use the word "young" more in contrast to my own seventy summers than to emphasize a life so cut short, for it was characteristic of Lion in the matter of friendship to take no account of age, which endeared him to many of my contemporaries. Perhaps he offered us the illusion of some kind of life after death.

There is a cynical side of my old crusty bachelor self that whispers that it may have been just as well that Lion died when he did. After all, there is something fine and noble in an early demise. We can always now see him in a halo of glory, with his gleaming blond hair, his laughing gray-blue eyes, his gracefully molded features, his splendid muscular torso; we can hear his excited tones voicing his high principles; we can feel that he has taken his proper place in the gallant and inspiring company of the slain English friends whom he met as a Rhodes scholar. Don't we glimpse through the darkness of today the broad green lawn of an Edwardian garden party and wonderful young men in blazers and white flannels talking of the great things they would do in a future they would never have?

The wrong people have survived this war. My own "sacred circle," as some envious folk have described it, came through without a scratch. How shall I describe the circle? It consists of a small group of individuals, more or less prominent in the arts — writing, sculpture, painting — all of whom live in Washington without being native to the city, and none of whom, with the notable exception of George Manning, has the least connection with government. All are old, of course, and none hail from the kind of background that might be expected to produce great art. Ella Robinson, the novelist, for example, was born of Boston Brahmins; Elihu Tweed, the sculptor, was the son of a New York governor; and my own father, siring a historian, was a United States Supreme Court justice.

We used to fancy that we represented a kind of American renaissance. In the two decades preceding the war, our country was emerging from its long dependence on European culture. The notorious low value that Henry James accorded the subject material which America offered to the writer of fiction had been totally revised; we now claimed equal rights, so to speak, on Parnassus. And the young man whom we all held as our joint heir apparent, who was going to be the great poet of the future, to whom we were all more or less John the Baptists, was Lion Manning.

Why does George Manning not write the life of his own

son? I have never much liked George. He is as deeply conservative as a Republican senator from Rhode Island can get;
he is shrewd, raspingly sarcastic, and basically mean. But he
exercises a hefty political influence, and he purports to be a
stout supporter of the arts. He had no patience with Lion's
ambition to be a poet, however. He wanted him to become
a lawyer, a statesman, a great man. He adored the boy but
never understood him and lectured him constantly on his
duty to follow in the paternal footsteps. Lion simply grinned
and didn't listen. He could always wind the old man around
his little finger. Yet I know he deeply loved his father. And I
think the reason the senator wouldn't write the book himself
may have been that he was a bit scared of the boy and would
have fancied him looking over his shoulder as he wrote.

It is perfectly understandable, at any rate, why George
should have picked me for the job. As an old bachelor who
at least professed high ethical standards and a longtime observer of the passing scene in the nation's capital, I had appealed to Lion from his boyhood as a counterpoise to his
father's political cynicism. I was the kind of avuncular mentor
he had never had. He read my long history of the Supreme
Court with a passionate and intelligent interest, and as always,
even with his elders, took independent and forceful positions
in his criticism. It was he who elicited all my memories of
my Washington past and hounded me until I put them in my
memoirs, *Life of a Voyeur*, on which such reputation as I have
gained will probably rest, even at the expense of my longer
and more exhaustive studies. That, anyway, is what I was to
Lion. What he was to me was simply the son I never had.

We all loved him, of course. I think Ella Robinson may
even have been in love with him, though she was almost old

enough to have been his young mother. But she seems to share some of my doubts as to the advisability of producing this life of him. I do not, however, quite believe in the excuse she has offered me for not participating in it. Here is what she has written me:

There has been no one in my life, dear Ralph, to whom I owe more than to Lion. It is odd that a woman of my age should have been significantly indebted to a man so much her junior. But I was. You may have suspected part of the story. Here, anyway, is it all.

As I was nearing my fiftieth year, I moved to Paris to try a winter there. I had separated from Ted Robinson after a long but tepid marriage, and I had reached a time of life when I assumed that the tide of romantic love, which had never reached far enough up my beach to touch me, would leave me permanently dry. Yet I was quite resigned. I had my work and a slowly expanding audience of readers; I had enough money and many friends. I enjoyed travel, and I loved Paris. I had no complaints.

And then I met Cyril Ames. He was actually brought to my house, to the small literary salon I had sought to establish, by Lion, who, having just finished his Rhodes scholarship, had come over to Paris to work on his epic poem on the murder of Agamemnon, which he hoped would establish his reputation as a serious poet. Cyril, of course, was a good fifteen years older than Lion, but as you know, Lion had friends of all ages. People were drawn to him. Cyril was a handsome dark-eyed and dark-haired bachelor who worked as the foreign correspondent for a small New York journal; he was a smooth talker with a reputation for philandering. But he spoke as if he was a man utterly disillusioned with romance. He professed an ardent admiration of my work, and he came to all my little gatherings with a flattering persistence. Soon he was sending me flowers and inviting me to dinner at delightful restaurants. I guess there's no fool like an old fool; he certainly made one of me.

I now know that he had a fetish of conquering distinguished women whose success in life, compared to his own lackluster achievements, aroused his spite and envy. And he cultivated the art of keeping them subjugated with desperate hope, even after he had discontinued carnal relations; it gave him some sort of jag to have them still pursuing him when he was defiantly courting others. I actually believed him when he told me that I was the first serious love of his life! We had a fast and furious affair. You've probably been spared, Ralph, the exhausting experience of being loved by a middle-aged woman who's discovered for the first time the joy of sex! It was only a few weeks before my new lover abandoned me.

In the agony of my despair I even appealed to Lion! Can you conceive of such degradation? I actually begged him to intercede for me with my ex-lover! The poor boy was appalled. He had never dreamed that anything would develop between Cyril and me. Cyril had been merely the most casual of Lion's friends, and he had only brought him to my salon because Cyril had expressed a great desire to meet me.

"It's sickening to see a first-rate woman in the grip of a third-rate man," he told me after I had related my sorry tale. "But I got you into this mess, and I'll get you out."

And he came to see me, for as much as two hours at a time, every single day! Think of the time he lost for his poem, listening to my endless ravings as I poured out my heart. But I don't know what I should have done without him. Jumped into the Seine, perhaps. I was almost mad. At length, after he had virtually ordered me to take up my writing pen again, I produced a short story about my affair to express what I had the folly to deem my new insight into the deeper emotions of life. I flattered myself that I had gained a new knowledge of the soul, that there was now a greater comprehension of love in my writing. Lion, reading my little effort, dispelled my illusion.

"It's not so much the artist's emotion, Ella, that goes into the making of great art. It's his imagination and persistent hard work. People who think Shakespeare must have been depressed when he wrote *King Lear* have it all wrong. He probably kicked up his heels when he saw what he'd done. This story is the one bad piece of prose I've seen from the hand of Ella Robinson. Back to your muttons, my friend! That's the word."

"You mean I should go back to all the petty snobberies of my old Boston tales? After I've learned at last about the heart?"

"Damn right you should go back. Boston is your field, Ella. Boston is your capital. And you mustn't waste a penny of it!"

Well, that was it. Lion simply took over my life. He sent me back to Boston, where I wrote the best-selling novel that made my real reputation, after which I moved to Washington, which would probably have been a mistake had there not been so many Bostonians there. Of course, I took as the model for my hero Lion himself. And that is my memorial to him. And my only one.

Was that her real excuse? Well, maybe. Elihu Tweed offered me a strangely similar one. He writes me that his post-

humous use of Lion's head as his model for the soldier leading
the bayonet charge at Château-Thierry in his war memorial at
Rock Creek Park is a sufficient tribute on his part to our young
friend. And of course he has a point. The figure of the warrior
is indeed a splendid one and well illustrates how Lion would
have looked and acted had he survived to take his part in the
war. I actually tend to think of him as a casualty in that conflict,
as if the heart that went back on him so cruelly early in life had
been a battle wound. And I like to think of the anomaly of that
heroic figure emerging from marble through the chisel of my
stubby, balding, passionate little friend Elihu Tweed!

Here is what he wrote:

> I really don't see the point, dear Ralph, of us old farts
> getting together to sing paeans in praise of the dear dead
> boy. Isn't there something repellent about a bunch of aged
> writers and artists, who've had their lives and successes
> perhaps beyond their deserts, warming their withered
> paws against the fire of Lion's flaming youth? Don't they
> seem to be scraping up every scrap of his abbreviated life
> to add to their own glory? They who had everything and
> he who had nothing? Ugh!
>
> However, I'll give you one thing you can use in your
> book if you care to. It's about what Lion did for *me*. As you
> know, I've been subject all my life to periods of black de-
> pression. When they hit, it's impossible for me to do any
> work; I have to suffer through restless days and even more
> restless nights until the cursed thing blows away, as inex-
> plicably as it came. But I had one such spell that seemed
> to be traceable to a cause. My statue group of the Rough
> Riders in Miami had received a poorish press. I had even
> been denounced by two major art critics as a totally de-

rivative sculptor, as a slavish follower of Florentine artists of the Renaissance, as a man who had nothing to say to the twentieth century that couldn't have been said better by Benvenuto Cellini! I had never been much concerned with critics before, but this really struck home. Because it was true! I might as well have been born in Florence at the time Columbus discovered America, in the shadow of the Strozzi Palace.

Lion was only twenty-one at the time, and he was often in Washington visiting his old man. He liked to drop in to my studio and watch me at work. Of course, then I wasn't working, but he came to cheer me up. Or to try to. That was like him, and eventually he actually succeeded. For after I told him about the critics, he gave me such a fight talk as I had never received in my life. This is the gist of it.

"Why is what they said so damning, Elihu? I don't see it that way at all. It strikes me, on the contrary, as the highest praise. They say you copy Cellini. But the truth is that you *are* Cellini! You have been given us straight from the sixteenth century, and now we have something just as good as anything even a Medici pope ever had. It is a unique possession, and we should treasure it and not reproach you for not speaking to your time. Why can't we live in any age we choose? We go on like crazy about old masterpieces; we dig up ancient statues and temples to adorn our museums. Why scorn a man who is producing the very things we spend fortunes on? Stuff and nonsense!"

So there you are, Ralph. He cured me!

Well, I shall certainly use Elihu's story. *If* I write the book at all. It is indeed exhilarating to contemplate how much Lion did for his older friends. Would I have ever written *Life of a Voyeur* without his urging? I doubt it. I had overdisciplined myself in the business of keeping my own quirky personality out of my history books, to the point of deeming it almost obscene to write about myself. Lion fixed all that when he told me, "The man who talks about himself at a dinner table is a bore. The man who fails to talk about himself on the platform is a greater one. The audience has come to hear about him." And think what he did for Ella, though of course I can't use her story! Nor can I use the incident when Lion kept his father from agreeing to endorse the appointment to the federal bench of a crooked Rhode Island politician. Which is too bad, as it graphically illustrates the strength of his character.

George Manning had summoned me to his house to intercede with his son. He explained that Lion was threatening to cease contacting his father, and even to cease receiving financial aid from him, unless he agreed not to support the unsavory proposed appointee.

"You've got to help me drum some sense into that stubborn head of his, Ralph," the anguished senator had wailed. "You've got to help make him see that the real issue is between me and my state's political boss. Mike O'Shaugnessy and I have formed a working relationship that, as you know, enables us pretty much to run Rhode Island. I've had to make some compromises, to be sure, but so has he. And it's been on the whole a good thing for the state. And now this business of making Lew Kraft a judge threatens to upset the whole applecart. O'Shaugnessy simply won't give in on it. Kraft has some hold on him that I don't know anything about, and he's adamant on the subject. What's got into Lion? He's about to marry his lovely Bella, and they won't have a nickel without my help, except for what he may get for his poetry, and you know what people pay for that."

I knew that George, a wealthy man, had always given Lion a large allowance but had never settled any capital on him. It was like George to wish to keep control of his family. But I also knew that Lion would not hesitate for even a minute to pauperize himself for a principle.

And indeed, when I faced him that day in his father's study, I found him impossible to budge. His manner to his father was perfect, even affectionate. He simply regretted that they should have come to this pass, but come to it they certainly had.

He interrupted me when I started to defend the principle of political compromise. "I know about that, Uncle Ralph. I am very much aware of Dad's alliance with O'Shaugnessy. But there still have to be limits. I have been up to Providence and talked to members of the legislature. Democrats, I grant you, but still men who know what they're talking about. Kraft has had a hand in too many purchased elections not to be known, among the Republican Party faithful, as the 'King Fixer.' I cannot sit by and see Dad stick his fine fingers in such slime."

What could I do? What could anyone do? Of course George surrendered, and the name of Kraft was not even submitted to the Senate. The alliance with O'Shaugnessy tottered, but it survived.

The beautiful Bella, Lion's brave and stalwart widow, who had been married to him for only a year when he died, was not enthusiastic about the proposed volume, but she muted her objections because her father-in-law cared so strongly. She came to me privately.

"The senator insists," she told me, "that the book contain a goodly number of Lion's poems. Indeed, I think he sees your text primarily as an introduction to them. Of course, as he is printing the volume and paying for everything, he can do as he pleases. But, Ralph, I'm sure you feel as Ella and Elihu and I do about the poems. We're hoping you can limit the number and not include any part of the unfinished epic. Need I say more?"

No, she needn't. Lion's odes and sonnets and elegies and even the famous epic are dead, dead, dead. You couldn't exactly call them bad, or even embarrassing; they are filled with noble thoughts and grave ideals. But they are lapidary. They are dull. Lion was one who could inspire genius without being one. Maybe his life was genius. But it had to be lived, not printed.

But yes, I will write the little book. Even if it bodes to be a work of contrived hagiography. After all, it will be read only by a few relatives and friends; it will be soon forgotten. I can feel Lion's eye on me. "Do it for Dad," he seems to be saying. "It may help him to remember me, as he passionately wants to."

Other Times, Other Ways

CAMILLA HUNTER HAD NOT thought that lightning could strike twice at the same family, nor that at age eighty she would be forced to relive in 1981 the same kind of Wall Street scandal that had disgraced her husband in 1937. Back then, David Hunter had been implicated in the embezzlements of his mighty boss, Jonathan Stiles. It was true that their lawyer had argued that David, as the most junior partner in the brokerage house of Stiles & Son, might not have been fully aware of the criminal aspects of the jobs he was carrying out for his boss, but the jury had thought otherwise, and Camilla had had to admit reluctantly to herself that her husband's raiding of her own little fiduciary fund, entrusted to his firm, could hardly have been at the instigation of the great Stiles. Both men, at any rate, had been sentenced to stiff terms in Sing Sing, and the presses of the nation had rung with denunciations of the guilty brokerage house. Stiles had been held up to the scorn of the society in which Camilla had been raised as a "traitor to his class," and backs had been turned on her husband even after he had served his sentence.

And now here it was upon her again, almost half a century later, as if the windows of the neat little parlor of her modest Madison Avenue apartment had been blown open by a black

storm and her small trove of lares and penates scattered over
the floor. Could a white-haired but impeccably trim and still
unwrinkled widow, who had managed to survive everything
with her dignity intact, not be allowed to relish the seeming
serenity that she had so precariously achieved? Evidently not.
Bronson Newton, the husband of her favorite niece, Genevieve, considered the star of the family for the vast fortune
he had made on the stock market in a scant five years' time,
had been indicted for using inside information in his trading
and sentenced to two years in jail.

"I can only thank God that my poor mother didn't live
to see this second disgrace in her family," Camilla moaned
to herself as she contemplated the headlines of the evening
paper.

But of course she couldn't just sit and sigh. She would now
have to help steer her poor niece through this crisis, drawing
from her own experience to teach her how to handle the falling away of friends, and even relatives, and how to maintain
the oasis of a cherished home when the condemned man was
released from incarceration. She wrote to Genevieve to ask
when it would be best for her to come and received an answer suggesting a wait of some days. Bronson was planning
an appeal, of course, but as a reversal of the conviction was
believed by his lawyers to be unlikely, he had opted to start
his jail term at once to get it over as soon as possible.

It was a week, therefore, before Camilla presented herself at her niece's splendid Park Avenue duplex. She found
the beautiful blond Genevieve, radiantly clad as usual, in the
front hall taking what seemed to be a lively leave of some ladies who had been calling on her. As they departed she turned
to her aunt with a cheerfully welcoming smile.

"Darling Aunt Millie, how sweet of you to fly to my side!
Come in, come in."

Camilla followed her into the great drawing room, done
entirely in gleaming white except for the ebony arms of
the chairs and table legs and the black jade of the lamps. On
the walls hung canvases of Picasso, Miró, Pollock, and Jasper
Johns. She declined all offers of tea or a cocktail and sat quietly
for a moment in an armchair, gazing sadly at her hostess.

"I had to come," she said at last. "I was waiting until the
first rude shock was over. I knew you had to face that with
Bronson and the children."

"And that was typically tactful of you, you old darling. But
as it happens you've come just at the right time to hear some
wonderful news."

"Really? Is it the appeal? They think it will work?"

"No, no, no. That's quite hopeless, I'm afraid. But what
our able lawyers *have* achieved is to get Bronson into a mini-
mum-security prison. One that's almost like a country club.
He can see me quite freely. He can even run his business
from there. And I know he'll be on his best behavior, so he
should be sprung in only eighteen months. And if there are
any nasty types among the jailmates—you know, you never
can tell—I'm told we can easily arrange to pay them off when
they come out, so they'll leave Bronson strictly alone."

"I see you're being very practical about this."

"Doesn't one have to be? Didn't you? And then, of course,
we have a couple of friends who've suffered through the same
rigmarole. They've given us some very helpful advice."

"And the fines? The ones I've read about? They seemed
so huge to me. Will you have to make changes in your lifestyle?"

"Not a bit. It sounds rather lordly to say it, auntie, but sixty million doesn't make that fatal a dent in Bronson's fortune. We may have to give up the place in Arizona, but we'll certainly keep Southampton, Jamaica, and this old flat. And to tell the truth, I was getting a bit sick anyway of all that sand and cactus."

"I guess not having to cut down may help assuage public opinion," Camilla commented, now in a drier tone. "People seem to have a great respect for money these days."

"These days? When didn't they? But what do you mean, auntie, by assuaging public opinion?"

"Well, when something like this happened to your uncle, we had a lot of trouble even with some of our oldest friends."

"You mean they were ashamed of him?"

"Well, yes. They seemed to feel he had betrayed them."

"You mean the ones who had lost money because of what he had done?"

"No, no." Camilla was beginning to feel frustrated and even a bit vexed. "I mean the ones who thought he had been dishonorable. That he had let down the system in which he had been raised." She paused, and then finally brought it out. "They thought he had given the New Dealers in Washington the chance they had been waiting for to destroy Wall Street in the public eye! Your friends don't feel anything like that, I take it?"

"Good lord, no!" Genevieve's laugh was perfectly good-natured. "You're talking about another era, auntie. Let's call it the Iron Age. No, the attitude of our friends might be described as 'There but for the grace of God go I!'"

"I see." What more was there for Camilla to say? She listened and let Genevieve rattle on about how best and how often to arrange for the children to visit their father, and took her leave as soon as seemed decent.

But she didn't go straight home. She was too upset. She had to talk to someone about the shock of this new experience, and who was there better than her oldest and dearest friend of the heart, Marielle Blagden, fellow widow, whose apartment hotel was only a few blocks south of Genevieve's dwelling? She turned her steps thither.

Marielle, after her husband's death, ignoring the concerned protests of her family and friends, had divided the bulk of his large estate, bequeathed to her outright, among their two sons, reserving just enough to maintain herself comfortably in two rooms. But the building she had chosen was a first-class one, and the two rooms were handsome and properly furnished with fine things from the big Blagden Georgian house in Long Island, so Marielle was not, as she had wisely planned not to be, to any degree an object of pity. "I am doing exactly what I want," she had answered all objections firmly, "and living exactly as I choose. Call it selfish, if you like. Indeed, I'd rather have you call it selfish."

But Camilla knew that her friend had always lived for Pedro, as Peter Blagden was affectionately known, and had adapted herself totally to the hunting and polo-playing tastes of that kindly, charming, but unimaginative sportsman, and had, losing him, adapted herself in turn to the needs of their two kindly, charming, but unimaginative sons, whose wives needed the money that their husbands were too busy hunting and polo-playing to earn.

Camilla thought, as Marielle opened the door, how marvelously preserved she was—tall, slim, elegant, with large, smiling brown eyes under a fine pale brow and sleek undyed black hair still only faintly lined with gray. And she seemed to sense at once that Camilla was troubled. She listened in grave silence as the latter described her interview with Genevieve and then rose to mix her a cocktail at a small bar table.

"I think you may need this," she said, handing Camilla a glass. "Let us drink to the new age we're living in."

"Must we like it?"

"Of course not. We must only accept it. For as long as it lasts. Ages don't last forever. This one, however, can be counted on to last our time. Yours and mine, I mean."

"What have I just told you that makes you think I don't accept it?"

"Your clinging to a bygone moral code."

"You mean that all these stock market shenanigans are no longer crimes?"

"No, they're still crimes. What has changed is the public attitude toward them."

"People approve of them now, you mean?"

"That's putting it rather strongly. But they recognize how widespread they are. How many others are involved who never get caught. So they don't judge too harshly. It might be *them* tomorrow."

"Yet people still go to jail for these crimes."

"Oh, yes. There have to be rules in any game. For that's what the stock market has become: a game. If you're caught inside trading or gambling with other people's money or making illegal investments, you're docked so many points, so to speak. But nobody thinks any the worse of you."

"So when you get out of prison, you take back your old place in society? Nobody snubs you anymore."

"Just so."

"And you approve of all that, Marielle?"

"Did I say that? You and I were brought up in a different school, Millie. There was a code that applied to everyone. The men downtown were supposed to be strictly honorable in their financial affairs. And their wives were supposed to give them moral support. Mr. Coolidge said that the business of America was business, and we were meant to uphold high standards. Wall Street was to set an example to the nation."

"Exactly! I remember that Mr. Morgan said he would never do business except with men on whose word he could entirely rely."

"Of course, the men on whom he relied may not have dared to give him one on which he couldn't."

Camilla began to sense that her friend might not be quite with her. It irritated her, because Marielle's Pedro, the heir to a considerable fortune, had never so much as poked his nose south of Canal Street. He and Marielle had lived isolated and protected lives. "Are you implying, my dear, that our parents' generation were hypocrites?" she asked.

"Well, there's always some of that quality around, is there not?"

"If it existed among us women, I never ran into it. We believed in our men, you and I! We lived for them. We thought it was our role in life to do so. Of course, you were not challenged. I was. I believed in a man who was weak. But I still had to live for him. As you did for Pedro."

"What do you mean, *had* to? Wasn't it a choice? I didn't *have* to do anything."

"Of course you did! It was the way we were brought up."

Camilla knew that her rising exasperation was liable to take her too far, but she went on. There is nothing as sharp as the irritation that one's nearest and dearest arouse when they do arouse it. "You deliberately squashed every artistic and literary taste you had in order not to embarrass in the smallest degree Pedro and his philistine friends!"

Marielle only smiled. "That's perfectly true."

"You even used to say, when you stole away to a concert or lecture, that you'd been 'naughty.'"

"I plead guilty."

"You mutilated yourself for a man! As I did!"

"And do you know something? Pedro didn't give a damn. I mean about whether or not I shared his obsession with sport. He was perfectly happy doing his own thing. His confidence in himself was unbounded. If I'd gone in for poetry or painting, no matter how extreme, he wouldn't have minded in the least. If I'd become as famous as Edna St. Vincent Millay, he'd have boasted about it in the locker room of the Racquet Club. 'You know, fellas, my Marielle has just won a Pulitzer. Isn't that great? How many of you are married to geniuses?' And then he'd have gone happily up to his court tennis game."

"So it was all for nothing."

"Not quite. For it made *me* happy. Doing what I thought would make him happy."

"And all the work I did to rehabilitate David was unnecessary? Does that follow? That he never needed rehabilitation?"

"Perhaps not as much as you thought. But what difference does that make? You were happy doing it."

"No, Marielle, I wasn't." Camilla shook her head somberly. "I wasn't at all. Perhaps it was all in the men we chose. You chose well. I less so. We were victims of our time."

"We were victims of ourselves."

"I don't think I can bear that. Anyway, I'm going home."

→>−◄⊦

Camilla did a lot of thinking that night. It seemed to her that from childhood she had seen the world about her through two very different eyes. One saw the myriad chocolate streets where a large clan of parents, uncles, aunts, and cousins dwelled in rather noisy conformity, where husbands ruled from a moneyed "downtown" and wives ruled the uptown expenditure, where marriages were either happy or never spoken of, and where children were granted considerable liberty so long as they seemed headed ultimately to a repetition of the parental careers. But the other eye embraced a world of fantasy where one grew up to be Geraldine Farrar singing Tosca, or Maud Adams playing Peter Pan, or Elizabeth Barrett Browning composing a sonnet to the Portuguese. The second vision was the one that she shared with Marielle Loomis, who lived just across East Forty-ninth Street in a house with a Beaux Arts facade that marked her family as richer, though not unbridgeably so, than Camilla's family, the Townsends, in their brownstone residence somewhat "gussied up" with supposedly Egyptian trimmings.

Camilla and Marielle always sat together, at least whenever it was allowed, in classes at Miss Chapin's School for Girls and reveled in the English poets of the recently ended Victorian era, in Tennyson and Browning, and, more adventurously, in Byron and Shelley. They loved the haunting music of Debussy and Saint-Saëns, and they particularly delighted in the new operas of Puccini when they went to matinees at the Metropolitan in Marielle's grandmother's box. They were daring enough to tell their parents that they

favored votes for women and might even have joined a suf-
fragette parade had not Camilla's mother, Eva Townsend,
suddenly frowned, shook her head sternly, and told them,
"Of course, you must realize that is quite out of the question."

But Camilla still liked to think that her Christian name
was derived from the Camille of Corneille's tragedy *Horace*,
though in fact it stemmed from a sweet and saintly grandmother who had had little enough in common with the fiery
Roman virgin who paid with her life for cursing her fatherland over the war in which her betrothed had been killed.
Camilla, in certain moments, had liked to imagine herself as
endowed with the guts to stand up against a family united in
defense of all the old ways and proclaim her independence.
She and Marielle even had the nerve, once, at least, to discuss
the possibility of a future in which they wouldn't marry at all
but would share a little house full of lovely things and live for
the arts, calling themselves a couple of *exquises*.

But whatever fantasies they allowed themselves, they
could never get away from the nagging suspicion that what
Camilla had called her first vision of their world was the true
one and that there would be no way of escaping their destiny
to become wives and mothers. That there were such things
as old maids in society was sufficiently obvious to them, but
these fell into two categories, both unthinkable, one beyond
their material means, even Marielle's, and the other too low
to be borne. The first category contained the rich old virgins
of New York and Newport, a strictly American phenomenon,
as in Europe they would have been married off no matter
what their disqualifications or reluctance. These included
Miss Anne Morgan, Miss Annie Jennings, Miss Julia Ber-

wind, Miss Ruth Twombly, and the Misses Wetmore, grandes dames who commanded wide reverence and respect. The second was the sorry residue of those too poor or too plain to catch a spouse, who were left to struggle for a living as teachers or paid companions or to haunt the upper stories of the houses of aged parents and dine on trays in their bedrooms whenever an extra man had dropped out of a dinner party below upsetting his hostess's *placement.*

That the ultimate power rested with men was the *donnée* of a woman's existence. It was dogma, having little to do with any innate superiority. Eva Townsend, in her daughter's eyes, was an abler, stronger, more practical, and more decisive person than her gentle, easygoing father, and nor had Eva herself ever been in the least unaware of this. She and her sisters and sisters-in-law had taken firm control of the areas of life allowed them by the other sex: the household, the costs, the schools, the summer resorts, and the makeup of society itself—who was in it, who out. But in the final court of appeal, where life or death was at stake, the male alone voted.

One could, however, always laugh at men. Camilla recognized that her mother and aunts liked to chuckle over men's foibles: their tippling, their falling asleep after dinner, their obsession with spectator sports, their bawdry, and their passionate anger at anyone who suggested the mildest control of free enterprise. But the myth had nonetheless to be maintained that the head of the family was fundamentally benign, an "old darling" at heart, gruff but lovable and pleasantly subject to female wheedling. How else was one to handle him? And handled he had often to be.

There were males, of course, in Camilla's and Marielle's lives: the youths of the neighborhood, if they got through the girls' mothers' social sieves, for the most part well-behaved, sometimes shy, even inarticulate, sometimes impertinent, sometimes almost coarse, always well dressed, at least at subscription dances, at times handsome, at times winsome, at times simply disgusting. There were flirtations, even kisses, but at least in Camilla's case, there was nothing really serious until her sophomore year at Barnard College, in 1919.

There had been a minor family issue over her going to college at all. Her mother, something of a reader of good books herself, had not been strongly opposed to it, and the end of the Great War had ushered in an era that was already showing signs of drastically changing the status of women, but the Townsend clan as a whole did not yet see the university as a necessary part of a woman's education. Did Camilla really want to be a bluestocking? But when Camilla, scenting a new independence in the air, found the courage to insist, objections were withdrawn, though on the condition that she should choose a college where she could still live at home. So she chose Barnard.

She had hoped that Marielle would go with her, but Marielle was now engaged to Pedro Blagden and already embarked on the career of preparing herself to share the life of a rich sportsman. Pedro had made one silly crack about her and Camilla training for an all-girls football team, at which his fiancée had promptly dropped all idea of further education. Camilla had rather pitied her for abandoning so easily the road to a higher culture and had entered enthusiastically into academic life, making several new friends among young women of backgrounds very dissimilar to her own. Indeed, she did well enough to be given a bid to the sorority Kappa Kappa Gamma and was not in the least put off when Pedro, now married to Marielle, referred to it laughingly as "Wrapper, Wrapper, Pajama." It was so like him!

But a major crisis arose at home when it materialized that the night of her initiation coincided with that of an aunt's dinner party which she had agreed to attend. She protested to her mother that she would have to back out, that Aunt Maud would surely understand, but Eva Townsend was unexpectedly rigid.

"It happens to be an important party: your cousin Willy's twenty-first birthday. But in any event, when one accepts a dinner invitation, one goes. Or sends one's coffin."

Her father, appealed to, of course backed her mother, as he always did in any social question, and Camilla had tearfully to explain to her sorority sisters that she would have to be initiated in absentia. At the party she found herself seated next to David Hunter, whom she was meeting for the first time. As her mother who, like many New York matrons of her group, had at first been much taken with this handsome young man, commented, "It goes to show that it pays to stick by the old rules."

David Hunter, at twenty-two, was certainly gifted with looks. Just before he had been sent overseas as a second lieutenant, his adoring mother, desperate at the idea that she might never see him again, had sent him up to Boston to sit for a charcoal sketch by the great John Sargent, so that she would at least have a perfect likeness to console her in the event of disaster. The master had done a wonderful job, and reproductions of his drawing of the curly-headed, wide-eyed, noble-browed, square-chinned youth had been used on enlistment posters as the epitome of the young American fighting spirit. David, on the distaff side, was the great-grandson of a giant railroad tycoon, but the tycoon's children and grandchildren, famous for their flamboyant expenditure, had

depleted his great fortune to a small fraction of its one-time glory, and this romantic-looking scion had been happy after the war to find a desk in the brokerage house of Jonathan Stiles & Son, where it was hoped that his looks and still stylish connections might attract investors.

He and Camilla hit it off at once. She was pretty enough to attract even a man who had his choice of her sex, and the badinage that she had learned from her new college friends struck him as livelier than that of the usual New York debutante. Besides, she was a good listener.

"Do you know what, Miss Townsend? The war hasn't just made the world safe for democracy, as President Wilson has said. It's made the world safe for young people, like you and me. We're not going to be confined as our parents were to all the petty dos and don'ts of the generation before us. We're going to be free to blaze new trails, to make our own rules for the game of life!"

Camilla had had enough of her mother's much-vaunted common sense pounded into her to suspect that this was the kind of thing that all the young men were saying, but she had also been indoctrinated in the maternal principle that a wise woman learns to tolerate, and even on occasion to applaud, banality in the opposite sex.

"A year in the trenches," she observed, "must have had the educative value of ten in an ordinary life. So it almost puts you ahead of the older generation."

"You see that, do you? It's because you're smart, Miss Townsend. I like smart women. The cute little 'you're so big and strong' type bore the bejesus out of me, if you'll pardon my French."

He had been only briefly at the front by the time of the

armistice, but he certainly made the most of it, and he had the gift of talking about himself without either boring his listener or appearing arrogant. Or was it just the charm of his youth and beauty? Camilla didn't care, and knew that she didn't care. She was already well on her way to being pulverized. He went on to tell her that he intended to make a fortune on Wall Street and that he would spend it in ways to make even his most flamboyant forebears look like cheapskates. He absolutely declined to turn to his other neighbor at the serving of the roast, as etiquette then required, and blandly insisted on monopolizing Camilla in the parlor after dinner, also in flagrant contradiction of the established practice of mingling. Obviously, she didn't mind at all.

She would have only too many occasions then and in later years to wonder why love is so often described as blind. It was certainly never so in her own case. She had been aware from the beginning of her relationship with David that however attractive she might have been, what had really immediately drawn him to her was the only too apparent effect that he could see he had made on her. But how long would that last?

For a while anyway, and that while was hers. He called at the house almost daily; he brushed aside her college commitments as so many flies and took her to expensive restaurants, where he held forth exuberantly on his great plans for a future in which he seemed to take silently for granted that she would play an admiring role. Camilla knew that she had tumbled to the bottom of the dark abyss of love and listened with controlled patience to her mother's now freely expressed doubts as to David's financial future. Eva's original enthusiasm for him had been qualified by later acquaintance.

"There's certainly no doubt as to his capacity to spend

money. He has inherited plenty of that talent. But I'm much less sure of his capacity to earn it. David wants to make a fortune in order to be able to squander it. He doesn't seem to realize that most of our great tycoons built their fortunes out of the love of building. Vanderbilt, Gould, Rockefeller — those men weren't interested in spending their piles. The accumulation was everything to them. It was up to their descendants to dispose of the loot. And the descendants were more than ready to take care of *that*. Mr. Morgan was different, but Mr. Morgan was *born* a rich man. And anyway, David is no Morgan. He's got the cart before the horse."

Camilla was perfectly willing to concede this, but she didn't care. She and David were married six months after their first meeting. Her parents had urged a longer wait, but she had found the force to resist them, pressing down in her mind the ugly suspicion that she dreaded the effect of a longer wait on David's volatile nature. And David's parents, who still managed to live with a certain splash on the remnants of the ancestor's fortune and who were relieved that their excitable and impetuous son had selected so sensible and reliable a mate, managed to scrape up enough cash to see the young couple at least through their first year.

Thus had started the decade and a half that was to elapse before the district attorney had issued his indictment against Stiles and Hunter and the last lights in Camilla's life flickered out.

The first years, at least, had had their pleasant side. In the 1920s, David's firm made plenty of money, and he was able to buy the shiniest and longest of foreign cars and the fastest and noisiest of motorboats, to rent large summer villas in the Hamptons and to go off with chosen Racquet Club pals on distant and dangerous mountain-climbing expeditions or on African big-game shooting safaris. Camilla had always feared that the time would come when his mercurial mentality might begin to tire of her so much plainer and more placid disposition and tastes, and she patiently acquiesced in being left behind with their son when he took off for far parts of the globe, seeking to console herself with the illusion that the limitation of his company to males would guard him from the allurements of her own sex.

He took for granted that she was totally content with her life. Was she not Mrs. David Hunter? What else could a woman want? "You know, Millie," he told her once, on his return from a fishing trip in the Arctic Circle, "it does a man good when he's freezing in below-zero temperatures to know there's a home fire always burning for him and a great little woman whose face will light up when he comes through the door. How's young David?" And then he looked for a corner of his mind not full of his latest adventure to devote briefly to David Junior, hugging him and spoiling him and buying him anything that he clamorously demanded at any price. And of course the boy adored him.

But it was, predictably, a very different David who survived—and barely survived—the market crash of 1929. He seemed to regard the long depression that followed it as a personal affront aimed at him by a vindictive fate, and when Camilla, with all the calm and resolution that she could muster, attempted to adjust their lifestyle to the drastic reduction of their income, he resented her disinclination to join in his shrill complaints, as if she were somehow in conjunction with the forces of evil. If she ever protested at his stubborn insistence on continuing to buy the most expensive

clothes for himself or at his refusal even to consider resigning from any of his clubs, he would ask her angrily if she expected him to take to the streets and hold out a tin cup. She
knew that he was seeing a lot of Paul and Gloria Davison,
at whose apartment he seemed to be always dropping in on
his way home from work without asking her to join him,
and she began to suspect that Gloria, the avid young blond
wife of a much older and notoriously gullible millionaire,
might be paying some of David's bills. Camilla remembered
having read in a life of the first duke of Marlborough that
he owed some of his amorous success as a dashing young
officer to his habit of borrowing money from the ladies he
seduced.

And then, suddenly, David seemed almost rich again. He
announced that he was renting a big house on the dunes in
Southampton for the summer of 1936. But they were never
to occupy it. David was fated to endure a very different kind
of housing.

He behaved well enough at his trial; he was always at his
best in the public eye. Camilla had even once wondered if
he shouldn't have been an actor; he might have lacked the
subtlety for the graver dramatic roles, but he certainly had
the looks of a movie star. He denied boldly all the charges
leveled against him. He had simply acted, he maintained, on
the orders of his boss, in whom he had had and continued to
have implicit faith. He even sneered at the prosecuting attor-
neys, who, in his lofty view, were simply misguided Marxists
incapable of detecting the grand and noble overall projects
of the Wall Street mighty behind the petty details of daily
trading, which were subject to malign misinterpretation. But
it was difficult for the jury—and for the sadly listening Ca-

milla — to believe that any grand overall scheme had dictated the plundering of his wife's little trust fund.

He even continued to insist on his innocence at home in the brief period before his incarceration. He openly resented his wife's downcast eyes and lachrymose silence, which, for all her head shaking, so clearly expressed her agreement with the jury's finding, and his bursts of temper culminated in his request that she not visit him in jail but leave him to such peace as he could find there.

This was Camilla's bitterest blow. She went up to the prison, of course, and he did allow her to see him. He craved such news as she could bring of the outside world, and besides, a refusal to see his wife might have been deemed by the authorities a demerit in his carefully sustained record of good behavior. He was indeed a model prisoner, even popular with his fellow inmates, who were not immune to the attractive note of democratic friendliness that he so easily knew how to assume. David had always known how to appeal to both sexes.

At home, during the Sing Sing years, Camilla reduced her living expenses to a Spartan minimum and earned some extra dollars by giving old friends lessons in bridge, a game at which she had always been adept. At first she received many dinner invitations from sympathetic friends and acquaintances, but as she felt it would be disloyal to David to go to any houses where she had reason to believe he had been roundly excoriated, and as most of her old world was of the unconcealed opinion that David and Jonathan Stiles had been traitors to their class, betraying it to the gloating mob of the new left, she spent most of her evenings alone. David Junior, who had had a nervous breakdown over his father's collapse and been expelled from Andover for drinking, was a bitter trial to her, but he ultimately emigrated to Hong Kong, where he was able to support himself as a bartender in surroundings where his name was not known.

Camilla had one opportunity to supplement her income substantially, but her sense of honor compelled her to reject it. Her lawyer advised her that the bank that had been cofiduciary with her husband of her trust fund was legally liable for the money it had negligently allowed him to embezzle and would replenish the account if requested. She could not see herself making the request.

Such, however, was by no means David's attitude when he was at last released, a coarser and moodier man. He professed himself utterly disgusted with the small apartment Camilla had taken in an unfashionable West Side district and was irate that she could not come up with the sum needed for his new wardrobe. And he really exploded when he heard from their lawyer what she had failed to do about her trust fund.

"Have you completely lost your mind, Millie? Do you realize the difference even that little income will make to us? Plus the fact that the income's been accumulating for three years. I'm going after the bank at once!"

"But, David, I can't touch that money! And you, of all people, ought to know why!"

"You can give it to me to touch, then. I'm not so finicky."

She gave in. He was her husband, after all. If she didn't look after him, if she didn't help to rehabilitate him, who would? She would have to see him through this crisis. And there would be others.

There were. The bank restored the embezzled fund without waiting for the suit that David threatened. But what she found even harder, for here her role was active rather than merely passive, was his insistence that she mend her bridges with all the people whose invitations she had spurned.

"My God, woman, don't you see what a hole we're in! We have no choice. I don't give a rat's ass at this point if you go to houses where I'm no longer welcome. We have to make do with what we have. And *you* at least have some goodwill left with people who swing a lot of clout. Well, *use* it! Use it to help a poor guy whom they're still mean enough to spit at. For doing what they all do. Or *would* do if they weren't scared shitless of being caught!"

So Millie, as he insisted, proceeded painfully to repair her social breaches. Nor did it ease her aching soul to find that she was good at it. Time had passed; prejudices had softened; pity opened the pocketbooks of men who were glad enough to help out without actually admitting David to their homes. They could be generous if they were allowed to be consistent.

Paul Davison went so far as to give David a modestly paying job as director of a small museum of ancient automobiles in Queens, and the Hunters were almost comfortably solvent when David died of a sudden stroke seven years after his release from prison.

⤖⬤⬅

When Camilla had sufficiently recovered from the shock of finding her friend Marielle so philosophically resigned to the readjustment—if that was the right word—of moral standards as professed by the younger generation, she agreed to resume their weekly lunches at the latter's club.

"I've done a lot of hard thinking since we had that illuminating talk," she told her friend after her first sip of the traditional Dubonnet that always preceded their meal. "And I've come to the conclusion that David may have been ahead of his times. That is, if his times were not, under the surface, pretty much what today's times are. It is I who may have been the blind fool."

"A fool you never were, Millie."

"But blind?"

"Perhaps a bit astigmatic. So many of our generation were. I certainly was."

"But he must have seen me as a fiend! Tormenting him with imputations of a guilt he didn't want to feel. That he wanted only to throw off. So that he might pick up his lost life! No wonder he hated me."

"Hated you? Oh, Millie."

"He was having an affair with Gloria Davison. I found it out from letters in his desk after he died. Did you know that?"

Marielle looked very grave. "We all knew that, Millie. And we rather assumed you did. It's not such a big deal, you know. With middle-aged men panicking over their lost youth. Many wives put up with it."

"Not you."

"No, not I." Marielle was firm about this. "But I hope I wouldn't have made too much a thing of it, had it been my problem."

Camilla sighed. "I suppose I must try to see it that way."

"How else should you see it but the way it is? Look, Millie. I happen to believe that what David did and went to prison for was a very bad thing. Perhaps even a wicked thing. But I also believe that he genuinely repented in his heart and that a merciful God will forgive him and take him into heaven.

There! Neither of my sons shares my faith, but they never give a thought to religion. I am perfectly aware that perhaps a majority of their generation consider my belief the rankest superstition, but should that bother me? Not a bit. Who knows? Maybe they're right. And maybe I am!"

"And we still have laws," Camilla observed doubtfully. "Criminal laws. I suppose that's something."

"'Tis something, nay 'tis much,' as Browning said. We don't have to do any of the condemning ourselves. It makes life easier, really. Though perhaps less fun?"

Camilla found herself wondering if it was going to help her to be able to laugh at this.

A Case History

As a retired md and former psychoanalyst, and a winter resident (yes, I have come to it like so many others) of the Florida beaches, I have also, like others, sought refuge from the golf course and cocktail parties—particularly the latter, as my physician forbids me alcohol—in writing my memoirs. But I soon came to realize that the autobiography of Lucius Carroll, MD, would attract only those who hoped it might enable them to peek into the psyches of some of my famous patients, which must, of course, remain shielded by professional confidentiality. Yet in reluctantly abandoning the idea of my memoirs, I have had some consolation in the conception of another project: that of putting together some of my more interesting case histories and leaving them to a medical library, which might one day, when all interested parties were long dead and buried, be able to make them available to qualified medical students.

The one I am now about to write does not concern a famous patient, but someone who was almost totally obscure and whose obscurity was largely the result of his own volition. Marvin Daly chose to remain obscure because he was homosexual, and it was this aspect of his personality that caused the nervous breakdown that brought him to my office. Obviously his trouble emanated from the era and the society in which he grew up, neither of which was favorable to diversity in sexual tastes, but there may still be profit to be gleaned from his story, as the Christian church derives edification from the plight of its early martyrs.

In my own not-so-humble opinion, we still have much to learn about homosexuality. The modern theory that it is a natural physical trait which cannot—and should not—be altered in any person in which it appears can be carried too far. It fails to take into account the prevalence of sexual duality in perhaps a majority of humans, of which every analyst has ample evidence, and that the percentages of male and female elements are different in each individual. In some men the predominance of the female marks them as homosexuals who will always be consistently that. But in others the balance may be so close as to offer them a choice, and that choice should not be dictated by arbitrary definitions or prejudices, pro or con.

I suspect that Marvin Daly, the subject of this report, might have been one of those who made the choice involuntarily at too early a date. I must state, however, that he always disagreed with me about this; he was convinced that he was fated to be what he became from birth and that nothing could have changed him. And he may have been right; one can never be sure. "Do you really and truly believe," he asked me once, "that if you had got hold of me when I was still in my teens, you could have molded me into a suburban commuter whose loving wife meets him on the evening train in a station wagon complete with three kids and an Airedale?" "Possibly" was my reply. He laughed scornfully, as if he was glad to have escaped such a fate, yet it was at least a better one than his own.

→>-<+

Marvin Daly was born in 1918, at the very end of the Great War, the fourth child and only son of Ezra and Lila Daly, who lived, when they didn't occupy their Italianate palazzo on Park Avenue, in a red brick Georgian manor house of surpassing beauty that dominated Meadowview, an estate of a thousand acres in Wheatley Hills, Long Island. The little boy, whose birth was joyfully greeted after a succession of three girls, was named for his late paternal grandfather, who had made his fortune in Pittsburgh steel with Andrew Carnegie. From the beginning the child was made much of, arrayed in velvet suits with lace collars, given sumptuous children's parties where real little silver cups were awarded to the winners of potato races, and painted or sketched by illustrious artists. But above all, certainly at least to him, he was the darling of his adoring and radiantly beautiful mother.

Lila Daly might have started the Trojan War had she lived in ancient Mycenae. Her finely chiseled features and heavenly blue eyes, her wavy gold locks and slender graceful figure were matched by a disposition so gentle and outgiving that the harshest Marxist of her day would have spared her in the extermination of her class. Yet she would have exasperated him in her complete acceptance of the privileged conditions of her life. She was perfectly happy to be the lovely center of the picturesque and elaborate setting that her devoted slave of a husband was always intent on creating around her. Lila Daly, smiling at the camera as she posed with basket and shears in her fabulous garden in Meadowview or receiving in her gold and yellow parlor on Park Avenue, seemed to justify the grossest social inequalities of the age of the robber barons.

But all the dryness of a mercantile era seemed concentrated in her husband. It was as if the beauty in which he enveloped his spouse, with lavish orders and commissions, had somehow drained every last bit of color out of his own personality, leaving him a balding, fussy little man, rigidly attentive to details and oblivious of the verdant forests whose trees he so accurately counted. Yet he was a good man, conscientious and charitable, whose large donations to schools and hospitals were usually anonymous and who saw little use in himself other than as the producer of the show that his wife exhibited to the world. Except with Lila, he found it hard, almost impossible, to express his affections, and his love for his children went largely untold, with the result that they neither recognized nor returned it. Marvin and his sisters respected their father and credited him with financial generosity, but that was all. After his death they were dismayed to find in his secret diary how intensely he had concerned himself with their problems and futures, but they could only try to love him in retrospect.

Marvin copied his father in one instance: he adulated his mother. As a small boy, he was allowed the privileged place on the divan, cuddled up against her soft silk-clad side, as one of her hands played idly with his curly hair, when she read aloud to him and his older sisters from Robert Louis Stevenson or Howard Pyle. The hero of the story became himself and his mother's knight. And as he grew older, he waxed more actively protective. He would show horror at her fondness for candy and sweet desserts and warn her about their baneful effect on her lovely figure; he would demonstrate deep concern about the wear and tear of her busy social life and its toll on her hours of sleep; he would urge her to take at least some daily exercise. Lila was touched by his caring but always laughed it off, kissing him or patting his shoulder while she went serenely about her business. "Marvin, my darling," she would sometimes protest, "if you insist on being my guide and mentor, what am I to do when you go off to boarding school? I shall become a worn-out fat old lady!"

It was indeed a good question, but not so much for her as for him. What would become of *him*? For Marvin received a rude shock when he arrived at St. Luke's, a meticulously regulated boys' academy, as strict and knobbly as the surrounding New England countryside was inconsistently soft and welcoming. As a "new kid," he was subject to months of verbal and physical hazing from boys who were not in the least impressed by the wealth of the Dalys, except to sneer at it, and for a time he felt that he was being singled out for particular abuse because of the "privileges" of which his father had always warned him not to be too proud. But he came to see that his treatment was no worse than that meted out to other new kids. In time it stopped, and his moderate good looks, his moderate competence in sports, and his moderate good nature caused him to be moderately accepted. And he always had Meadowview, of which the lovely land around the school nostalgically reminded him, to dream about, and the vacations to look forward to.

Meadowview, I must here point out, occupied a central position in the mind, or perhaps I should say the imagination, of my patient. Marvin adored the place and knew every one of its thousand acres. On vacations from school, and later from Yale, he would insist on staying there even when his parents and sisters were residing in the city, happily living alone in the great empty house, deserted by all but the silent old caretaker and his silent spouse. He would wander over the fields and through the woods, across meadows where the herd of Black Angus grazed or over the flagstoned paths of his mother's wonderful gardens, or he would sit and muse in the little porticoed Greek temple that she had had constructed on top of a small hill commanding four views down grass paths lined with statues of gods and goddesses. From there he could see the long soft-red brick façade of the two-story mansion, which seemed to melt into the countryside, the work of an expert landscape gardener who had blended to perfection the things of man—house, farm, stable, out-buildings, even the ancient windmill in the distance—with the things of nature.

However much it was his life, Meadowview, of course, was a shrine to his mother's beauty. It seemed to him that her spirit permanently inhabited the Greek temple, silently and benignly present, worshipped by all who approached. Her actual appearance at Meadowview struck him at times as faintly out of key, for she moved briskly about the grounds, checking efficiently but smilingly on this and that, uttering her gently phrased but perceptive criticisms to gardeners or farm workers who obviously adored her. And she was always adequately terrestrial with her adoring son.

"Sometimes, child, I think you're a little too fond of this place," she would tell him. "You're missing out on the subscription dances in town I've signed you up for. You must learn to pay more attention to social life."

To some extent, however, he was doing that. At least in school. He was finding friends there. He had now attracted the attention of some of the leaders of his class. Few of the boys had as yet become worldly or socially snobbish, but there were those who had been impressed by the long yellow rattling Hispano-Suiza town car and its scarlet liveried chauf-

feur when it had borne Lila Daly on one of her weekend visits to the school. By the time Marvin was fifteen, the gray
Gothic buildings of St. Luke's and the heavy rounded arches
of its Romanesque chapel had begun to lose some of their
grimness, and the red and golden glory of a New England
autumn had bathed the campus in a new and softer light. He
had begun to relish Keats and Shelley and was learning "La
cathédrale engloutie" in his piano lessons.

It was at this time that he first fell in love. Billy Lansdorf
was a seemingly shy and reticent boy with dark, rather sultry
good looks. Actually, as Marvin was later to discover, Billy was
anxious to join the popular group of the class leaders, but he
didn't know how best to put himself forward. He had noted the
Hispano-Suiza and learned that Marvin's grandfather had been
one of the "lords of Pittsburgh," and as he was a scholarship
student whose family had lost everything in the great market
crash, he had begun to regard Marvin as possibly just the social
asset that he needed. Finding that his overtures of friendship
were readily, even gladly, received, he was soon Marvin's daily
companion, taking long walks with him in the countryside and
patiently listening to his enthusiastic chatter about music and
poetry. It was particularly agreeable to Billy to find that his
new pal was eager to have him visit in the approaching summer at the Dalys' famous estate on Long Island, a welcome
alternative to the exiguous Lansdorf family flat in Brooklyn.

To Marvin the friendship was a very different affair. It simply illuminated his life. His attraction to Billy, which had preceded the latter's interest in himself and consisted originally
of moodily casting covert glances at Billy's handsome profile, now burgeoned into a flame that seemed to consume his
whole being. He chose to deem their now more intimate re-

lationship a high and noble union of souls; they were Damon and Pythias, or Orestes and Pylades, and he did not hesitate to fill his weekly letter to his mother with glowing accounts of his new idol. Lila wrote back to urge him to invite Billy to stay with them at Meadowview.

That July the two boys ranged over the whole of the Dalys' vast estate. They fished in the ponds; they climbed to the top of the old windmill; they ran away from the angry Black Angus bull, whose field they had invaded; they captured and killed snapping turtles. And then one afternoon, finding themselves alone at the swimming pool, Marvin suggested that they dispense with bathing suits. Stripped and lying on their bellies in the sun after a swim, Marvin felt the swelling in his groin and rose boldly to expose himself to his friend. Billy, grinning lewdly and not in the least surprised, jumped up to reveal himself in the same condition, and the two embraced.

For Marvin what ensued was a supreme moment, a kind of near sacred ritual appropriate to the Greek temple on the little hill above them. It even seemed to fit in with Meadowview, even with his mother's beauty. For Billy it was simply the dirty nocturnal game that he had played with others in his dormitory at St. Luke's.

Let me put my patient's reaction to what happened when the boys went back to school in Marvin's own words. I had a tape recorder in my office which I could switch on at particularly revealing moments of a patient's free association—always, of course, with the patient's permission.

That September I found that Billy had considerably changed toward me in the month that had elapsed between his visit to Meadowview and the reopening of school. He had been invited in August to visit Dicky Brown, one of the more popular and outstanding leaders of our class, in nearby Oyster Bay. Dicky was not a particular friend of Billy's; his bid had really come from Mrs. Brown, Dicky's mother, who was some sort of cousin of Billy's father. She had been reminded of Billy's existence seeing him at a lunch party at Meadowview and had insisted that Dicky ask him to stay with them, as the poor boy would otherwise be stuck in the hot city when his visit with me was over. So I had, after all, proved of some social use to Billy.

Billy had succeeded in worming his way into Dicky's affections as he had into mine, and back at school he was taken into Dicky's set, of which I was only a fringe member. We continued to be on outwardly amicable terms, but our intimacy was over, and there was certainly no idea of any repetition of the incident by the swimming pool. Such an incident did take place, however, between Billy and one of his new pals, and so indiscreetly that they were caught in the act by a snooping master, who reported it to the rector of the school. It might have been grounds for expulsion but for the extremely unpleasant publicity that such an action would inevitably evoke, and our whole class was summoned before the headmaster for a severe lecture. He excoriated the guilty pair in violent terms and thundered against what he called depravity and decadence and unmanly conduct. I was appalled.

To me it was as if the big dirty paw of some huge brute dipped in shit had smeared my mental vision of Meadowview, of the Greek temple, of love. But it was not any brute who had done it; it was *I* who had done it! I had defiled my home, my haven, my ideal, my mother! And I had had the ultimate gall to see beauty in what I had dared to call love! I was awash with guilt.

That Christmas vacation something happened that made me feel even worse. My family had decided to spend the holidays at Meadowview, and one evening before dinner, when my sisters happened to be all out of the room, Father availed himself of the moment to tell Mother and me something not fit for young girls to hear. As in many Long Island estates, we had a night watchman who circled the house in the dark hours armed with a revolver. Ours was a dear old boy who couldn't have hurt a fly, whom Father, in his kindly way, had employed because he was on relief, saying that his mere presence might act as a scarecrow. But the poor old fellow had been arrested in the village on a morals charge, having approached a young man in a public washroom with an indecent suggestion. Father had appeared as a character witness for the unhappy defendant and persuaded the local magistrate to be as lenient as possible, but of course he had had to discharge him as a watchman.

I can never forget how Mother raised her clasped hands in a gesture of fervent gratitude to a benignant deity and exclaimed, "To think all these years we've been at the mercy of an armed pervert!"

Father simply chuckled at an emphasis so undue, but I was far from doing so.

My patient believed now that he was doomed to live chastely. Though his sins were as scarlet, they would be as white as snow. If, returning to school, he sometimes succumbed to the temptation to masturbate at night, he would attempt to lessen the black feelings of guilt that he knew would assail him afterward by fantasizing that he was making love to a girl. At Yale, where he matriculated after graduating from St. Luke's, he allowed himself what he hoped was the harmless pleasure of reading the works of Oscar Wilde, Walter Pater, and John Addington Symonds and seeing his own repressed idealization of a certain kind of love condoned.

In his summer vacations while he was an undergraduate, Marvin became interested in the daughter of Meadowview neighbors, a lively, good-tempered, dark-haired, wide-eyed girl called Barbara Shields. She loved fishing and hiking and riding to hounds with the local fox hunt; the latter sport was also a favorite of his. The other girls he had met at Long Island parties had by no means been indifferent to him. He was at least passably handsome, though shy with them; his manners were modest, at times even charming; his family, of course, was socially prominent. His mother indeed had found fit to warn him, although smilingly, to be careful about girls who might be "after his chips." But he didn't think Barbara was. She had none of the coyness, the affected shyness, the faintly feline glitter that he saw, or fancied he saw, in other girls of their opulent neighborhood. She was too much the outdoors sort for that, too much a good sport. He found himself at ease with her as he had never been with any member of her sex except for his sisters, who "didn't count." It only bothered him slightly when he heard from his sister Cynthia, the one closest to him, that people were beginning to speak of him and Barbara as a possible match.

The reason that such talk didn't frighten him more was that Barbara didn't appear to expect him to play the game of sex, which all young men and women seemed expected to play, whether they wanted to or not. It was like football at St. Luke's, a rigid sports requirement until a student's last year, when he could elect, braving a slight sneering, the alternative of tennis or squash. But to Barbara being pals seemed quite enough. No matter how frequently they saw each other, there was no talk of a more intimate relationship. They shared hikes and rides and books and swapped anecdotes, sometimes hilarious, at the expense of each other's family. Marvin began to enjoy his new reputation of having a "steady" girlfriend, and Barbara was highly approved of by his mother. He even began to entertain warmer thoughts about her; at night in bed he would imagine what it might be like to hold her naked in his arms, causing him to have erections of which he no longer had to be ashamed.

What happened next engendered a grave crisis in Marvin's life, and I turned on my recorder to catch his exact account of it.

It turned out, doctor, that Barbara's failure to initiate a sexual relationship with me sprang not from her inexperience in such matters but from a familiarity with them considerably more sophisticated than my own. She was taking her time and knew what she was doing. In 1939 there were a lot more virgins in our Long Island set than there would be today, nor was there any stigma to it. Indeed, rather the reverse. If a girl was "fast," she didn't brag about it. Which is why I didn't know that Barbara had had an affair with a married groom attached to the stables of our country club. But some mothers knew about it, and it had not made her more marriageable in the area. Barbara was twenty-three, a bit older than I, and her father's financial reverses in the Depression had made penniless matches, however romantic, less tempting. Oh, I don't mean that she was really mercenary, but her friends were all married or getting married, and she wanted to get away from her family and be on her own, and she liked me and liked to be with me, so why not? I was what is called a catch. And she knew she would be a good and loyal wife, which is indeed just what she has been—to Frank Cooper.

She had the acumen to understand that sexual timidity in a virginal young man was not necessarily fatal to his becoming an adequate, even forceful, lover. She also had the rarer sense, usually possessed only by older women, to know that gentleness was the way to handle such cases. We began to kiss on meeting and parting, at first cheek-to-cheek, then on the lips. Soon we were hugging and even necking. There was a children's playhouse on her family's estate, long disused, as she and her brothers were grown, and we sometimes met there. She at last dared to consent to lie naked in my arms on the couch if I agreed to remain dressed and would only stroke her. Startled but excited, I agreed.

I grasped her tightly as soon as she was bare, almost as if I were trying to cover her up to spare her the shame of her nudity, but when my hands glided over her soft back and buttocks, I felt a surge of ecstasy with a stiff erection. I started to pull down my pants, and then it happened. Far from urging me to desist, she cried, "Hurry! Hurry!" with a shrillness in her tone I had never heard before.

Of course, it was the urgency of her cry that revealed the full force of her expectation. She wanted it! How she wanted it! And wasn't it her right? But being her right made it, alas, my obligation. All my old doubts about my masculinity, plus the hideous fear that I was presuming to play a role I was not fit to play, rose up to throttle me. My erection was lost, shriveled beyond hope of revival, and I could only abjectly apologize.

Thinking back now, I can wonder what would have happened if Barbara had been able to laugh and pooh-pooh the whole thing, if she had got up with an air of insouciance and said, "Better luck next time." She certainly had the intelligence to know that that might have been the way to handle me, and she tried to act accordingly later. But then it was too late. At the time, the poor girl was so aflame with readiness that the frustration was actually physically painful, and she could not help bursting into tears. I was shattered.

Despite all her efforts, we were never the same again, and when she started seeing Frank Cooper, a handsome hulk of a man who had nothing like my money but who held down a big job at a big bank, I did not feel I had the right to interfere.

As I have pointed out, this was certainly a grave crisis in my patient's life. Had Barbara been able to make light of it immediately afterward, who knows what might have happened? The next time they might have tried it with him stripped and her clothed. It could have worked. The question Marvin was to put to me sarcastically when he became my patient—could I have turned him into the commuting husband with the wife in the station wagon—might conceivably have been answered in the affirmative. As a psychiatrist I have seen stranger things.

At any rate, the war intervened, and Marvin, as a naval officer on the staff of the admiral in command of the Eastern Sea Frontier—a position that his father, unknown to him, had wangled for him—spent four years at a desk at 90 Church Street in New York. He put in again and again for sea duty, but his work was good and the admiral wouldn't let him go, and Marvin suffered all the pangs of the noncombatant as his classmates departed for combat zones, some never to return.

His sense of isolation was rendered much worse by the loss of both his parents during the war, his father first of heart failure and his mother a year later, at only sixty, from ovarian cancer. Stationed in New York, he was at least able to be at her bedside at the end, which she faced with all the charm that had characterized her life.

"Dear child," she said, holding his hand in both of hers and shaking her head sadly at the sound of his sobs, "you must try not to grieve so hard. I've had a lovely life and done all the things I wanted to do, and I don't think I'm really missing too much in missing old age. Some women age wonderfully, but others become old crones. You wouldn't want your ma to be that, would you? But I worry about you, dear boy. Your sisters are all married and taken care of. You must promise me to try to find yourself a nice girl. Wherever I am, if I'm anywhere, I'll help her to watch over you."

Peace found Marvin rich but homeless and alone. Meadowview, devised not only to him but to his sisters, had been sold, at their insistence, and was now a golf club. He had wanted to keep it, but he had had to acknowledge that it would have been absurdly large as the residence of a single man who had no interest in entertaining or giving house parties. Besides, it was too evocative of his mother, whom he was going to have to learn to live without.

He had little idea what to do with the dreary gap of life that remained to him. He had finished one year of law school before being called into the navy, but he had found it a dry field, where words were used so differently from the romantic literature in which he reveled, and he had no desire to return to it. There was Wall Street, with its banks and financial houses with plenty of openings for one with his capital, but their sole purpose, so far as he could see, was to make money, and money he already had. His classmates were engaged in reconstructing marriages formed before the war or entering into new ones, but he continued to feel that his disastrous experience with Barbara foreclosed that solution to his loneliness. Would he end up as one of those perennial bachelors, the friend and confidant of both husbands and wives, the recipient of conjugal complaints, the constant single guest at holiday dinners, the godfather to a multitude of godchildren? Heaven forbid!

In the meantime, anyway, there was the narcotic of travel. Spending a year seeing the world might widen the area of possible careers to choose. Early in 1947 he flew to Italy, which he toured from Milan to Naples, ending in Florence, where he decided to remain for an indefinite number of months. He suggested to me that the presence there of Michelangelo's nude *David* and Cellini's *Perseus* and the cult in art of the unclad male, with an infinity of arrow-pierced Saint Sebastians, may have had something to do with his choice, but he insisted that this was not a conscious motivation at the time. He rented a studio apartment overlooking the Arno and set himself up as an amateur painter. It was at least an occupation that could explain his choice of temporary residence to his critical but loving and constantly inquiring sisters.

For his next crisis I return to my tape.

I went every night for a cocktail at the rectangular bar at the Hotel Excelsior, which was a favorite meeting place for many young American expatriates, including writers, painters, sculptors, and more or less disreputable idlers. A regular patron was Sylvester Seton, a former classmate of mine at both St. Luke's and Yale, whom I had never particularly liked but who, in a town full of strangers, struck me as an oasis of friendliness. Even his homely, sarcastically grinning, equine countenance was welcome after a long day of daubing and wandering the streets with a guidebook, and as he had been living in Florence since the war, he was easily able and willing to identify the various characters at the bar and acidly spell out for me the reasons, often scatological, that explained their preference for life in Italy over life at home. Sylvester, or "Silly," as he was inappropriately known, for the nickname hardly suited his agile mind and mordant wit, exhibited a sly but unsatisfied curiosity as to my motives for being in Florence. Obviously, he harbored lurid suspicions, but he was amusing and instructive, and I had no one else to play with, so to speak.

At Yale he had been considered something of a fairy or faggot—those were the terms we used—but as he was funny and genial and rigidly persistent in his flattering cultivation of the class leaders, and as he had no visible discreditable sexual attachments, he was accepted into the "in" circles, though never considered eligible for such "real" Eli honors as the sacred senior societies. But Silly was content to be a kind of court jester.

In Florence, except with visitors from home, he

made no pretense of concealing his sex life and lived quite openly with an Italian youth, who tactfully disappeared when a Seton relative or Yale classmate (other than myself) appeared in the Grand Hotel. His candor with me showed only too clearly that he suspected my inclinations, whether or not they happened to be repressed. "So long as you don't throw it in people's faces," he assured me, "it doesn't matter a hoot what they surmise or even know. Life can be a simple matter if you follow a few rules."

It fascinated me that he felt not the slightest twinge of guilt at his behavior. In his opinion, to have exposed his habits to the gaze of convention would have been like going to a black-tie dinner in a blazer and white flannels. I even wondered if he were not wicked. Yet I found myself seeking his company nightly at the Excelsior Bar and listening fervently to his racy tales of all that went on in Florence. Was he trying to convert me? Why? Was he playing Mephistopheles to my Faust? He had rather the appearance of a devil. Or did he simply want to set me free to enjoy myself, to express myself? Or did he want to tie me to him by a bond that would enable him to dip his hand into my pocket? For Silly, though possessed of a modest trust income, had been well known among his many rich friends at home for being a constant borrower and not a constant repayer. It had been his one flaw as a successful social climber.

At last, one night when he invited me for supper at his flat, which he rarely did, I usually being the host, I found there not only his Italian boyfriend but one of the latter's pals. He was a handsome olive-skinned youth of eighteen or nineteen called Tonio. We had a pleasant evening of much red wine and idle chatter—the boys were hardly intellectuals, and my Italian was still up to only simple expressions—but when I rose to take myself home, Silly took me aside and muttered, "Take Tonio with you. He's primed for anything. And be generous with the poor boy. He has to help support a mother and three younger sisters." He paused as he took in my gaping expression. 'Now look, Marvie. For once in your life don't be an ass. You're going to love it. Live it up, fella!"

Well, of course I did take Tonio to my studio, and he started me on the career that has brought me to this couch. For a brief time my life was ecstasy. Those Italian boys are nothing if not sophisticated in sexual relations with either sex, and even when they do it for money they can still derive pleasure from it, provided that their partner is not old or fat or otherwise repulsive, which makes them different from prostitutes in other climes. For weeks I lived in a feverish blaze of amorous activity, seeing Tonio every night. He was my John the Baptist in the realm of sin, and I gratefully bought him anything he wanted, including a Bugatti roadster, which made all the noise he loved and which infuriated Silly, who said I was ruining the market for others. I was happy, but it was the happiness of one living in a dream.

What awakened me, like the jarring clang of a strident alarm clock, was the visit to Florence of my favorite sister, Cynthia, only two years my senior, with her husband, Ernest Fowler. Cynthia had always been a spoiled but very special darling; she was pretty, sweet-tempered, affable, and always ready to see the best in everybody, even in a kid brother who refused to settle down in a regular job and showed distressing signs of becoming an expatriate. To say that her husband was clean-cut would be an understatement. Ernie was the epitome of what some people consider the Groton-Harvard type: cheerful, breezy, clad in gorgeous tweeds, manly, handsome, and oh-so-determined to be fair about the many things he inwardly but obviously disdained, including a wayward brother-in-law.

They both tried to be enthusiastic about my drab paintings of street scenes, dead fish, and bowls of fruit. Of course, I had put away the few sketches I had made of the nude Tonio—the only things I had done that actually showed even a scintilla of talent. Seeing my other things now through their eyes, I ruefully recognized that I would never be an artist of any note. They were not art critics, but still, it was enough.

I had an even worse time that night at dinner in a restaurant with the Fowlers and Silly, even if it was the best, or certainly the most expensive, café in Florence—trust Ernie for that. He and Cynthia had known Silly for years and liked him, and the three of them chattered away about the feasances and misfeasances of New York friends, but I was little inclined to join in. Silly, of course, knew just how to deal with them and just what sort of gossip they wanted to hear, and he avoided any reference to subjects dear to his and now to my heart, though his occasional double-entendres, accompanied by a sly glance in my direction, made me squirm. When he left us later with the excuse of having to attend the reception of a certain principessa—Silly's double life did not for a minute keep him from cultivating fashionable Florence—the three of us stayed on for a nightcap. Ernie in talking to me now allowed himself a longer rein.

"Silly's good company, even if he is a fag. *Chacun à son goût*, I suppose, even if it's not yours or mine. And I guess plenty of that sort of thing goes on here." He cast a dubious eye over the other tables in the room. "I daresay half the Yanks in town are given an allowance by their families on condition that they don't live at home. If you go to Silly's more private parties—the ones he doesn't ask principessas to—you'd better keep your back to the wall."

And despite his wife's reproachful "Oh, Ernie," he indulged in a coarse chuckle.

Something in me snapped. I mumbled a word about an early art lesson the next morning and took my leave. The moonless cloudy night perfectly fitted my state of mind as I walked slowly home. It seemed to me that I at last realized that the black gulf that yawned between my old life and my present one was going to be too wide for me to bridge. By every standard that I had learned from childhood, my Italian existence was a sordid failure. I had no real home, no real family, no job, not even a decent hobby, and my absorbing concern was what I was doing every night with a young man who could offer me nothing but that. If I would be a horror to my sisters if they knew, what would I have been to my mother? It was unthinkable!

In the weeks that followed, I sank into deep and deeper depression. I gave up seeing Tonio, writing him a check that was undoubtedly much too large but that utterly contented him. It was probably enough to allow him to marry the girlfriend of whose existence I had been faintly but uncomfortably aware. To avoid Silly and his importunate calls, I went to Siena and holed up in a hotel there. I had to recognize that I was in the grip of a major nervous breakdown.

My patient then came back to New York, escorted by the solicitous Sylvester Seton, who had embraced the occasion for this act of compassion to make a long-due visit to his old and ailing parents, charging the first-class air travel there and back to Marvin's account. It was through Cynthia Fowler that Marvin, staying in her apartment, came to seek my professional services. He was now willing to submit himself to a lengthy psychoanalysis.

He was with me twice a week, for one-hour sessions, for two years. He was an articulate and humble patient, even a charming one. I was perfectly clear from the start that my job would be to reconcile him to his homosexuality; he was far too deeply committed even to think of any alteration. My trouble—it sounds odd to say—lay in the fact that *intellectually* he saw nothing morally wrong with it. He was utterly free from popular or religious prejudice. With other patients, removing their intellectual doubts as to its morality can help, but he had no such hang-ups. His problem was that emo-tionally, deep, deep down, his inversion struck him as unpardonably wicked, even if he was in no way responsible for it. He was like an early Calvinist who believed that he might be damned through no fault of his own. God arbitrarily selected those who were to be saved and those who were not. Marvin's god, if that was his word for whatever force or demiurge created the universe, was entirely capable of saving Sylvester Seton and damning Marvin Daly for doing exactly the same thing. Heaven for him was Meadowview and Mother; hell was Florence and Tonio.

But we made progress. He managed to crawl out from under the thick, stifling blanket of his depression, to look around at the world again, to purchase a brownstone for his residence, and to adjust himself, more or less, to a prosperous bachelor's life in New York. He couldn't return to Italy while he was undergoing my treatment, and he spent some of his copious supply of spare time putting together quite a fine art collection, mostly of French eighteenth-century paintings: Lancret, Pater, van Loo, and Hubert Robert. They probably suggested to him, particularly the last named, some of the grace, the ease, the delightfulness that he associated with his idealized memory of Meadowview.

Nor did he feel required to live a chaste life, however sinful the alternative might be. I had at least liberated him from that. Through a friend of Silly's, he found himself invited to some all-male parties in Greenwich Village, and he engaged in a couple of discreet affairs. He could even be almost lighthearted about them. "You got the St. Luke's out of me, doctor," he told me laughingly once. "But after an operation as drastic as that, there was no question of my resuming a normal life. The best you could do was to sew me up and make me as comfortable as possible."

In the dozen years that elapsed between his release from my care and his premature demise, I saw him only infrequently, when he suffered sharp returns of agitation. I really believe that had he gone back to Italy and taken up permanent residence there he might have had a happier and certainly a more productive life. There his past would have been absent and his present peopled with a friendly acquaintance to whom the sexual habits of a rich American were a matter of total indifference. But in New York he found himself increasingly adopting a hermit's life rather than mingling with the world of his family and old school friends, who were occupied with businesses and children and clubs and sports in which he had no real part or interest, and from whom he felt compelled to hide tastes that at the very least would have invited their pitying disapproval. And it only made things worse that whenever he did run into one of them, he would be greeted enthusiastically with cries of "Marvin, where have you been? Why do we never see you? Come to dinner! Yes, anytime, do!"

What kept him there, when his analysis was finished, was the Korean youth he met at a Village party and with whom he became deeply involved. It was indeed the love affair of his life. He finally induced Hai Kwan to move into his brownstone, though he took care to set him up in a separate garden apartment so he would look like an ordinary tenant. He would gladly have taken him to Italy and lodged them both in a Venetian palazzo, but Kwan loved New York, where all his friends were, and Marvin at last gave him a gallery of his own, where he sold, with some success, Korean art.

Marvin had always dreaded Cynthia's finding out about his love life, but when she did—and it didn't take long before the peculiar position of Kwan in his household became known to her—it was almost worse than he had thought. Her easy handling of the situation showed the amused scorn beneath her seeming tolerance. "Put him in a white coat," she advised her brother. "And then nobody'll mind."

Even so, his life might have worked out had Kwan remained faithful to him. Marvin might have been able to give their relationship, even in his censorious heart, some of the dignity of a marriage, might even have seen it achieve a kind of acceptance in his old world. But Kwan liked boys, and as Marvin visibly aged, he had no idea of confining his nights to his patron. I should make it clear that Kwan was not a bad fellow at all—I met him a couple of times when Marvin asked me to his house. But however devoted he was to Marvin—and he never left him—he made it clear that both of them were free to form other intimacies. Their relationship became a platonic one; Kwan became Marvin's "family."

Which left Marvin to seek sexual gratification elsewhere, and he took eventually to the streets. The partners whom he found were not like their Italian counterparts; they were tougher and more mercenary and often didn't even pretend to enjoy what they were doing. As Marvin's life became more sordid, his compulsion to shield it from his old connections became even more obsessive. He was soon almost a complete recluse, and except when he appeared in art galleries or auction houses to add to his collection, he virtually disappeared from the world. His sexual preoccupation had come to encase his entire existence, as a skin cancer can cover a whole face.

The sense he must have felt of being mercilessly encircled by quixotically hostile gods who had picked him as their victim for no explicable reason may have been like the one expressed by Racine's tragic heroine in *Phèdre:*

> Wretch that I am, how can I live, how face
> The sacred sun, great elder of my race?
> My grandsire was, of all the gods, most high:
> My forebears fill the world and all the sky.
> Where can I hide? For Hades' night I yearn.
> No, there my father holds the dreadful urn.

He died in his fifties, an early victim of AIDS. His sister Cynthia, who was with him at the end, told me of his last grimly humorous mood. "Plenty of people regard this terrible disease as God's punishment of the wicked," he murmured to her. "Of course, it's no such thing. It's his judgment of me."

He finally recognized that his was a very special case. He was too intelligent not to. He saw that he had seen himself as the victim of a Calvinist god. Perhaps that was all that a Calvinist god was good for.

Lady Kate

I DON'T KNOW whether or not it's a national mood of nostalgia, brought on by this seemingly endless economic depression that started on that fatal October day of 1929 — now four years back — but my friend at the corner bookstore on Madison Avenue, who claims to know the literary tastes of old dowager ladies like myself, keeps sending me memoirs of the Mauve Decade, often written by persons I actually knew in that bygone era. Are readers today really interested in the idle doings of those obsessed hostesses, with their big pearls and big hats, their bigger villas and bigger parties? Oh, I know, I'm hardly one to talk. It's all very well for me to scoff at them now, but the glaring fact that I was an integral part of the whole silly game is flung in my face by the frequent appearance of my name in these very memoirs and the repeated likeness of myself in that celebrated photograph, crossing a lawn at a garden party in Newport, a thin maypole swathed in Irish lace with a long, plain face and a huge wide-brimmed black hat, "in full sail" as the phrase was, and accompanied by the short, dumpy figure of Mrs. Astor herself.

Yet can't I make out — or is it part of a desperate self-delusion? — that there is something in that tall figure which in part redeems it from the pomposity of that gaudy age? Isn't there a hint that the woman it represents is turning herself into a deliberate caricature of the opulent grande dame who constituted the logo of the era? Isn't my hat too grotesquely large, my laciness overdone, my hauteur too pronounced? Isn't the mocking laughter that I liked to think of as always bubbling out of me showing a bit of its froth? After all, no one who knew those times can deny that I was known and even feared for my sharp tongue and dry oral portraits and that I was even dubbed the enfant terrible of Newport. Or was that, too, an act? Was my whole life an act, and perhaps, after all, not a very good one?

I was certainly born for better things. My family was not nouveau riche, like the Vanderbilts and Goulds, but of old colonial stock. Our tree boasted eight passengers on the *Mayflower* and a signer, and my late lamented husband, Bayard Rives, was the son of a Rhode Island governor and the heir to a large textile fortune that had its respectable origin in New England mills long before the rise of the robber barons in railroads and steel. And before we inherited from his mother the grim old Rives "castle" that beetled over the sea in Newport by Fort Adams, we lived a more civilized life in Washington, where my husband occupied a minor but responsible position in the State Department and where we entertained at our lovely Greek Revival house in Georgetown such luminaries as the Henry Cabot Lodges, the John Hays, and Henry Adams himself. My portrait of those days, in which I am clad in a luscious gold evening gown, standing tall and haughty, presumably ready to receive distinguished guests, a fan clasped in one hand as if ready to strike the countenance of some unwarranted intruder, was considered one of the finest of Sargent's finest period and is now in the National Gallery.

And yet. Must I not admit that if I try to glean an interesting insight from my photograph on the Newport lawn, I can also spot a hint of the future dowager in the hostess of an intellectual salon depicted by Sargent? And I have to concede that Henry Adams, on first viewing the oil, exclaimed with a hoot of laughter, "Sargent has done it at last! He has immortalized the wife of the goldbug!" The goldbug, of course, was his term for the species of male who, in his constantly reiterated opinion, had begrimed American culture.

But I'm certainly not going to let the old cynic have the last word. He always professed to believe that women were the superior sex—in sensitivity and perceptiveness, anyway—and maintained that any astute observer would rather be ruled by Edith Roosevelt than Theodore and by Nanny Lodge than Cabot. He even went so far as to argue that the dullness of American history was accounted for by the scanty role it accorded to women, of which his own history of the administrations of Jefferson and Madison is dry proof. But what I should have asked him is, how could the American woman play any important part in the American dream if the American man slammed every important door in her face? In a country where the male devoted all his energy to business, from which the female was excluded except in degrading factory tasks or secretarial functions, what could the latter—at least the upper-class ones—do but grab hold of the one thing allowed them, which was, quite simply, the money? For the American male, unlike his sex the world over, was unique in caring more for the game than for its prize, more for the toil than for its profit. So long as he was allowed to spend his life in the office, his spouse could pretty well spend his dollars as she chose.

Which, of course, explains the phenomenon of Newport, not only the watering place in Rhode Island but its lesser counterparts across the nation. Alva Vanderbilt Belmont, a recreated Catherine de Médici, was only the most conspicuous of the lavish female builders who covered our seaboard with derivative European palaces, packed closely together so each could envy the glories of the others. Even I, on a more modest scale, when my husband's health forced his retirement from government and we moved to New York, erected a gray French Renaissance chateau on a long narrow plot running down East Seventy-ninth Street, pushing its slender front onto proud Fifth Avenue. Ignorant souls criticized me for employing in the city a style supposedly designed for large domains of landscaped fields and forests. Had they never seen the urban mansion that the bourgeois Jacques Coeur placed in the very heart of fifteenth-century Bourges?

"Society," as it then existed, was entirely the creation of women, and they clung to it, their one fief, with an understandable possessiveness, which is why they guarded it so fiercely from climbers, at least until those climbers had accepted their disciplines and code. The etiquette, the moral standards, the dress, the styles of living and entertaining were their exclusive prerogative, under rules rigidly enforced. The role of the husband and father was simply to pay. With Washington behind me and middle age reluctantly accepted, I looked about me for a new occupation and found only the social game sufficiently challenging. I didn't have anything like the fortune of the principal players, but I had enough to make a goodly show, and a show was all it was. My family offered no obstruction.

My only daughter, Ethel, who prided herself on the mo-

dernity of her views and was always quoting Veblen, scorned
such ambitions and had married a Stanford economics professor and moved to California, and my only son, Tim, a scholar,
had become a dedicated archeologist and spent his share of
the Rives fortune in distant digs. My husband, a quiet, gentle,
intellectual man who tolerated most things and admired few,
and who enjoyed frail health, simply smiled at my new project and told me, "Go to it, Kate! You have to work off some
of that excess energy of yours. I'll pay the bills as long as I can
and watch from the sidelines. But don't make me go to your
parties."

And indeed, after I had occupied and renovated the old
Rives castle in Newport, he spent most of our summers on
his yacht, resting his eyes on the eternal bobbing blue-gray of
the ocean and no doubt considering me a silly ass.

Newport, obviously, was my chosen battleground. Few
observers have understood it as did the French novelist Paul
Bourget, who in *Outre-Mer*, the account of his American
travels, pointed out that it was entirely dominated by formi-
dably respectable middle-aged or elderly females, the wives
or widows of largely absent husbands, who had rid the summer colony not only of bohemian artists and writers but of
anything remotely resembling a demimonde. The extra men
at their parties were a dressy bunch, more or less epicene, and
any husband who kept a secret mistress to entertain him on
his rare visits to Aquidneck Island dared not lodge her any
closer than Narragansett.

Mrs. Winthrop Chanler, in her memoirs *Roman Spring*,
related that the so-called four hundred would have fled in a
body from a poet, a painter, a musician, or a clever Frenchman, and she described well its organizer and acknowledged

leader, Mrs. Astor: "She always sat on the right of the host when she went out to dinner parties; she wore a black wig and a great many jewels; she had pleasant cordial manners and unaffectedly enjoyed her undisputed position."

Yet it was from the side of this great matron that I seduced the young or youngish man who became what he himself liked to term my major-domo and court jester. Beverly Dean, despite his long and rather messy blond hair, his mocking blue eyes, and his screeching laugh, might have struck an observer as a regular and even almost sturdy American youth had not his habit of overgesticulating and nervously twisting his shoulders and torso seemed to indicate that he was warning one against any overestimate of his masculinity and strength. He had wit and impudence and a species of charm, no known occupation or source of income or even family, and he was a fixture at every party. He was generally supposed to be trying to occupy in Mrs. Astor's court the place of her late guide and mentor, Ward McAllister.

The conversation that led to his brief reign over my equally brief social endeavors occurred after a dinner party at Alice Vanderbilt's Genovese palazzo, The Breakers, when he and I were sitting in a far corner of the vast marble hall to which we had retreated so that we might chat without disturbing those guests who were listening to a rather mediocre string quartet.

"Our hosts have certainly made the grade," I commented drily, glancing toward the crowded and respectfully listening audience in the parlor. "But then there is really no resisting the Vanderbilts. Such a numerous clan, and each member richer than the one before. And actually quite amiable, too. And handsome, unlike the Astors, who are so plain. Yesterday there was no knowing them, and today you can hardly tell a Vanderbilt from a Van Rensselaer. But where, after all, have they got to? Now they're as dull as the rest of us."

"Nobody had called *you* dull, dear lady."

"Not to my face, anyway, and God knows, you're all welcome to my back. But what in the name of Lars Porsena and his nine gods have we or the Vanderbilts gained, my dear Beverly, by housing ourselves in the borrowed glory of the Italian Renaissance? Think of what the marble walls of a palazzo like this would have witnessed in the days of the Borgias! Murder and poison, no doubt, but also passion and great art! And what do they see today but a bunch of over-dressed old women lost in a snowstorm of cards, both playing and calling?"

"Write up that onslaught, will you please? It should make your name in belles lettres." And he crushed my incipient retort with his high cackle of a laugh.

"But seriously, Bev, what is it that gives Newport its peculiar deadness? For some of the architecture is not so bad, really, and the air and sea are delightful. Not to mention the matchless gardens. Why do I want to scream?"

Beverly resorted to his favorite nickname for me. "It's just your good taste, Lady Kate. You see the summer colony as a farce. It has nothing to do with what is really going on in America. Tiaras and porte-cochères. Emblems of royalty. It's a court without a sovereign, a religion without a deity, a ritual without a cause. At fancy dress balls how do the guests dress up? As kings and queens! As Mary Stuart and Marie Antoinette!"

"You mean they lose their heads?"

"But not their headdresses."

"Yet isn't that the way with fancy dress the world over? You remember all those pictures of the British peerage at the famous Devonshire Ball? They all came that way."

"True. For the Brits suffer from the same disease. Their lords and ladies try to kid themselves into believing they have some of their old power left by strutting about a ballroom in the glad rags of the glorious dead. Except they still have a monarch and an upper house to give them a kind of sham glitter."

I was struck by the comparison. "But if you see it so clearly, my friend, why do you spend your life in it?"

"A good question. But I didn't always see it so clearly. It's only recently that I have become bright-eyed. And that is why I have cultivated *you*, dear lady. You thought it was *you* who found the apple in Eden. But it was I who put it there, right under your keen and curious nose."

As a matter of fact, I had half suspected this. His many crossings of my social path could not have been entirely accidental. "And what was your purpose in attaching yourself to a woman almost old enough to be your mother?"

"Oh, quite old enough to be my mother!" he retorted with another outrageous laugh. "I was looking for a woman who had the brains, the imagination, the genealogy, the wit, and the coin to turn Newport on its heel. And if she could turn Newport, wouldn't she turn the hundred lesser Newports across the nation that devour our social doings in the evening press?"

"And you found such a woman in me?"

"I did. And you had another virtue as well. You were a rebel. I gleaned that from the famous photograph showing you and Mrs. Astor at a garden party. The great Caroline is plodding ahead with the placid conviction of a dedicated princess performing her function at some idle ceremony, while you, with that tall lean lacey figure, are bending down, probably to murmur some heresy in an ear that will never understand it."

That was where he had me. Knowing that I wanted something different. Knowing that I hated to be classified with the group I was killing myself to lead.

"It's keen of you to have spotted that," I admitted after a thoughtful pause.

"Well, Falstaff said he was the cause of wit in other men. You're the cause of it in me, Lady Kate. We could be a great team. The parties we could throw would set the colony on its ear."

"And how would you dispose of Mrs. Astor in all of this? Hasn't she a first claim on you?"

"The great Caroline would have to give up her place. Her sun, anyway, is setting."

"Isn't that rather disloyal? Like those little brown creatures that have such an aversion to leaky vessels?"

"Not if it's a case of *sauve qui peut*, We have lived in the last days of great queens. Victoria and Tzu Hsi. It is only realistic to turn one's gaze to the future."

→►◄←

Thus my famous summer partnership with Beverly Dean began. He was constantly at the "castle," ever at my side, escorting me to parties almost as if we were a recognizably united couple. But like what? A dowager sovereign with her minion? Or the old British queen with her gillie, John Brown? Or even Elizabeth and Essex? I didn't give a hoot how people saw us; I was amused, and that was enough for me. He organized and gave life to my entertainments, and it is not too much to claim that, between us, we altered irretrievably the revels of the summer colony.

To start with, we reduced the time spent at the dinner table from three hours to one. We instituted parlor games and elaborate charades with dazzling costumes. We abandoned place cards and adopted Thomas Jefferson's rule of pell-mell. We played tricks on our friends, picking certain guests in advance of a party to dress as maids or footmen, to prove that people never really look at servants. We organized tableaux vivants in which some of our prettier young people appeared almost (but not quite) scandalously unclad. I gave a party for an "unknown Russian grand duke" and introduced a chimpanzee in full regalia. At the dinner table, Beverly would sometimes scream for silence and call on people to confess their most shocking secret, with uproarious results. And sometimes, aloof and exhausted, I would retire with a chosen few to my bedroom suite to sip champagne and tear our other guests apart.

Of course, there were reactions. Mrs. Astor, piqued by Beverly's desertion, let her opinion be known that we were fatally lowering the tone of society, that we were undermining the orderly hierarchy that she and Ward McAllister had been at such pains to rear. I was denounced as a female Attila, scoffing at the ruins of the noble Roman temple I had blown apart. It was all great fun, and as my cynical husband observed on one of his rare visits, using a marine term, perhaps it was the sanitary hosing of a greasy deck.

Beverly had now become one of the principal figures of the Newport social scene; his blazers and cravats were louder and louder, and his high chortle could be heard up and down Bailey's Beach at noon when he visited the cabanas of his adoring women friends. His jokes and gibes waxed freer and freer, and though he continued to amuse me, there were moments when I wondered if I were not going to have to caution him to treat me with more reserve. It was all very well for him to call me his adopted mother, but his behavior at times bordered on the too impudently filial, or even resembled the impatience of an aging heir apparent enviously eyeing the crown of a too-long-surviving monarch.

I never knew what he lived on, though it was bruited about that he received commissions from the caterers in town whom he recommended, but I didn't like it when he began seeking loans from me. Twice I supplied him with moderate sums, but on a third occasion, when the amount requested was considerable, I suggested an alternative.

"Why don't you marry? I can think of at least three widows who would jump at the chance. And you wouldn't have to perform any prodigies of romantic passion, either. They'd settle for a black or white tie to escort them to parties."

"Lady Kate, you're wonderful! You know what's on a man's mind before he even tells you."

"A man? You wouldn't even have to be that. Though I don't doubt you could take care of any appetites that you aroused. No matter how tough the old bird." Beverly, of course, was widely supposed to be homosexual, a matter of small concern in society, but I rather imagined that he could handle either sex—if it was to his advantage to do so.

"What would you say, Lady Kate, if I told you I had already cast my eye on a *princesse du sang*? Of your *sang*, too. Can a cat be so bold? Can even a kitten?"

"A princess? Here in Newport? I thought we allowed only princes and that we kept them for our richest virgins."

"I don't mean a European one. I mean a Yankee princess closely allied to my queen. Your charming cousin Adelaide."

So he was ahead of me! He already had his candidate. I didn't know why, but I didn't quite like it. Adelaide Welldon, fair, fat, and forty, was the widow of a wealthy steel heir who had died of alcoholism. She was the daughter of a first cousin of mine, and although dull and a bit on the silly side, I had included her in my larger gatherings because she was kin and amiable and flattered me.

"You'd be calling me Cousin Kate, I suppose," was my rather dry comment, after a moment's silence.

"That, of course, would be one of the principal motives for the match!"

"Hmph. Would you be kind to her?"

"Kind to Adelaide? Why, I'd adore her!"

"She might prefer to be loved."

"Never fear. Our attachment is quite mutual."

"Oh, you've found that out? You've asked her?"

"I have been so bold."

I viewed him skeptically. "You couldn't hold yourself back, I take it. Passion overwhelmed you? Then where do I come in?"

Beverly's features assumed what seemed almost a businesslike expression. "She won't marry me without your blessing."

"That's a condition?"

"She says it's an absolute one. I take it, dear lady, you won't let me down?"

I was about to give him the nod, but some impulse made me pause. "I'll talk to her," was all I could promise.

Adelaide came to me that very afternoon. She seemed divided between a palpitating self-satisfaction and a dread that I would laugh at her. Her round, bland, fair countenance was puckered with agitation, and she kept clasping and unclasping her hands until I told her flatly to stop.

"Of course, I know that my money is something of an inducement," she said defensively.

"Well, of course. He couldn't marry at all without that."

"But I think he also cares for me. Somewhat, anyway." Her eyes were suddenly alarmed, almost beseeching. "He has a heart, hasn't he, Cousin Kate? You must know!"

"We all have hearts, surely, Adelaide."

"And he wouldn't say he loved me if he didn't, would he? If he didn't at all, I mean?"

"My dear, I'm sure he's very fond of you. Who wouldn't be? But you don't want me to tell you he's Romeo, do you? We're not in Verona, after all. This is Newport!"

"Oh, I know! Which is why I've come to you. Because you know us all so well. Of course, I'd be happy to be able to buy all the things for poor Beverly that he needs. And I do love him, Cousin Kate, I really do! And although I don't expect him to be a Romeo, I don't want to have what they call . . . or what the French call . . . what is it?"

"A *mariage blanc*?"

"Yes, that's it! It wouldn't be that, would it?"

"My dear, what a question to put to me! You're not asking what *my* relations with Beverly have been, are you?"

Adelaide's face was at once drawn with horror. "Oh, my goodness, no! However could you ask? Oh, Cousin Kate, what you must think of me!"

"Well, you needn't take it so for granted that I'm as neuter as an old rock," I retorted. And then I stopped. Perhaps it was just what I was! But I knew, as clearly and vividly as if I saw Adelaide stretched, absurdly and expectantly, on the nuptial bed, her hair tied in pink ribbons, her too ample white flesh tingling, that she would never be the bride she dreamed of being. Any performance on Beverly's part would be, at best, perfunctory.

We were sitting on the veranda, and I turned my eyes now to the sea and the racing sailboats, white specks on the gray-blue. Adelaide watched me anxiously.

"What is it, Cousin Kate? What are you thinking of?"

"Oh, nothing in particular." I closed my eyes for a moment. Why should I make a fool of myself? Why should I deprive this foolish creature of a husband with whom, after the mild initial disappointment of a fumbling wedding night, she would settle down to a life of laughs and trips and parties? Wouldn't Beverly brighten up an existence stifled in a widow's dreary routine? I was taking her too seriously, Beverly too seriously, and myself too seriously. He and Adelaide would be a perfect case of symbiosis. Maybe even God had planned it that way.

"Don't worry about the bed side of things, my dear. Beverly's a man, and men can do anything. I'm told they even like it!"

Adelaide laughed and hugged me so tightly that I had to push her off. She even made me give her away at the wedding.

→>-<←

The honeymoon lasted only a week, for Beverly had promised to return for a bachelors' dinner given for one of Newport's rare old bucks who was getting married at last at age fifty. What was very odd was that neither Beverly nor his bride saw fit on their return to call on me or even to drop a card. Such a pointed omission could have only a serious reason, and I waited, with some curiosity and even a mild apprehension, to learn what it was.

My explanation came one day at noon when I was seated alone in my cabana at Bailey's Beach with a novel that was hardly amusing enough to distract me from gazing at the sea and the bathers. It was generally known that I did not welcome visitors at this time; Newport was accustomed to my matutinal grumpiness, and I was a bit surprised when Adelaide, fully dressed for some luncheon party, with no concessions to the sea or open air, asked if she could join me for a chat. "Chat" was the word she incongruously used, though her tense, set, flat, stupid face boded no such trivia.

"It's not my chatting time," I answered gruffly. "But you're welcome to a seat if you need a rest."

Adelaide plumped herself down on a stool and was silent for a long moment. At length she spoke up. "You may have wondered, Cousin Kate, why I have not called on you before."

"When I start wondering, my dear, you may say I'm wandering."

"And why," she pursued, ignoring my comment, "Beverly has not consulted you on your end-of-season ball."

"There's plenty of time for that. And I'm not even sure I'm going to give one."

"That's just as well, then. For my husband says he's not going to have any part in it. He says that the time for the kind of party you and he gave is past. That the job of breaking up the old ways has been done, and it's now up to him to create a more serious and stable society."

"Fancy! And one, I take it, in which I'm to have no part? The old nag is turned out to pasture?"

"Well, he didn't put it quite so crudely."

"Adelaide," I said severely, "you came here to say something even more disagreeable than that. Well, say it!"

I was interested at last. The woman, for once, was almost interesting. She had some spirit, or at least spite, in her, after all.

"It's this, then. You sacrificed me to a man you thought was your protégé. Your property. Well, now he's going to sacrifice you for me! He's going to make *me* the Mrs. Kate Rives of Newport!"

"Well, well!" I let my novel drop to the ground. "This beats fiction any day. How have I sacrificed you? To what strange deity have I offered so untempting a morsel?"

"To the god of your own pleasure!" Adelaide's face had turned a bright pink. "You knew what awaited me. Do you want to hear what happened on my wedding night?"

"Avidly."

"I'm sure you do. It was all that your jaded, decadent curiosity could have asked. My husband of a few hours made it very clear to me that he had no interest in me physically, that he offered me instead what he termed a 'congenial partnership' which would take us both to the top of the social ladder."

"Wasn't that more or less what you might have expected? Wasn't it what Newport rather took for granted?"

"I expected the partnership, yes, but I expected more. Because you had assured me there would be more. That I was marrying a man! And you *knew* he wasn't! You knew all about him!"

"What makes you think that?"

"Because you reek of such things! Do you deny it?"

I paused a moment. "No," I said at last. "Because any way you take him, he's good enough for you. You were nobody, and now you'll be somebody. Unless you're a complete fool, you'll learn to enjoy it."

"I'm going to try, anyway. And half my fun will be knowing that I'm undoing half the stupid things you made Beverly do."

"Oh, get out of here. I want to read my book."

By the time I had picked it up, she was gone. I had little compunction about her. No, my disgust was all with myself, for having so long put up with such a little rat as Beverly Dean, whose only ambition had been to replace Mrs. Astor with me and me with himself. Of course, he had no loyalties; the women he betrayed were only fantasies of himself. I had no doubt that he pictured himself, in his mind's eye, as a despotic hostess, dazzling in diamonds and ruling a world turned court. Adelaide would be his bank, not his hostess. And he would never leave her, as he would never find a richer or more compliant wife. He would grow fat and shrill, autocratic and occasionally obscene, with bigger and bigger jeweled cufflinks and studs, and when the social world ultimately tired of him, as they tired of every new favorite, he would become bitter and misanthropic, and Adelaide would have her ultimate revenge by supporting him in his lonely luxury and ignoring his sour complaints.

That night, at home, I was glad when my husband arrived for one of his rare Newport weekends. He listened politely, over a bottle of the finest Burgundy, while I voiced my grim little tale.

"Well, my dear, you have had the dubious privilege of presiding over the decline and fall of Newport society. But do not think you can be a Gibbon. If its golden age was a fiction, so will be its twilight. It really is hardly worth recording."

"But couldn't you say that of any period of history?"

"Perhaps. But if history, as has been said, is only biography, your Beverly is at best only a small footnote."

Which is what this memorandum is. Later that year we turned the Rives castle into an orphanage and took a cruise around the world.

The Attributions

When Mrs. Winthrop Chanler paid her last visit to my little *pavillon* in the Forest of Fontainbleau in the early 1950s, she had already passed her eightieth birthday and was the last survivor of what I like to think of as the galaxy of the American Renaissance. She had been dubbed by Henry James the most intellectual American woman (or had he said the only intellectual?); she had sat with Henry Adams under the blue brilliance of the windows of Chartres; she had motored in Italy and in Spain with Edith Wharton. As a girl, she had played the piano by listening to Liszt; as an equestrian, she had studied *manège* in Vienna. Tall and serene, she had gazed down the little green slope that unrolled from my terrace through geometrical garden plots to the *pièce d'eau* in the middle distance and asked me, "Tell me one thing, Leonardo Luchesi. What have you done to deserve so much beauty in your life? Have you sold you soul to the devil?"

"Not quite. I may have mortgaged it. Let us hope that I shall have paid it off before my time comes."

Have I? I'm afraid not quite. But I wasn't going to tell Mrs. Chanler that. She wouldn't have understood. Or should I say, she wouldn't have sympathized, for she understood many things. My point is that she had never encountered poverty or need. Her galaxy may have been, in my opinion anyway, the finest group that the culture of the New World has ever produced, but they were still a small, privileged, and even snobbish circle. If *they* had sold their souls for beauty, the bargain was well hidden. At least there was no trace of it. The same could not be said of mine.

I thought that day of baring my mortgaged soul to Mrs. Chanler, but I repressed the impulse. She would have been a wonderful listener, but I was not to forget that she had been raised by American expatriates in the Rome of Pio Nono and was the most devout of Catholics. Was there anyone who would see me quite as honestly as I saw myself? Not now. Since Mrs. Leila Warren is dead, and her personality lost in the glitter of the great art collection that I helped her put together, I can address these thoughts only to her shade.

→>—<←

I was born in Apulia, in the lower part of the Italian boot, in the poorest section of what was then a very poor peninsula, in the 1880s, in the coastal town of Trani. The book *Christ Stopped at Eboli* was later to describe vividly the dark poverty of that area, but I still cherish the mildly compensating memory that we had of the glory of the Adriatic at our doorstep. As a boy, lonely and dreamy and uncongenial with my clamorous siblings and schoolmates, I used to take long walks down the beaches and ponder what marvels might lie across the sea. My particular musing spot was by the plain bare Gothic church, standing by itself away from stores and habitations, on the very edge of the shoreline, like some great stranded wreck raising its lofty campanile over the long sands and the infinite stretch of blue water. There, with the ever circling, squawking gulls, I had beauty to myself as a solace.

A solace for everything. It was there that I resolved that if I could have beauty in my life, I should have all that I needed.

My father, Antonio Luchesi, who as a bartender made a bare living for a large family, had an older brother who had emigrated to New York and achieved there a degree of economic independence as a tailor. He had married but had had no children, and as his wife was no longer of an age to have any, he offered to take one of his nephews as an apprentice and possible heir. My parents, relieved to be freed of at least one of their demanding brood, picked me as the one who was brightest at school and the most likely to learn a new tongue and new ways, and also as the child least likely to adapt to the rough-and-tumble of Italian village life, and so at age fifteen I was duly dispatched to the New World. I was not to return to my native land until I was equipped to deal with it as a source of art rather than the home of misery.

My uncle was a kindly but stolid and wholly unimaginative man who saw in me an able enough assistant and a docile schoolboy, but who hardly conceived that I would need anything beyond an elementary education to be a good tailor. It is to my dear aunt that I owe everything. She had all an Italian woman's longing for motherhood, and she clasped me to her bosom as her adopted son. It was she who persuaded my uncle, with much difficulty, to hand over enough cash to supplement the meager scholarship I had won at a city college, on the theory that a more literate tailor would attract a classier clientele. And of course she knew, as my constant confidante, that my only passion was for art and that I had chosen all the courses that bore on it and was reading every book on the subject I could get my hands on. My uncle never asked me about my classes or my reading—the university was a closed book to him—and when, graduating at twenty, I had to tell him that I was seeking a job in an art gallery, he exploded in wrath, called me an ungrateful scoundrel, and kicked me out of his home. Never mind. My faithful aunt had her own savings and helped me until I was able to take care of myself. I am happy to say that I was able ultimately to repay her many times over, and in his old age I made things up with my uncle. A good Italian will always forgive success.

On my early years I need not dwell. At first I performed every kind of task for a Chelsea dealer in pictures, bric-a-brac, and antique furniture. I swept the shop and cleaned it; I acted as a packer, later as a salesman and buyer, and eventually, with my aunt's financial backing, as a very junior partner. I read and studied at night; I explored other galleries on weekends and visited every museum in town; I was a totally dedicated student and never married. I moved in the course of time to other and much more important shops, and I began to acquire clients who retained me to find them beautiful things. I always had faith in my star, and I was sure that I would at last encounter what I thought of as the ultimate collector.

When I met Erastus Dunlop, I believed for some years that it was he. I met him at an exhibition of the paintings of a deceased collector, which were about to be offered for auction at Parke-Bernet. A gallery employee had respectfully pushed up a chair before a painting that the great collector wished to study at his leisure, and the stout, stocky, impressive magnate was silently contemplating it as he smoked a cigar. I took my stand beside him and watched his profile intently.

The painting might have been by Gérôme or Delaroche; it was one of those academic historical scenes painted with vivid colors and painstaking realism to tell, of course, a dramatic story. Stretched on cushions spread over the floor in a dark, richly paneled chamber is the gaunt gray figure of the aged and dying Queen Elizabeth, whose haggard eyes and gaping mouth show that she is desperately trying to communicate something to the young Robert Cecil kneeling assiduously at her side. Standing behind these two figures is a small group of elaborately dressed courtiers, contemplating the grave event in silent awe. One could imagine Cecil uttering his famous plea, "Your Majesty *must* go to bed," and her haughty reply: "Little man, little man, the word *must* is not used to princes."

At length Dunlop turned to me, whom he didn't know from Adam, as if he took for granted that anyone standing so close to him was on his staff, or ought to be, and asked gruffly, "What do you think of it?"

"I don't think. I react. It's melodrama, isn't it?"

"Is it? Why do modern critics say this sort of thing isn't art? It states precisely what the artist wants to state, doesn't it? Could it possibly be clearer or more accurately shown? Of course, I'm not going to buy it, because collectors, the real ones, anyway, don't buy this sort of thing anymore. But can you put it in a few plain words just why that is so?"

"Because it's not a painting. It's a play. Or a scene from a play, at least. It refers to something you've read about. It reminds you of something. Its effect, so to speak, is through your mind and memory, not your eye. A true painting should be an ocular experience."

"It can't ever tell a story?"

"Well, it can, but that's not the point of it. Not the real point, anyway. The real point is to excite emotions that may have little to do with thinking."

"Like music."

"Very like music."

"But what about all those Italian Renaissance paintings that illustrate stories from the Bible? You're not going to junk Leonardo and Raphael, are you?"

"Far from it. They had to bow to church demands if they were going to sell anything. But it was not the subject matter that was important; it was what they managed to do with it. In a Saint Sebastian you see more than a saint stuck with arrows—you see a glorious study of the nude."

The great collector nodded as he turned back to the canvas before him. "But you'll admit this is well painted."

"Certainly. Indeed, it's so well painted that you can see that the models were all contemporaries of the artist arrayed in fancy dress. They're no more Elizabethan courtiers than I am. He has faithfully delineated exactly what he saw before him. It might as well be a color photograph. But it's not art."

Dunlop grunted and rose. "Let me take you to lunch. What's your name, anyway? Who are you?"

And so that chapter of my life began. Erastus Dunlop was an unusual type of American tycoon, though not as unusual as he thought he was. He liked to point out that he had started life on a higher social level than most of his contemporary magnates—he had been a successful lawyer from an upper-middle-class Cleveland family—but the bulk of his fortune, like that of so many others, had been the fruit of good luck. He and his law partner had quit their practice to drill successfully for oil on a tract of western land deeded to them by a cash-poor client for a fee, and in selling the tract to a giant monopoly and taking stock for the purchase price they had multiplied their original investment many times over. It was also true that, although Dunlop prided himself on having a shrewd collector's eye in amassing the great art now in his Cleveland gallery, he brushed over the early years before he sought professional advice and had filled his mansion with Burne-Jones, Bouguereau, and Boldini.

He was a big, craggy, fierce-eyed man who liked to dominate and impress dealers when they brought their wares to his office, where Dunlop, seated below a Pontormo portrait of a grim-looking condottiere, would glare at them. Yet he could be as quiet as a cat, and as stealthy. He reminded me of an old repertory ham who would play Shylock one night and Hamlet the next. Always acting. What was he hiding? Perhaps the fact that he was fundamentally something of a son of a bitch.

I do not mean to minimize him. Some of those tycoon collectors *did* have sharp eyes for art, or at least they managed to develop them. Nothing teaches a man who is not a fool (and whatever these tycoons were, they were not that) like the discovery that he has just spent a fortune buying a fake. Dunlop in collecting soon learned to rely on professional experts. But never entirely. He made constant use of his own tastes, and one can certainly pick this up in his fondness for the lavish and spectacular in royal portraits, interiors, palaces, and pageants. His inner vision of himself as a collector must have been closer to Lorenzo il Magnifico than to a shareholder of Standard Oil.

Like many able financiers he made up his mind quickly, and it was not long after he had invited me to inspect and evaluate the art he had amassed that he hired me as a regular consultant. It proved a giant step in my career and led directly to my establishing an international reputation as an art connoisseur. I had become Dunlop's regular companion on his foreign excursions in search of new treasure.

I can see now that the first crack in our unity came in Constantinople, where we were examining the recently excavated sacramental vessels of a fifth-century Christian church. I did not, however, recognize it at the time. We were seated in the dark back parlor of a famous Turkish dealer while he brought out the pieces one by one, placing them, silently and almost reverently, on the velvet-covered stand before us: the golden reliquaries, patens, and communion cups of that early Christian service. But what particularly dazzled my eyes was his final offering: a set of huge silver plates on which were enchased scenes of the battle between David and Goliath. It was the finest and most impressive silver work I had yet seen of the Byzantine Empire.

If it *was* of the Byzantine Empire. Dunlop suddenly turned to the dealer and asked him, with his customary gruffness, to please leave the room. "I wish to talk to Mr. Luchesi alone," he deigned to explain. When the dealer had promptly vanished, he explained to me that a servant at the hotel where we were staying had tipped him off that the David plates were modern work introduced into the treasure by the crooked dealer.

"Take me to the man who made them," I promptly exclaimed, "and I'll buy everything he's got!"

"Even if they're fakes?"

"Why are they fakes? There they are, right in front of you, in all their beauty! *They* are not saying what they are or aren't."

"You think I should buy them? *Knowing* I'm being hoodwinked!"

"How can you be hoodwinked when you know exactly what you're buying? You're buying *those* plates."

Well, my client did buy them, and they turned out to be a genuine part of the early treasure, and to this day they are proudly exhibited in the Dunlop gallery. The hotel servant was found to have been working for a rival dealer who hoped to destroy his competitor's credit. But unbeknown to me, Dunlop's faith in his consultant had been seriously undermined by this exhibition of a preference for beauty over provenance. Had the plates been modern work, their value would have been a small fraction of what it is today.

My break with the great man came only a year later and was caused by his having relied on my attribution to Jean-Marc Nattier of a portrait he had purchased of a daughter of Louis XV. The picture, perfect in every respect, was a smaller version of one hanging in the Salle des Madames in Versailles, representing Madame Infante, as she was known after marrying an infante of Spain, *en costume de chasse*. Trouble came when a French scholar and the greatest authority on Nattier let it be known that there was no record of Nattier's having ever done a replica of any of his portraits of the royal family other than that of the queen, and that Dunlop's painting was presumably the work of one of the four painters who worked for Nattier in the royal atelier.

"Well, if it's not by Nattier, it's by a better painter!" was my indignant response when my client confronted me with this new evidence. "You've got a perfect thing. Shouldn't that be enough?"

Dunlop smiled. I had already learned that when he smiled, he was at his most ominous. "That doesn't alter the fact that I've spent a considerable sum on a picture I now couldn't even give away," he said softly.

"How can anyone assert it wasn't painted by Nattier?" I

demanded hotly. "It came out of his atelier. He and his assistants presumably used the same materials. If the king of Spain had asked for a copy, do you think Nattier wouldn't have done it himself? And your lady, Mr. Dunlop, was the king of Spain's daughter-in-law!"

But it did me no good. Erastus Dunlop allowed a man not even one mistake. He never used my services again, but as he didn't want people to know he had ever been misled, he never mentioned the matter, and though it became known that I no longer worked for him, the damage was contained. I even implied to other clients that our difference had sprung from my disapproval of some of his later purchases, which brought me the sympathy of the Warrens, who had feuded with Dunlop over a painting they felt he had unfairly grabbed from under their very eyes, and the Warrens became a far bigger presence in my life than Dunlop had ever been.

What had a profound effect on me was my realization, engendered by the Nattier crisis, that art collecting by the rich was often simply an amusing way of reinvesting and even substantially increasing their wealth, a diversion that also paid off in dividends of public recognition, highly gratifying to egos which had not been small to begin with. Being known as the owner of a Leonardo or a Raphael might entitle one to a patch of the painter's fame. And mightn't one steal a leg of their immortality by giving a specimen of their work to a public institution, or better yet, to a museum like the Frick or the Morgan or the Guggenheim named for oneself? At any rate, it seemed to me that I had some right to a private moral code of my own, where the only criterion was the beauty of the object in question and not of where or how or by whom or for whom it had been made.

It was in Paris, where I now established my principal residence, that I had my first contact with Hank and Leila Warren. They were originally from Troy, New York, but they had moved to Manhattan and had purchased a mansion on Fifth Avenue, primarily as the repository for a growing art collection and which would, after their deaths, be converted into a museum. They already, when we met, had the beginnings of a distinguished accumulation, and they had come to Paris en route to Spain, where they hoped to snag a first-rate El Greco. As I had already obtained a wonderful repenting and weeping Magdalene for a Baltimore collector, they wished me to accompany them on their Iberian expedition, which I was glad to do.

They struck me from the start as an oddly mismatched couple, yet their mutual tolerance and understanding was clearly evident. She was small and dark, with rich raven-black hair and a pale face of rather pinched features that might have once been briefly pretty. She rarely smiled, and one was slightly uncomfortably aware of the rather grim sobriety of her countenance and the acerbic intelligence betrayed by her carefully chosen remarks. Yet I soon had reason to feel the reassuring grasp of her strong willpower and the intense emotions that she kept chained up like a watchdog. If she was on your side, it was great. He, in contrast, was big, bland, cheerfully effervescent, expansively and expensively clad, redolent of big gold chains, rings and the finest cigars. His rumbling laugh could also be the crater of bursts of temper that made all but his wife quail. If she took the lead when it came to buying art, it was he who paid, and he was very much the American tycoon in his insistence on getting his money's worth—every penny of it.

How had they met? Well, they hadn't. They had grown up together as first cousins. Their fathers had been brothers and partners in a prosperous western mining operation; each had been an only child, and their ultimate union had guaranteed the continuing solidity of the family business. Indeed, from what I could make out, they had taken for granted from childhood that they were destined to wed, a fate apparently entirely acceptable to each. Had they always been in love with each other? Had they ever been? Who knew? They never quarreled, and they were always together. They had one child, a daughter, long married and independent, with whom they seemed on good but not intimate terms. Someone told me that she was a dull but amiable ass, wed to a dull but faithful spouse; her parents had settled a fortune on her, and that was that. The rest could go to art. Leila's share might be equal to Hank's, but he had legal control of the whole.

The painting they were after was owned by a grandee in Burgos, and to Burgos the Warrens and I now directed our steps. It hung in the dark and decayed parlor of a dark and decayed palace, where its owner, obviously anxious to make a great sale, left the three of us alone to study it.

It was another version of the *Martyrdom of Saint Maurice*, of which the best-known hangs in the Escorial, even though Philip II had not cared for the artist or his work. El Greco, of course, had a custom of doing different studies of the same subject; there are several *Saint Jerome*s, *Cleansing of the Temple*s, and *Agony in the Garden*s. In the picture before us the saint, in the regalia of a Roman officer, is depicted as engaged in a serious discussion with his presumably accusing fellow officers. In the background we see the two scenes that will follow his condemnation for his Christian faith: his exposure, stripped of all clothing, before the legion and his beheading. The striking thing about the painting is that the officers engaged in the discussion with the saint do not appear in the least vindictive; one can only suppose that they are trying earnestly to induce their friend to abandon his religion and avoid the penalty that they are otherwise bound to inflict on him. And the saint seems touched that they should care and genuinely sorry that he cannot oblige them.

At dinner at a restaurant that night the Warrens and I had a long discussion about the painting and then about the artist. Leila did not for a minute believe that he had been a devout Catholic.

"You have to remember that all his life, wherever he was, he was an alien. In Crete he may have been a native Greek, but the island was ruled by Venice. And when he moved to Venice and then Rome, he was still under the sway of Italians. And even after he had spent the better part of his lifetime in Toledo, he was always known to the Spaniards as 'the Greek.' His life was painting, and in Spain what did the Inquisition want you to paint? Religious iconography, of course. Oh, you could do portraits, yes, and even now and then a landscape, but saints and martyrs were the order of the day, and don't anybody forget it! El Greco had occasion to see how the Holy Office treated Moors and Jews. He had no idea of being burned alive. And he wanted to prosper. So he conformed. Let us be thankful that he did!"

I protested. "But you can't deny, can you, the passionate faith you see expressed in the heaven-seeking eyes of all those ascending virgins and carved-up saints?"

"Of course not. The man was a mystic. He had a deep sense of another world around us, a greater, more wonderful world, whether morally better or worse than our own we don't know, but which our spirit, if we are open to it, may touch, though our reason denies it. And he saw that gifted men may live on two levels, even if some of them attain the greater level through what seems to us terrible means. For even an inquisitor who believes he can be saved by burning heretics may be touched with this sometimes cruel inner fire. Look at that old cardinal Mrs. Havemeyer has bought. The average man isn't capable of such exalted feeling; he can only look on in mild bewilderment like those noblemen in *The Burial of Count Orgaz* or the Roman officers in the painting we've just seen. A Catholic, even a bigot, may be blessed or cursed with these otherworldly visions, but the Catholic Church and its dogma have nothing to do with them. That, gentlemen, is what I believe El Greco saw. He could transmit the sense of beauty that seized him through a Christ on the cross or a Laocoon in the coils of a serpent or a storm over Toledo. That is why he was always an artist. Bowing to the organized fanaticism of the Holy Office gave him no trouble at all. Why should it have? The church was simply irrelevant to everything in life that was vital to him."

The *Saint Maurice*, anyway, became the gem of the Warren collection. Hank, of course, insisted on my attribution, as there had been a number of El Greco copies hawked about, and I had no hesitation in this case in giving it to him, nor has it ever been questioned. But our conversation at the restaurant had an interesting impact on my relationship with Leila. It cemented my conviction that the bond that tied us so securely together was that we were both aesthetes who lived primarily for the satisfaction of our artistic tastes. Nothing really mattered to either of us but the quest of the perfect thing. Leila would have bought that picture had its authenticity been challenged by a hundred experts. The thing was in itself perfection.

Subsequent revelations of my private negotiations with art dealers over the provenance of paintings they sold to the Warrens have raised doubts as to whether the price paid didn't sway some of my convictions, and it is certainly true that my concern has been more with the quality of a picture than with its origin. Indeed, I have never thought the law should protect a purchaser who questions the latter. He bought *that* particular object, didn't he? He could see it and feel it and smell it, couldn't he? The future will probably contain methods of reproducing masterpieces so faultless that no expert will be able to distinguish them from the originals. Indeed, that time has almost come. The doctor in whose sanatorium van Gogh languished so long did copies of his patient's work that baffle the keenest eyes today. Yet the difference in the price can be high in the millions. What nonsense!

Have some of my attributions been affected by the lure of profit? Could I have been tempted, for example, to promote a Francesco Pesellino to a Fra Filippo Lippi to satisfy a lover of Robert Browning's famous monologue? I suppose it's possible. The subconscious is much played up these days, and the lifestyle of my later years has certainly been costly. But I have never recommended anything but great works of art.

Once and once only have I given an opinion that was directly contrary to what I truly believed. As it caused my ultimate break with Hank Warren, though his wife took no part in his decision to cancel my retainer, I will relate here what happened.

Once again we were faced with an El Greco, or what purported to be an El Greco, supposedly an early example of his Venetian period. It depicted the taking of Christ's garments by the Roman soldiers, a subject later more magnificently treated by the artist in his famous *El Spolio* in the Toledo cathedral. But the treatment in the picture in question was very different.

The hall in which Christ was about to be stripped had the ornate grandeur of a Veronese palace, and its great arches opened to a sky of a lovely cerulean blue. The soldiers laying their hands on the patient, heaven-gazing Jesus were scantily clad, some actually naked, and very handsome and muscular, totally unlike the grotesque, skinny, sexless nudes of the later El Greco, but in making my attribution I had to take into consideration that in his Italian period he was almost a realist. What convinced me that it was not an El Greco was that the soldiers were not shown as either cruel or indifferent. They appeared to be fascinated by the very garments they were tearing off their victim, particularly the scarlet robe that dominated the center of the picture like a great glittering ruby. Despite all its action the painting had some of the serene stillness that Poussin was later to bring even to such scenes of carnage as the massacre of the innocents. The spirit of the artist's conception was totally unlike anything El Greco had ever done, so, despite the similarity of many of its details to his early Venetian paintings, I was convinced that it was not the work of the Toledo master. But it was a masterpiece. It might even have been a Titian.

Leila was not of my opinion. She was totally and enthusiastically convinced that it was a genuine El Greco, and she had to have it.

"It bears out my theory!" she exclaimed. "The soldiers are not capable of receiving the inner flame, but they are able to sense its presence in one who does. They might be trying to warm their hands against the fire of that red robe!"

The price demanded was stiff, and Hank insisted on my unqualified opinion. I gave it. I wanted his wife to have that beautiful picture. Hank accepted my attribution and bought it. Later, when a dealer whom I had mistakenly regarded as a friend but who was actually intent on stealing the Warrens from me betrayed to Hank the doubts that I had indiscreetly admitted to him, Hank never mentioned the matter but ceased forever all business dealings with me. Leila, to whom I am sure he confided his outrage, continued as a friend to discuss her collection with me. If she knew about the El Greco, even if she had come to my conclusion about it, she didn't care. She had what she wanted.

She and I were soul mates.

An Hour and a Lifetime

Linda Griswold had always rather tended to assume
that by age twenty-seven she would be a comfortably wed
matron, the mother of a couple of tots, with an attractive
apartment in New York, a cottage for summers and weekends in a fashionable New York suburb, and a handsome, or
at least charming, husband who worked "downtown": a life,
in short, that was a replica, if on a minor scale, of her family's
rather grander one. And yet in 1943, in the middle of a world
war, she found herself married, and to a handsome husband,
it was true, but he was not downtown: he was a naval officer
on sea duty in the North Atlantic, and she, still not a mother,
was hard at work as the civilian secretary-assistant to the district intelligence officer at the headquarters of the Pacific
Sea Frontier, in Balboa in the Panama Canal Zone. It was a
kind of success, perhaps, for a woman of her protected background, but certainly not the one she had envisaged.

Yet the significant thing in her life was that she had always expected success. From her teens on she had been in the
habit of giving herself over to private gusts of exhilaration.
Life was not only going to be good; it was going to be better and better. Let war clouds gather over Europe, let Hitler
and Mussolini rant and rave; at home in a nation that had so

gallantly pulled itself out of a deep depression, the future was still secure from foreign isms. She had beauty and health and money and, what was much more important, the will to enjoy them.

She had known Thad Griswold all her life; their families had adjoining country estates in Westbury, Long Island. He was blond, handsome, athletic, and of a sunny disposition; his innate decency and the evident sincerity of his admiration for intellects superior to his own—and she certainly recognized that such existed—went a good way to make up for his deficiencies in wit and imagination. Not that he was stupid. Far from it. He had common sense and industriousness, and he knew how to apply himself to any given task. As her father said, such a man might go far in a bank, and he had taken Thad on in his. The very appropriateness of his and Linda's union seemed to further her habitual optimism, though she privately admitted it might well have had the opposite effect. She was sure when she married him—a virgin, as were most of her friends—that the physical side of wedlock would be all a girl could hope for. She imagined that this would cover a multitude of other things, and for a good while it did. She indignantly thrust into the back of her mind the nasty crack of a cynical old bachelor friend: "An excellent first marriage."

As war broke out in Europe not long after their wedding and the eventual entry of America into hostilities was generally expected, the young Griswolds agreed to postpone starting a family, and when Thad, a reserve officer, was called up for sea duty, Linda decided to take a job. She knew shorthand and typing, and when a cousin of her mother's, a regular navy captain stationed as an intelligence officer at the district headquarters on Church Street, suggested that she work for him as a secretary and general assistant, she jumped at the chance. Was it not patriotic as well as interesting? And so absorbed did she become in the job and so indispensable to her boss that when he was ordered to the Canal Zone to become district intelligence officer there and asked if she would go with him if he could arrange it, she cheerfully agreed—though to her family's distress and Thad's mild but distant objections. With Thad on the waves and she overseas, what a striking war couple they would make! Success might have strange ways of showing itself, but here it was!

The shimmering heat of Balboa and the dull green military buildings of the headquarters of the Pacific Sea Frontier, so little relieved by the brash pink and yellow of neighboring Panama City or by the too-distant lush greenness of the isthmus jungle, were disheartening to her, but the real blow came when, after only a year in his new job, her boss was transferred to sea duty. Linda thought at first that she would go home, but the new district intelligence officer, whom she liked, begged her to stay on, and she decided in the end that it was her patriotic duty to do so.

Left alone, as she felt it, in the Canal Zone, she soon wondered if her first idea had not been the right one. All around her the atmosphere was becoming as dry as the air in the months of rainlessness. What had been a gallant and united military outpost excitingly threatened by a cruel oriental power had become the routine station for supplies and transport for victorious American forces driving a distant foe to greater distances. The officers and men who guarded the canal from a less and less likely repetition of Pearl Harbor had never had, and now never would have, and probably didn't even want, combat duty. They idled through their humdrum tasks and spent their evenings in bordellos in Panama City or in bars talking about sex. Everlastingly about sex! Linda had given up going out at night even with respectable-looking officers who knew or pretended to know connections of hers at home. Such engagements, despite her announced married state and usually their own, seemed invariably to end in a spurned pass. She had no friends among the female staff at naval headquarters; they were all—or at least they so struck her—dull Canal Zone daughters intent on catching a husband to take them to the blessed North when the war was over. Besides, they regarded her as a snob. And they were right!

Making matters worse was the daily transit from the Caribbean to the Pacific of the great gray vessels of war on their way to swell the now invincible flotillas sweeping the Japanese from the seas. Linda's boss sometimes took her with him when he called on the commanding officer of one of these, and her spirits would rise at the sight of so many fighting men. But when she returned to her office, her brief elation would be punctured. For what cause were they risking their brave young lives? For the sleaziness of the zone, which she was beginning to equate with what she saw as the sleaziness of America, of the West, of everything? Were those bleak historians correct in thinking, like Brooks Adams, the subject of her major thesis at Vassar, that human civilization was glorious only in its fighting warriors, that peaceful eras degenerated into mere money grubbing and sexual incontinence? Even the New York of her younger days now took on in her fantasies some of the aspects of an academic painting of Rome in decline, with men in togas and women in less lolling on couches at a banquet, waiting fatalistically for the barbarians to arrive.

It was through Stuart Fraser that she met Conrad Vogt. Fraser, whom she had known in New York in her debutante days, was a third secretary at the American Embassy in Panama; he was bright but pompous, witty and self-important, and so much the gentleman that she would never have to tell him to keep his hands to himself. His conduct was always scrupulously correct, and on the rare occasions (his social calendar was a busy one) when he asked her to dine with him at the Union Club, she accepted with mild pleasure. At least she would not have to frown and shake her head at unwanted solicitations.

Once he brought with him an old college friend in transit of the canal, a lieutenant attached to a submarine temporarily delayed in Balboa for minor adjustments. Vogt immediately struck Linda as a man of considerable magnetism, exercised mainly by large and rather brooding dark eyes in a very pale skin under a high brow and thick, shiny, ebony hair. His figure was a bit slight but well formed, and she could see, when he rose from their table to answer a telephone call from his ship, that he moved with the coordinated grace of a Gallic or Italian aristocrat. His voice was soft and low; he gave the appearance of a controlled gentleness that in no way suggested weakness or pliability but rather their opposite. In the course of a rather animated conversation between the three of them, he managed to redeem for Linda much of the disgust into which her Panamanian *séjour* had sunk his sex.

She liked to play a discreet game of seeing how much biographical data she could glean from a new acquaintance without resorting to the crudity of direct inquiry. Now she was able to put together that Vogt had been a teacher of English at a private boys' boarding school near Boston of which he himself was a graduate, that he had already spent two years on submarines in both the Atlantic and the Pacific, that his parents had a summer cottage in Bar Harbor, Maine (from which she deduced that they were well-to-do and could afford to let him be an instructor if he insisted), and that he had been unhappily married and divorced but had no children. He was intensely male and intensely conscious of her. Yet he gave her an odd sense of absolute security. Her mind, full of a romanticism that she scorned, was already dubbing him Bayard, *sans peur et sans reproche*.

She was pleased but hardly surprised when, the conversation turning to books, he told them that the war had not interfered with his reading but rather intensified it.

"No matter how much there is to do on shipboard," he said, "there is still time to read. Long periods in port for repairs and so forth. You can't work all the time, even when you're on duty, and when you're not working there's often nothing else to do. We were in Attu, for example, for two whole months. My mother can never understand why in her letters I'm so interested in even the trivial events of her life at home. She imagines that people involved in a big war must be taken up with big things. She can't understand that the twenty minutes in my bunk when I'm reading Henry James's *The Spoils of Poynton* is the high point of my day."

"I can't say that I rise as high as that," was Linda's comment. "But I readily admit that Trollope has got me through some rough times in the Canal Zone."

"Well, of course, I'm fortunate in having the daily drama at the embassy before me," Stuart put in with his customary condescension. "Keeping an eye on the devilish international intrigues of Latin America provides a shelf of whodunits for me. Some may think we're a remote post in this war, but the German agents are everywhere."

Conrad had a jeep at his service and took Linda back to her hotel after dropping Stuart off.

"War was made for the Stuart Frasers of this world," he told her, but in a tone devoid of spite. "They can enjoy every minute of it, and when it's over and we've won, can't you see His Excellency Ambassador Fraser telling off one minor Latin dictator after another? Oh, Stuart will always be magnificent. Some men have to develop an air of greatness to go with their achieved importance. Stuart will develop greatness to go with his already achieved air of it."

"I didn't imagine you were the best of friends."

"Oh, don't get me wrong. I'm very fond of Stuart. He's a friend from boyhood, and we always have special tolerances for such. Besides, he's basically well-meaning. But I like to take him in small doses. Not the way I like to take you, Mrs. Griswold."

"Linda, please."

"Unlike you, Linda. May I see you again? For dinner? I know you're married, and I'm sure happily married. I wouldn't be such a silly ass as to think I could cause even a ripple on that. But just a friendly dinner?"

"You're not married, I take it."

"No, my wife, like Henry VIII in Shakespeare's last play, found 'metal more attractive.'"

"She had little taste, then. Of course I'll have dinner with you."

"Not just to keep the navy happy?"

"Well, that too."

In the following fortnight they dined together four times,

always in the same little restaurant chosen by him. They avoided the Union Club and Stuart Fraser; nor did they see fit to tell him of their meetings. The embassy secretary had ceased to exist for them. The bond they shared was a past, a past of blessed things that, brought up in lively but nostalgic discussions, seemed to illuminate a dreary war-torn world. It was not, for either of them, so much the past that had immediately preceded Armageddon; it was rather the past of childhood and the loss of innocence, which now seemed almost the loss of everything. Linda's husband, for example, despite her long acquaintance with him, figured as a near stranger to her reminiscences; it was as if this beautiful and pensive and mildly melancholy submarine lieutenant had been the sole companion of those days of yore.

"My wife used to say I was Peter Pan," he confessed. "And she didn't mean it kindly, either. She hated my being a schoolteacher. She had taken for granted when we were married that I would eventually have a job in my father's brokerage house. But when I got that sudden offer to teach at Saint Jude's and jumped at it, she accused me of crawling back into the nursery. Perhaps I was."

"And she hated Saint Jude's?"

"*Hated* isn't strong enough. She didn't last there a year. She bolted and shed me and married an old beau of hers who *had* gone into Daddy's firm. And I have to be fair to her. The happiest days of mine *were* my schooldays at Saint Jude's. It was there I met Shelley and Keats and, of course, Shakespeare. I loved the friends and the sports and the lovely green campus and the tower of the Gothic chapel. Oh, I was like that poem of Matthew Arnold's, 'Rugby Chapel'! I even had a religious phase."

"How I see it!" she exclaimed. "I was that way at Saint Timothy's. The springtime of life! We should have known it couldn't last. Maybe you *did* know. For you'll never be a poet, Conrad. An unhappy childhood is an essential preliminary to great art."

"You're so right!" he retorted with a laugh. "Happiness is fatal." He looked at her for a quiet moment. "And I'm happy right now."

What saved him from any diminution in her eyes was a nostalgia that she recognized as even greater than her own; what guarded his masculinity from the least tint of weakness was the only too obvious fact that he was a warrior who had been tried and tested in combat, that he was able to master the complicated machinery of an undersea vessel, that if he had ever known fear, it must have been largely overcome. At night she shivered even in the Panamanian heat at the suffocating sense of being trapped in that cigar-shaped tube deep below the surface as depth charges detonated around it. Yet he never talked about it, nor did she presume to ask.

After their second dinner, she knew she was in love with him and felt not the smallest twinge of guilt or the least pang at her disloyalty to Thad. What she was going through was so utterly her own affair that it seemed to have nothing to do with the past, or even, for that matter, with the future. It was an interlude, an elating interlude, and she was determined—well, perhaps not so much determined as resigned—to let it have its full sway over her.

She was hardly surprised on their third evening together when he said suddenly, "Of course, I'm in love with you. How could I not be? But you needn't worry. Nothing is going to come of it. Your husband is never going to get a 'Dear

John' letter as a result of anything I do or don't do. And don't feel you have to comment on this. I just had to let you know, that's all. And that's bad enough of me. Now let's talk about anything else. How long, for example, you plan to stay in the Canal Zone."

Linda, her heart full of joy, knew she could take him at his word. He was too much a gentleman to extract from her the avowal of a love of which he was only too well aware. She took a long sip of her wine and then replied, in the flattest voice she could muster, "Pretty soon, I think. But not, certainly, before you sail."

He nodded slowly as he took this in. "Thank you, my dear. But that should be any day now."

And it was. On their fourth evening he announced that his vessel was due to sail on the morrow. But she was ready for it.

"Then this is our last night together. Do you have to spend it onboard?"

"No. Everything's ready. I have till eight tomorrow morning."

She had rehearsed her lines. "Then there's something I think you and I ought to do. It may be our last time together."

He reached across the table to take her hand. "You're sure?"

"Of course I'm sure. Aren't you?"

"On one condition only. If you can promise me it won't break up your marriage."

"It has nothing to do with my marriage!" she exclaimed, almost with a note of shrillness. "Oh, I know people say that. But it still can be true!"

He closed his eyes for a silent moment. "I can't fight this," he said simply. "Let's go to your place."

It was, God knew, if God were watching, a simple enough and common coupling, but it was still unlike anything she had imagined, and certainly unlike her unions with Thad. Nor did she feel the least shame or regret afterward, when he had left her; it was almost—however odd this might seem, and indeed it seemed very odd—as if she had been to church. She didn't regret that he hadn't come into her life before, that he had not been her husband. She felt only a fierce gratitude that he had come at all.

Linda stayed on in the Canal Zone for several months after the departure of Conrad's submarine. She had been earnestly persuaded by her boss to remain at her post, and besides, the war was coming to a conclusion. She and Conrad had agreed not to correspond; it was part of their resolution—or at least part of *his*—that they would do nothing more that would tend to break up her marriage, and she thought a period of continued isolation in Central America might help her to adjust her spirits to taking up her life again with Thad when peace came.

Thad's letters had been cheerful and newsy; he had been taken off convoy duty when the submarine threat had eased and assigned to shore duty as the executive officer of a naval section base in one of the English Channel ports. He wrote a good deal about Britain and some of his new British friends; he was still apparently his old tolerant and accepting self. She wondered if going back to her old life wouldn't be like awakening to a rather dull and routine but certainly not disagreeable existence after a blissful but fantastic dream.

And then one morning Stuart Fraser, calling on the Admiral on official business, stopped by her desk on his way out.

"Do you remember Conrad Vogt, Linda? The submarine officer we dined with some months ago at the Union Club?"

She stared; her heart seemed to stop. "I remember him," she half whispered.

Stuart noticed nothing unusual in her response. "His submarine was lost off the coast of Okinawa. Blown up, of all things, by a kamikaze that caught it on the surface."

"He's lost, then?"

"Oh, yes, with all on board. Horrible, isn't it? But then everything in this war is horrible. Thank God it'll soon be over. Would you be free for dinner some night this week?"

"I'll see," she muttered. "I'll call you." And he left.

She didn't plead illness and flee to her quarters. She simply sat dumbly at her desk for the rest of the afternoon. Fortunately it was not a busy day; her boss was in conference, and she was left to the silent entertainment of her agony. She kept saying over and over to herself that at least she had had that night, that single night; she clenched her fists as if she were holding their time together tight. There was that, only that. The rest of the world, the rest of her life, was something altogether separate. But she knew that the crash of a hissing sea as it burst over a stricken vessel was never to be muted in her inner ear.

⤞⤝

When Thad came back to New York, released from the navy, she had already reoccupied and redecorated their old apartment. Their reunion had its awkward, its inevitably stiff moments, but both had the intelligence to recognize that many of their friends were undergoing the same experience, and on the whole the thing was managed pleasantly enough. He professed to find her unchanged—"as beautiful as a movie star," as he rather tritely observed—and she found in him some of the old exuberance, but a bit chastened. He was thinner and paler and inclined to sudden silences. They agreed to take their time before renewing old intimacies. They would not, for example, sleep together for the first few nights.

And then one evening he told her, almost solemnly, that he had booked a table at a very expensive French restaurant. "I have something to confess to you that needs the best of food and wine."

"Some limey gal, I suppose," she retorted with what she intended to be a sophisticated shrug. "I've seen what you men were up to in Panama. Don't worry. The war has taught me a perhaps excessive tolerance."

"Well, you'll see," was his enigmatic reply.

She wondered whether this might not be the time to tell him about Conrad. Wouldn't it be something of a fraud to conceal from the partner of her life—as Thad was destined now to be—that a substantial part of her soul and being did not, and never could, belong to him? That even if she were forever faithful and became the mother of his children, it still behooved her to build their joint lives upon a declared truth? But she would hear him first on the subject of his limey hussy or hussies. As if she cared!

At their table in a secluded alcove, with a bottle of Haut Brion and two martinis apiece already consumed, Thad slowly and with difficulty told his tale.

An English woman serving as his secretary at the section base in Falmouth, whose husband was serving with the Royal Navy in the Indian Ocean, had become his right hand in administration, then his close friend, and at last his mistress. She had broken off their relationship abruptly when her spouse had been unexpectedly invalided out of the service and came home and had passionately vowed never to see him again. Nor had she. The break had been final.

"The reason I'm telling you this, Linda, is that it was no fly-by-night affair. I was in love. Deeply in love. It was unlike anything that ever happened to me before. Now it's over. But it was a part of me that I thought you ought to know about. If you choose to leave me now, I'll make it easy for you, financially and legally. But my hope is that we might build a new life together."

Linda was so startled by the clash of emotions within her that for several moments she felt almost dizzy. It was as if she had walked into her old life and collided with a stranger. Under her surprise was a kind of muffled anger, a resentment that he could so complacently tell her of his wonderful experience. Resentment of the English woman? Not in the least. The woman had no reality to her; she could hardly be jealous of a wraith. No, it was resentment that he—the likes of *him*—should aspire to something as precious as she had had with Conrad! That he should intrude himself in the same heaven as her! For if Thad could have such a love in his life, couldn't anybody? Was her one exquisite night with Conrad to lose its unique magic in the desert of her wartime disillusionment? Would it have to take its place with all the Canal Zone couplings, with all the scatological chatter at the bars and barracks, with the appalling nothingness of military stagnation?

"Are you totally disgusted with me?" Thad asked. "I can't blame you if you are."

"No, it's not that. It's just something I need a little time to adjust to. Perhaps I should even be glad that you had something like that to make up for what the war has done to all of us. Perhaps it is right that *everyone* should have the blessing of love. Only there has to be a part of me that begrudges it to you."

"I'm glad of that part, Linda. Very glad. It gives me a ray of hope for our future."

"Because you think it shows I care?"

"Well, mightn't it? Just a little? I know I can care for you a great deal if you can care for me the least bit."

He reached for her hand, and she allowed him to take it.

"And now," he pursued, "do you have anything to tell me?"

Again she was silent for several moments. But she knew now that she was never going to tell him about Conrad. She was sure, with a sudden spasm of conviction, that the only way to preserve that throbbing memory alive within herself—and maybe even to live on it—was to share it with no one. Oh, maybe one distant day with a beloved and sympathetic daughter—who knew? Did that mean it was too frail to subject it to the common stare? Perhaps. What of it? Frail things can be precious.

"No, my life down there was very dull. Very commonplace. I'm afraid I have nothing glamorous to tell you."

She saw that he didn't believe her but that he wasn't going to—and never would—pry. And for that she almost loved him.

Her next remark was delivered in her flattest tone. "You know what I think we both need more than anything else? To raise a family. And we might start this very night."

The Artist's Model

JOHN EPPES GLANCED about the big studio that he occupied on West Forty-first Street to be sure that it was in
reasonable order to receive his next sitter, Mrs. Harold Ames,
whose husband owned almost as many city blocks in Manhattan as Colonel John Jacob Astor. There had not been many
things to clear away, as the large, square, high-roofed chamber whose three great windows overlooked Bryant Park contained mostly empty space, space that Eppes loved now that
he was prosperous enough to afford it. Aside from his easel
and the marble-topped Italian Renaissance table on which
he kept his paints and brushes, and the spectacular Persian
carpet, there was little but the unfinished canvases stacked
against the walls, the different period armchairs in which he
sometimes seated his customers, and the various rolls of cloth
and curtain that he used for backgrounds in his pictures. He
turned a second easel so as to make visible to a visitor the
charcoal sketch resting on it of former president Theodore
Roosevelt, now on a much publicized safari. It had been the
preliminary sketch to an oil portrait hanging in the Capitol
in Washington.

Eppes, age fifty, though still the fine strong figure of a
man, with large staring eyes and a full head of sleek black-

and-gray hair, was at a crisis in his career. He had gone as far as one could go in the painting of fashionable portraits, and he was beginning to wonder if there might not be a higher goal to attain if he were to achieve any really lasting fame. Even though he received the highest fees of any portraitist and some of his works now hung in museums, he was only too bitterly aware of what younger art critics were saying about him: that he was slick and superficial, that his skill in detail was mere trickery, and that his flattering portraits of society matrons were fashion plates. The English critic Roger Fry had even gone so far as to state that it was hard to believe Eppes had ever been taken seriously.

Of course, much of this could be written off as jealousy or the resentment of plutocrats by radicals, but he suffered from the uneasy suspicion that there was still some basis for it. Had the gorgeousness of his dresses and interiors in his paintings of women manifested a too complacent acceptance of the vulgar values of a mercantile society? Had he become the apologist of the early-twentieth-century goldbug?

He had liked to think of himself as a Velázquez or Goya, able subtly to suggest the faults of an era in the very countenances and poses of the aristocrats who represented it, but wasn't it possible that he was actually more like Nattier, whose bland French court beauties gave little hint of the guillotine that awaited their like in the near future?

His reverie was interrupted by his sudden realization that Mrs. Ames had quietly arrived and was standing in the doorway.

"Are you ready for me, master? I hate to break in on great thoughts."

Really, she was lovely. A painter's dream. She had eager,

darting, gray-blue eyes, a pale oval face, thin scarlet lips, and a small, perfect nose ending in a tiny hook, with hair a rich chestnut, and she was clad in red velvet with gold trimmings, an evening dress in which, quite rightly, she evidently wished to pose. She apologized for her lateness, for her presumption in choosing her attire, for her nervousness at meeting "so great an artist." She paused before the Roosevelt sketch and raised her hands in gratifying admiration.

"Imagine painting silly me after doing *him!*"

Eppes decided to paint her sitting, and he selected a gilded eighteenth-century Venetian armchair for the initial sketch. She adapted herself quickly and gracefully to each pose he suggested, and he finally chose one in which she was leaning slightly forward, as if to be sure to catch every word of the man—of course it would be a man, and a charming one—who was engaging her in conversation at a soiree. Her expression was amused, receptive, delightful.

She professed herself enchanted with the rapidly executed sketch and accepted cheerfully his invitation to stay for the tea that his manservant, rung for, now brought in. Eppes asked her what sort of pictures she liked.

"Oh, you'll think me a terrible philistine," she protested. "I love all those big academic historical paintings that tell stories. Of course, I realize that makes me totally out of fashion."

"You shouldn't be ashamed of anything you really like. Liking something is the start of appreciation in art. Liking can always be extended. It's indifference that can't be. Tell me about some of the academic pictures that you like."

She took him up enthusiastically on this. "Well, I remember one that particularly thrilled me. It showed Catherine de Médici coming out of the Louvre on the day after the Saint Bartholomew's Day massacre to view the dead bodies lying about, half stripped, on the street. Her ladies, obviously compelled to follow her, exhibit every kind of horror and disgust, turning their eyes away and putting handkerchiefs to their noses. But the queen mother, stalwart in widow's black, strides ahead, taking in the bloody scene with a calm and glacial satisfaction. How terrible, but how unforgettable!"

"I know the picture. It's by Pinson. What else did you like?"

"There was one of the execution of Lady Jane Grey. Oh, you must find me very macabre. But they're so exciting, those scenes. In museums you always see a lot of people in front of them, until they're scared away by remembering the art critics. But this one was so pathetic. You see the poor girl, who was only fifteen, blindfolded, on her knees and reaching about for the block, helped by a kindly older man, while the headsman stands mutely by with his terrible ax."

"That's by Delaroche. He was very good. He also did the little princes in the tower."

"But you know everything, Mr. Eppes!"

"I know that, anyway. But you needn't be ashamed of liking those pictures. They're competently executed."

"*Executed* does seem the right word. And do you know something? I think there are stories in some of your portraits."

"Really? Can you give me an example?"

"Yes! In your rendering of the duke and duchess of Ives. She's so tall and proud and fine. The captive American heiress sold against her will to an impoverished peer. Talk about slave markets! And he's so short and plain and arrogant. You can see that he'll never even try to appreciate her!"

Eppes was amused. He had not thought of the duke so meanly. "Dear me. I had no notion of such a drama. And how do you think I have rendered, as you put it, the doomed duchess?"

"Oh, as bravely determined to make the most of her bad bargain. Which, by all reports, she has. One hears she is the toast of London. And that the duke is small enough to resent being cast in her shadow."

Eppes found this implausible, though he was flattered. After two more sittings he allowed a friendly art critic, Frank Shea, to come in for a private view.

"The pose is fine, and the colors quite up to your usual splendid standard," Shea assured him. "Of course, you're still developing the face. It will be interesting to see what you will finally do with her. Will she be at last your definitive study of the wife of the American goldbug? Lost in the silly pipe dream that she has affinities and aspirations nobler than those of her commonplace husband?"

"What's the husband like, have you heard? Pretty grim, I suppose?"

"Oh, not such a bad guy. But you know: stolid, stout, and dull."

"I might have guessed."

He had discussed several topics with Mrs. Ames in their sittings, as she was always lively and interested, but she had tended to shy away from questions about her life, preferring more general subjects. But at their next session he resolved to be more personal.

"I tell you frankly, Mrs. Ames, that you baffle me. I haven't been able to decide how to get the essential *you* in your likeness. You tell me that you see stories in some of my portraits. What story would you like to see in yours?"

She seemed to be thinking this over for a long moment. He had the notion that she was not going to dodge the point. Yet when she answered, with a sudden bright smile, he was not sure that she hadn't. "How about that of a perfectly happy woman?"

"Isn't that a conclusion rather than a story? It's like that last line: 'They lived happily ever after.' After what?"

"Do you have to know? Is it that important?"

"I don't *have* to, no. But let's put it that it might help."

Again she was silent for a time. "Is a painter like a priestly confessor? Are your lips sealed by professional discretion?"

"No, but they are by my word of honor. Which I freely offer you."

She nodded now with sudden decision. "That should be enough. Particularly as I shall be telling you nothing that my husband doesn't already know. And who else's business is it?"

"I can hardly be the judge of that."

"Hardly. Anyway, leave your easel and pull up a chair. I'm going to tell you my story."

He did as she suggested, turning away from her, at her further request, so that she could address his impassive back.

"My family, Mr. Eppes, was what you call old New York, but we were fearfully impoverished by my poor father's lamentable investments. He was one of those dear idealistic, impractical men who didn't realize that he could not afford to work. Had he sat back and simply cut his inherited coupons, we would have happily prospered. But no. He succumbed to the old American rule that a man must *do* something. So he did—disastrously. My mother spent her life trying desperately to claw her way back to the top. There is no one more ravenously ambitious than a woman who has had it and lost it. Mother was a woman of powerful personality. Her rages were terrifying. Had I not accepted Harold Ames when he emerged from the clouds, like the deus ex machina of Greek drama, to offer me his golden chariot, I think she might have murdered me. At any rate I was simply glad to be able to pull my father out of the creek in which he was drowning. And Harold was so kind and nice, and he always wanted to give me everything under the sun. What did I care that he was constantly off on hunting and fishing expeditions and that his heart belonged to whatever was at the end of his rifle or rod? There was plenty to amuse me at home. I had one child, my son, now fourteen, but others didn't come, and I had nurses to look after him day and night, and all New York and Newport in which to amuse myself with money and dogs and horses and new young friends in handfuls as rich and idle as myself.

"Harold had a cousin, younger and handsome and dashing, with a share of the family fortune as large as Harold's, who seemed more than willing to act as my escort to parties during my husband's frequent and prolonged absences. He was married to a dreadful woman who cared only for his money and refused adamantly to give him a divorce—besides, the Ameses were all devout Catholics, including Harold—and for a long time I thought his attentions were innocent and that I was simply a diversion for his loneliness and he for mine. It is the old story, Mr. Eppes. By the time he revealed his true feelings for me, I was already caught, violently in love for the first time in my life, which can be a terribly strong thing when it happens as late as at twenty-five."

She paused here for a moment, but Eppes knew better than to utter a word.

"We were soul mates," she resumed, "or so I assumed. He wanted me to leave home and child and flee with him to Venice, where he would buy a palazzo on the Grand Canal and we would live on love and beauty. There was no way, we both knew, that our spouses would ever free us or that Harold would give up his son and heir. We would be ostracized, of course, by New York society, but abroad we would associate with people of larger views. I was enraptured. I agonized at the idea of giving up my darling child, but I tried to persuade myself that when he was older he would understand and forgive me. I had to break my golden chains! We were not yet lovers, but we were obviously on the brink. I told my admirer that I had to think it over, but he was clearly convinced that he had already prevailed and that I would go."

The pause that now followed was so long that Eppes ventured to break it. "But you didn't go."

"I didn't go. Harold came home at just this time from a trip to the Arctic Circle. He summoned me to his study, very grim and stern. His old mother had written him about my goings-on. His cousin and I were causing a public scandal. He told me solemnly that he had no alternative but to insist that I give up seeing his cousin altogether. He turned quite black when I told him that I was in love with his cousin. I said I would give him his answer in the morning, fully intending that I would decamp that night. He left the room without a word.

"The miracle that saved me was that my cynical brother, Tim, a Harvard sophomore in love with himself and what he assumed was his wit, was staying with me at the time. I loved him dearly despite his airs and nursed the idea that if he cared for anybody, he cared a little bit for me. In my sudden desperation I went to his room, where he was dressing for a dinner party, and told him what I was going to do. You'll never believe what he said and what an extraordinary effect it had on me."

"Well?"

"It was like him to quote Oscar Wilde, even though Wilde's name at the time had been blackened by his trial and conviction. Tim obviously cared nothing about this. He quoted a line from *A Woman of No Importance.* 'To be in society is simply a bore; to be out of it is simply a tragedy.' And it changed my life!"

"That glib quip? How, in God's name?"

"I repeated it over and over to myself in that long night, when I didn't sleep a wink. I came to see that it contained the moral essence of our time. Isn't it *Anna Karenina* all over? When being out of society ceases to be a tragedy, our whole class system must fall. Not that that would necessarily be such a bad thing. But it hadn't happened yet. Or at least it certainly hadn't happened ten years ago, when we were still in the nineteenth century. I saw in a blinding flash what my life would be like without my dear little boy, surrounded by the Venetian riffraff that illicit lovers attract. Was it too late? Would I ever be able to make it up to the decent husband who was giving me one more chance?"

"So he wasn't so bad, after all, the great hunter and fisherman?" Eppes saw that the moment had come when he could be facetious.

"Well, he was pretty bad for a while. How could he not have been after my confession? When I went to him the following morning and told him that I would never see his cousin again, he assumed I was up to some kind of trick. But in the days that ensued, I took him the desperate letters that my frustrated lover sent me, and he had to concede that I was serious. We took up our old life together, but it was a cold and formal one. Harold spoke to me only when he had to, about some detail of our daily schedule, and then as briefly and curtly as possible. I ignored this completely. I was wild with relief and passionately resolute to win him back. It was a task that took every minute of my days and nights and obliterated my love for his cousin — it became an obsession, but a happy one. I had to win! I knew I would win! I never missed one of his mean old mother's 'days' or protested at going to his sister's boring evenings. I insisted on going to his Canadian camp with him, even though I had to spend long days in our cabin alone, reading novels while he shot moose or wolves with his pals."

"But he came around at last?"

"After six months, yes. What a time! One day, when his old cat of a mother snapped at me with some only half-veiled crack about flirts in the family, he suddenly turned on the old girl and shouted, 'If you're referring to my wife, you should have your mouth wiped out with soap!' Never had anyone heard him use such violent language before, and to *her*, of all people! Our real marriage began that very night."

"You must have always loved him. Deep down."

"That's romantic twaddle, Mr. Eppes. I hadn't at all. I simply saw where my true happiness lay and grabbed it — literally only hours before I should have lost it forever. I have been a very lucky woman, that is all."

But that was not what Eppes finally put in his famous canvas. He couldn't bear it. It would never have redounded to his fame. It made mock of every great love drama of his time. The interior behind the figure of Mrs. Ames glimmered with gold and scarlet, but it hemmed her in. She was beautiful; she was loved — one saw that—but she was also confined. In her radiant eyes, in the near ecstasy of her expression one might have made out her vision of the life she had missed, the passion that could have enveloped her. It was not the portrait of an unhappy woman; it was the representation of a dreamer.

It was thus that the critic Shea interpreted it when Eppes first permitted the picture to be seen. The artist could not resist the temptation to temper his friend's admiration with the true story of the sitter. But Shea had the last word.

"So that's it, is it? Well then, Mrs. Ames is not unlike one of those Renaissance madonnas. The model need not resemble the conception. A saintly virgin of Raphael may have a streetwalker for her model. Is that the trick of great art? To make us worship a lie?"

Pandora's Box

AMOS HERRICK HAD NOT thought as a boy, or even as a Harvard undergraduate, that he would ever become a lawyer. He had once eminently respected the distinguished old Wall Street firm that took care of his family's much dwindled but still good income-producing Manhattan real estate, but he had tended to regard legal counsel as he did doctors and business managers: as necessary supporters of the managerial class, which in a well-regulated republic should watch over and guide the multitude. What a young heir of such a class should do with his life ought to be something more important. Just what that was in his own case he had still not decided on his graduation at Cambridge. But he was able to take his time and, in the meanwhile, to look around. How he came in the end to choose law will be the subject of what follows.

At twenty-two Amos was a highly reserved and very sober young man, with a personality that some found serene and others merely impassive. Nobody denied his evident intelligence or the tenacity of his memory; he had earned a Phi Beta Kappa key in college and was deemed by his family and friends to be a near genius in the higher mathematics, which had been his undergraduate major. There might, however, have been more of a question as to the scope of his imagination or even the very existence of his sense of humor. In person he was slight and trim, very straight in posture, with slick dark hair parted in the middle over a round pale countenance and calmly gazing, faintly quizzical gray eyes. It may be hardly necessary to add that he was always impeccably clad, in black or somber gray, and that his only concession to brighter colors was in his silk Laotian ties. He lived harmoniously with his parents and two sisters in a large brownstone in the Murray Hill district and in a rather formidable stone pile by the sea in Bar Harbor, Maine. He saw no need, despite his ample means, to seek bachelor diggings. The Herricks were a closely united clan.

They were also old Knickerbocker New Yorkers. They had been Tories in the Revolution until the surrender of Cornwallis and Confederate sympathizers in the Civil War until General Grant had turned the tide in favor of the North, but ever since they had been staunchly patriotic and prided themselves on their public spirit. Herrick men had always sat on the boards of worthy civic institutions — Trinity Church, Columbia College, the public library — and their wives, selected without exception from their husbands' social milieu, were admirable examples of feminine decorum. Unlike many in their group, they never succumbed to the temptation of supplementing their diminishing funds by alliances with the new money that threatened to inundate their island. Had any of them aspired to draw a Thomas Nast cartoon of Christ cleansing the temple of money changers, he would have shown the lash falling on the backs of Vanderbilt and Gould.

Amos, as far back as his schoolboy days at Groton, in the early nineteen thirties, had taken in not only what his family was but what it was in relation to the rest of the world. He totally sympathized with their ideals and their feeling of responsibility to a community in which they still regarded themselves as leaders. He shared their belief that the nation should be governed by what John Adams had called "the rich, the wise and the good" and that by "rich" was meant the old rich. But Amos differed from the other Herricks in one important respect: he saw that their influence, social, moral, and political, had largely passed, and that whether it could be brought back or even preserved in its diminished state was gravely in question. What, however, he never questioned was that it would be his duty in life, no matter what the odds, to fight for it. Even in an ultimate defeat he would be like a Stuart devotee in Scotland and continue to raise his glass regretfully to the king across the water.

More intelligent, however, than conservatives who indulged in angry and idle vituperation, Amos saw that opposition to a superior foe required an icy calm and careful research. He had to be ready to rebut socialistic argument with cutting, deadly, and accurate replies, and always to maintain the appearance of goodwill with a bland gaze and even a faintly sarcastic small smile. Emotion was not to be shown, and appeals to emotion, in all fields, were to be regarded with suspicion.

Much of this attitude was hardened at Harvard, but it had been born as early as Groton. At the age of fifteen, when he was attending an Episcopalian confirmation class, a young priest who was assisting the headmaster, and who was passionately and enthusiastically devout, had taken a particular interest in this seriously attentive but never questioning boy who sat so quietly through every session without joining in any of the discussions of the creed or its implications. Perhaps sensing in Amos a future cleric — or even a future atheist, for who could tell with a thoughtful adolescent? — he took him aside for a private chat.

"You seem to have no questions, Amos. That's all right, of course, if you're satisfied with the creed. Is that it? Because if you're not, I'm here to help you. And you don't *have* to be confirmed, you know. Maybe you'd like to put it off for a year. And have a chance to think it over."

"No, sir. I'm ready now."

"You have no trouble with any parts of the creed?"

"No, sir. Do you imply that I should?"

"Oh, not at all. Though it's perfectly natural to wonder about some of its assertions. The descent into hell, for example. That bothers many people."

"It doesn't bother me, sir."

The minister seemed faintly shocked. "One way to mitigate the horror of the idea is to believe, as some do, that if there's a hell, there still may be nobody in it."

"It seems to me, sir, that if there's a hell, there must be people in it. What else would it be for?"

"The unimaginable sinner, I suppose. I confess that the idea of hell troubles me. Could one ever be really happy in heaven, *knowing* there were people in hell?"

"Perhaps one wouldn't think about it."

"Heaven would be oblivion?"

The boy faintly smiled. "Perhaps that's all one would need."

The minister soon saw that he was going to get nowhere with Amos, and he sorrowfully abandoned the quest. He could not penetrate a mind where two opposite points of view could exist tranquilly side by side. Amos was perfectly ready to accept the Nicene Creed as true for everyone but himself. And he was already learning that if one could keep one's thoughts strictly to oneself, one had taken a long step toward impregnability.

This meant, of course, that he had no truly intimate friends, persons, that is, with whom he wished to share his motivating ideas. Even his devotion to his parents did not induce him to do this. His mother was a small, gentle, graying lady, always perfectly neat and simple, who was happy to believe the best of everyone, especially of her "darling boy," as she always called him. Amos felt little need of words to supplement the deep sympathy that existed between them; he was satisfied to recognize that she lacked, and was quite content to lack, the clarity of vision that would enable her to comprehend him more fully.

His father, though equally loved, was a very different affair. His stout, rather formidable looks and the heavy gold objects attached to his watch chain seemed to deny the devotion and benevolence that he manifested to his wife and offspring and especially to his only son and heir. Disobedience to the rigid rules that he laid down for the government of his household might well have brought violence out of hidden places in his heart, but this he never encountered, as his family subscribed in all sincerity to his conservative moral and philosophical creed.

And to his political one. Mr. Herrick, like all his relatives and the bulk of his acquaintances, regarded the advent of the New Deal as an ancient Roman might have regarded the onslaught of Attila. "A traitor to his class" was the mildest of the terms that greeted any mention of President Roosevelt's name in the halls of his clubs. When the Supreme Court took to overturning what he denounced as "Bolshevik legislation," he wrote his friend Justice Van Devanter, "You are guarding the pass at Thermopylae with all the heroism of Leonidas." Amos, of course, was in entire agreement.

But the storm that now burst on the Herricks might have been the revenge of an outraged liberal god. In the fall of 1936 Mr. Herrick died of an apoplectic stroke, and Amos, as his executor, found himself in a desperate struggle to mitigate the impact of what threatened to be almost confiscatory estate taxes. The distinguished old firm that had for so many decades represented the Herricks proved to have been woefully deficient in preparing for what to them had evidently been the new and unfamiliar thrust of federal levies. Trusts that had been deemed immune from inheritance duties were found to contain powers that swept them into Mr. Herrick's taxable estate; gifts to Amos and his sisters were held to have been made in contemplation of death, and the final assessment of what was due Uncle Sam had to be raised by the sale of securities at an all-time market low. In the end, the widow and her offspring might still have been considered by some to be well-to-do, but the bloom was certainly off their rose. The house in Maine, with its gardens, pier, and small steam yacht, had to be sold, the staff in the townhouse slashed to a mere three, the charities drastically reduced, and the list of poor relatives to be helped stricken to almost nothing.

Amos, at least, now knew just what he had to do with his life. His career problem was solved. He would enroll in Columbia Law School and prepare himself for a lifelong battle with the commissioner of Internal Revenue, representing the unfortunate who were threatened with the same fate that his family had suffered. His determination was grim, but it armed him with a certain inner exhilaration. He now had a cause.

He was a few years older than the average student in his class, and he had never taken an interest in law before, but his aptitude with figures stood him well in tax courses and his high marks there brought his final average up to a respectable middle-of-the-road status. But taxes were all he cared about. His brother-in-law, Dexter Post, who had married his pretty (as opposed to his other) sister and who was forging ahead as an associate in the great firm of Coverly & Day, advised him that his marks and failure to make the law review would put him out of the running for the big downtown firms (such, indeed, as Dexter's) and that he might do well to seek employment with the old family counsel.

"After the way they manhandled Daddy's estate?" Amos retorted coolly. "Do you realize, Dexter, that they don't even have a tax partner? All that work is handled by a superannuated accountant who thinks Franklin is Teddy Roosevelt's son! And taxation is the only field in which I propose to practice."

His brother-in-law proceeded patiently to give him a list of smaller firms that had less exacting standards for their proposed associates to meet. Amos listened to him without interruptions, for it was not Amos's habit to interrupt. Besides, he highly esteemed his brother-in-law. The Posts were no "better" than the Herricks in Knickerbocker society but they were just as good, and the brilliant Dexter, handsomely hefty and well tailored, was considered the star of his family. He and Cora had extended their social sphere considerably beyond the limited pales of the Herrick-Post world, and their names were associated with those of "yesterday millionaires" as patrons of charity balls.

Amos's respect for his brother-in-law was in part generated by his deep devotion to his sister. Cora did everything well: her perfect manners were the same in all gatherings; she never seemed to be too callously abandoning the old or to be too eagerly cultivating the new. Did that mean she saw no difference between them? Amos did not think so. He knew that Cora would have been content with the social environment in which she grew up, but her husband was ambitious, and she had seen that compromises had to be made. The Herricks' high rung on the old Jacob's ladder could be an asset, but only if tactfully and astutely handled. Amos, she liked to point out, used it as a fort, she as an underground tunnel into the enemy's dens of the new rich. But their differences did not mar their deep attachment.

When Dexter had finished his little survey, Amos simply stated, without commenting on it, "Thank you, Dexter. You've been very kind. And I know you're right about the reception I would receive if I should apply to Coverly & Day. Nonetheless, I should very much appreciate it if you would use a touch of your undoubted goodwill there to procure me an interview with one of the tax partners."

Dexter was a bit taken aback by this, but he knew how stubborn his wife's brother could be, and he managed, not without some difficulty, to arrange the interview requested.

Amos, a few days later, seated in a paneled office before the paper-laden desk of Mr. Snell, the firm's junior tax partner, surprised the latter by opening the interview with a terse, obviously rehearsed little speech.

"I know your time is valuable, sir, so I shall take very little of it. I am fully aware that my Columbia Law School record is not what your firm expects of a new clerk. But I can point to my top grades in every tax course I took, and I took all that were offered. I am not interested either in the amount of my salary or in any future partnership. I have an income adequate for my needs. All I am seeking is the opportunity to match my wits and skill against those of the commissioner of Internal Revenue. I am bold enough to think that I could make it worth your while to employ me in that capacity at whatever stipend you see fit to pay."

Mr. Snell was intrigued. He had never met such an applicant. After only an hour's further talk he took it upon his own responsibility to hire Amos on the spot. Of course, he had already learned from Dexter that his new clerk was entirely respectable.

And so started Amos's highly individual career in the great firm. It was not long before his aptitude made its mark. The tax department was quick to realize that for all his rigid conformity to somewhat outdated habits of formal wear and speech, he had a mind always open to a new approach in seemingly doomed situations where every path appeared to have been explored. After he had reversed on appeal a decision in favor of the Treasury that the entire tax department of the firm had deemed unbeatable, he was given his own small office with his own full-time secretary and allowed to operate virtually unsupervised. He was in his office promptly at nine and left on the dot of seven at night, never wasting a minute in idle chatter with his fellows (he kept his door closed) and lunching on a sandwich sent in from a local grill.

Clients began to like him. Even corporate officers known for their tough business ways developed a kind of affectionate

respect for the cool, trim figure of their tax counsel, with his
jacket neatly buttoned and his collar still unfastened as he sat
on the hottest summer day at a conference table where all else
were in shirtsleeves, motionless except when he made a brief
calculation on his slide rule. And he earned the admiration of
many of Uncle Sam's auditors as well. For his manners were
always, like his sister Cora's, though drier, perfect. He never,
by so much as a flicker of the eye, betrayed that he deemed
himself engaged in a holy war against the forces of nihilism.
On the contrary, he gave the impression of taking part in a
kind of sporting gentlemen's duel, with face masks and épées,
artistically manipulated and inwardly exhilarating.

He had good reason to be home for dinner every night,
for he was now married. He had always planned to be, though
his relations with the daughters of family friends had never
gone beyond a cool and pleasant amity, and he had kept an
eye out for the spouse he was sure would suit him and whom
he would suit. It would be part of an orderly life, and she
must not object to living in the commodious and independent apartment into which he had converted the upper two
stories of the brownstone where his mother and sister Thyra
dwelt. Miriam Duer, small, blond, adequately pretty, and of
a sweet and sober disposition, and of course of the Herrick
world (though a little poorer), was just the person. He was
quite perceptive enough to sense that she was after exactly
the same thing that he was: a quiet, orderly, and respectable
life, very like that of her own parents, but he deemed that an
advantage, and he was right, by his own lights anyway. For
Miriam was one of those rare creatures who not only know
exactly what they want but who are perfectly content when
they get it. She knew very well that Amos wanted to be near

his mother, and she didn't mind so long as Mrs. Herrick ascended to her apartment only when invited, to which rule Amos's mother had the good sense to adhere. Everybody got on with everybody else in this ordered brownstone life, and Miriam and Amos even came to love each other in their own quiet way. One child, a son, was born to them.

Amos Jr. would eventually be a problem, because Miriam now had something not merely to love but to adore. All the hidden fire in her nature suddenly blazed with this infant, and its mother for the first time conceived of ambitions beyond the scope of her upbringing. The boy had to grow up to make his mark in a much larger world. She had taken no interest in her husband's tax work; his income had satisfied her limited though very definite needs and wants, but now she began to look ahead and wonder just where her spouse's brilliant mind was taking him. He was in his early thirties, almost past the age when most clerks were deemed eligible for partnership in Coverly & Day, and he was still an associate. Dexter, a year younger, was already a member of the firm. What was going on?

Miriam talked to her brother-in-law, who was eager to confide in her. Dexter was of the opinion that she might be a real help in the matter. Amos, it seemed, rarely took his advice, but he would have to listen to his wife. Dexter was very anxious to see Amos made partner; he had visions of their ultimately running the firm together. What he didn't tell Miriam was that he visualized himself as the senior partner, with Amos as his trusted executive officer. Every great leader needs a loyal number two. But Amos showed no interest in partnership, and there were some members of the firm who, knowing that because of his lack of ambition they were not apt to lose him as a clerk, questioned if he were not too odd a duck to place in their front rank. As one of them had put it to Dexter, "Do we really want a partner who's that far to the right of Louis XIV?"

And then Dexter told Miriam about the Connelly brothers.

⇥⟨⟨

There were three brothers, and they formed a partnership in the ownership and management of apartment houses and hotels in New York City that constituted a considerable empire. They were among the most important clients of Coverly & Day, their work occupying the major part of the time of two partners and half a dozen associates. Amos did most of their tax work. With two of the brothers he got on very well. They expected nothing but expertise from him, and that they got. They may have thought it odd that in two years of frequent conferences they and he had never reached a first-name basis, but this was hardly a matter that concerned them. They could joke among themselves with Irish bluntness about "the little tax prick" and sneeringly liken him to the haughty Brits who had once misgoverned their native isle. But his brain was at their service, and that was all that mattered.

Aloysius Connelly, however, was different from his brothers. The ablest and cleverest of the three, he was also the least attractive. While the other two were big and bluff and hearty, he was small and mean. The weighty log on his shoulder, begotten no doubt of his diminutive stature and unlovely features, bred in him the suspicion that he was being snubbed as a "mick" by any of Anglo-Saxon origin. When he asked Amos, at the end of one conference, with a slight but fixed grin that seemed anything but hospitable, if he and his wife would dine one night with the Aloysius Connellys in their sumptuous penthouse atop one of their apartment houses on Central Park West, Amos replied politely that it was his fixed policy never to have social relations with clients.

"I do not wish anything to interfere with the total independence of mind that must accompany my legal opinions," he explained smoothly but unconvincingly. "Even gratitude may do that."

Aloysius frowned, but he accepted it. When sometime later he encountered Amos at a cocktail party given by one of the Hudson River Livingstons, who was selling a lot to the Connellys and hoped to up the price, he challenged Amos to defend his theory.

"I see there are clients and clients, Mr. Herrick. Isn't our host's mother's estate administered by your firm? I believe I've been told so."

"Quite so," Amos replied without visible embarrassment. "But she was a second cousin of my grandfather Schuyler. One has to make exceptions for family."

Aloysius bristled as he took in the implication that the Connelly brothers could never by any stretch of the imagination be included as "family." But he still bided his time. At last, when he spotted Amos at a large Christmas reception thrown by the Bank of Marine Commerce, a principal client of Coverly & Day, he knew he had him trapped.

"Well, Mr. Herrick, is your blood so blue that even the azure of the ocean flows in it? Do you address our host as 'Grandpa Bank'? And will you deign now to dine with Mrs. Connelly and myself? Name your day, my friend."

But even this did not perturb Amos. His eye was cold. "You must forgive me, Mr. Connelly, if Mrs. Herrick and

I limit the number of houses at which we dine out. Our schedule is ever now too full. Social life takes a heavy toll on energies that should be preserved to service clients like yourself."

Aloysius turned his back on Amos, and the next morning he summoned Dexter Post to his office and had a serious talk with him, following which Dexter telephoned Amos and forcibly insisted that he give up his daily sandwich and join him for lunch at his downtown club. When Amos got there, he found that Dexter had had time to get Cora to join them. The three were soon engaged in a tense discussion.

"I have already told you, Amos," Dexter pointed out emphatically, "that there are still members of the firm who, for all their appreciation of the great work you've done, shelter doubts as to whether your social and political convictions aren't too out of step with the times to justify their taking you in as a partner. I have been doing my darnedest to argue them out of this, and I think I can say I'm on the brink of success. But if this Connelly thing breaks, you've had it."

"Breaks?" Amos inquired. "What do you mean?"

"Simply that Aloysius Connelly has told me, in no uncertain terms, that he doesn't know how much longer he and his brothers care to be represented by a firm that assigns their tax work to a lawyer who regards them as social pariahs."

Amos shrugged. "Which perhaps they should be, but which they certainly are not, in the amoral world we live in today."

"Oh, Amos, dear," his sister Cora exclaimed, "don't be like that! If the Connelly brothers walk out, the firm will never forgive you, no matter how hard Dexter pleads for you. You've *got* to learn to live and let live. Dexter tells me that if you will simply ask the Connellys to dinner, he thinks he may be able to smooth the whole thing over."

"The price is too great, Cora."

"But why, Amos, why?" Dexter demanded, exasperated. "What's so great about one silly dinner party? You should see some of the types your heroic sister has asked to the house for my sake!"

"That's your affair and hers. I don't interfere with that."

"But why can't you do likewise?"

"I shall tell you. It is because the Connelly brothers engage in shady deals and in tax evasion that is close to criminal."

"Not under your aegis."

"That I concede. Everything I do for them is strictly aboveboard. But there are aspects of their multifarious business dealings that are never brought to our attention. I have been told this on reliable authority. For these dealings they employ other lawyers. Less reputable ones."

"What business is that of ours? We're not even their general counsel. We represent them on particular deals, and those deals are fair and square. Why do we have to inquire into what else they may be up to?"

"We don't. We even make a point not to. An ethical doctor may remove an appendix even if he knows the patient to be engaged in illegal drug trafficking. But he doesn't have to dine with him. I don't choose to dine with dishonest persons."

"Even if your partnership is at stake?"

"Even so."

Cora now played what she appeared to regard as her trump card. "Even if Miriam asks you to do this little thing?"

"Miriam never would."

"Ask her!"

"There's no point. Miriam and I see eye to eye."

"Ask her!"

Amos was startled by her vehemence. At last he nodded. "Very well. I will."

His discussion with his wife that night did indeed contain a shocking surprise. He knew well that Miriam, usually so compliant with any expressed wish of his, could be on rare occasions absolutely unyielding, but he had never anticipated that anything in his office work, about which she had always been content to profess absolute ignorance, should prove one of these.

"You say that your partnership may depend on our asking these people to dinner?" she demanded in what for her was certainly a sharp tone.

"That has been suggested, at least."

"Then what are we waiting for? Ask them!"

Amos began patiently to explain the reasons he had offered to Dexter and Cora, but Miriam uncharacteristically interrupted him before he was halfway through.

"That's the silliest thing I ever heard! Who cares what these horrid people do in matters that don't concern you? You have no right to put such idiotic scruples ahead of your family!"

He gaped. "My family?"

"Well, your son, anyway."

"My son?"

"Yes, your son. You have one, you know. And I want him to be proud of his father. And I wonder how proud he'd be of a superannuated law clerk long passed over for partnership and hanging on to his job by his teeth!"

Amos, stunned, had nonetheless time to take in that this sorry description of his future self must have come from Dexter. Miriam would never have thought it up herself. Was the whole world against him? He drew a deep breath. "Don't you think, my dear, that a decision like this one should be made by me alone?"

"No! Because it doesn't concern you alone." And here Miriam actually jumped to her feet. "Amos, if you won't do this for me and our boy, I don't know what it may drive me to do! I might even leave you!"

Amos rose and silently paced the room as she stood by, anxiously watching him. What she proposed was, of course, unthinkable. It could never be mentioned again. But there was only one way to be sure that it never would be.

"Ask the Connellys, my dear, for any night you wish."

"Oh, Amos, dear one, you'll never regret it!" She hurried over, once again uncharacteristically, to throw her arms around his neck. "You'll be a partner in the new year! Dexter almost promised me that!"

He smiled, but there was a trace of grimness in the smile. "And maybe one day the senior partner. Who knows?"

"Don't we have to leave that for Dexter?"

"Who says we have to? Dexter has taught us the new ways. Unless they're really the old ones. Anyway, I've learned my lesson. He may find that he has taught me more than he planned to."

Miriam beamed her approval.

Her Better Half

No wicked fairy godmother was present at the christening of Evalina Lane in the beautiful spring of 1900 at the fashionable Church of the Madeleine in Paris. No babe could have entered the world under more auspicious stars. Her father, Schuyler Lane, a handsome, dashing, yet finely cultivated and gentle-mannered American sportsman, had inherited a fortune of many millions from his railroad magnate grandfather while suffering no taint of the vulgarity or coarseness so often ascribed to the new rich of the New World. On the contrary, the Lanes were one of America's oldest families, and Courtland Lane, the grandfather, himself the grandson of a trusted aide of General Washington in the Revolution, had had the wit early in life to associate himself with the Union Pacific and had become a rare *Mayflower* descendant in the ranks of the so-called robber barons. About whom, incidentally, he had written a famous and scathing memoir. That was the way of the Lanes: they had their cake and ate it too.

On the maternal side, baby Evalina was even grander. Her mother, Eliane, had been born a Bourbon-Brassard, a family that claimed seniority to the House of France, insisting that only the unreasonable refusal of Louis XI to recognize the marriage of an ancestor had robbed them of the crown which

Henri IV had deemed worth a mass. Indeed, Schuyler Lane may have been subject to a similar impulse when he had easily (and some said cynically) acquiesced to the demand of his proposed in-laws that he change to the older faith in wedding their daughter. He had even gone further and agreed, for a time anyway, to adopt his wife's native land, sumptuously remodeling the lovely but dilapidated family *hôtel* in the rue de Grenelle as well as the ancestral chateau in Normandy.

Gathered in the church for the christening were some of the greatest names of ancient France, the most respectable of the American expatriate community, several ambassadors and statesmen, and a sprinkling of the father's intellectual French friends. The infant would have several worlds to choose from.

But if there was no wicked godmother present, there were a few skeptical observers who clung to the very private opinion that the child's own mother might do for one. Eliane de Bourbon-Brassard had been born in Frohsdorf, the cold and lonely Austrian chateau where the exiled Comte de Chambord, the uncrowned Henri V of France, had presided over the gloomy little court of nobles, who loyally took their turns "in waiting," leaving their fine Gallic homes for a bleak season of dull and pointless etiquette. When Eliane's poor mother had died there of lung disease and her grief-stricken father had at last brought the child back to Paris, he was determined to fill her life with all the cheer it had so far lacked, and he satisfied her every material want at whatever cost to the sad remnant of his always diminishing capital.

Beautiful, clever, and vivacious, Eliane grew up the prey of moods of frenetic exuberance from which she could plunge into the blackest despair. She was convinced in her high periods that she had everything a woman could possibly want or need: no blood was bluer, no wit sharper, no features more winning, no mind acuter, no soul more imaginative. But at other times she would be convinced that the slightest symptoms of physical malaise were ominous and that she was doomed to an early demise. Only one thing was sure: she had to have her cake while she was still young and gobble down every last crumb of it. She shared at least that resolution with the Lanes.

The Bourbon-Brassards had too little capital to attract the dower-hungry sons of their peers in the Faubourg Saint-Germain, and rather than choose among the eagerly proffered ones of the *haute bourgeoisie*, they cast their net for a rich American. These had the advantage of belonging to no recognized class in the French hierarchy, so it was possible to squeeze them into even the *société la plus fermée*. Schuyler Lane, a first secretary at the American Embassy, with a supposedly brilliant future ahead of him, fitted their every requirement, except for his religion, and that he proved reasonable about. It was true that his mother hurried across the Atlantic to make a noisy fuss about this, but what could she accomplish against the will of a son so in love?

That son was not unaware that his betrothed was subject to violent changes of mood, but he had the male vanity to believe that the deep mutual love which he assumed bound them together would stabilize her and permit what he had no doubt was the noble side of her character to predominate. And to some extent this at first had seemed to be the case. But when he began to differ with her in her fixed notions of where they should live, what people they should see, and what kind of career he should carve for himself, he encountered a

resistance the force of which he had certainly never anticipated. The storm which finally crashed in his ears erupted
when he announced that he was resigning his post at the embassy. He had been corresponding with friends at home who
wanted him to seek election to the New York State Assem-
bly.

"You mean I'd have to live in America?" she cried.

"For some part of the year, anyway. We'd keep a base here,
of course."

"And you'd be a politician? You want to be president?"

Schuyler smiled. "I might have to start a bit lower. But
it is essential for me first to establish a definite residence in
New York. Later on we might move to a western state. If I'm
ever to aim at Congress, it would be more feasible to live in a
less populated area."

"But you never told me all this!"

"I haven't been clear about it in my own mind. Until quite
recently. But I never planned to give up my country. I've always had a political career in the back of my mind. Did you
really expect I'd spend my whole life dawdling in Paris?"

"Dawdling, you call it! And you want me to live with cow-
boys and be scalped by Indians? When we're privileged to
live in the most brilliant city in the world! And belong to the
most brilliant society! Darling, have you gone mad? Look at
the success you've been here! Why, Tante Marielle was telling me just the other day that you spoke better French than
she did. She said no one would take you for an American!"

"Is that the ultimate compliment? I guess it is indeed time
I went home."

"No, no, *mon cher*, it's out of the question. You don't know
what you're asking. There's no limit to the things you can

achieve here. Uncle Pierre tells me he's even going to put
you up for the Jockey. Now, let's not talk about it anymore.
And it's time, anyway, that I dressed. We're due at the Roth-
schilds' at eight."

He let the subject drop, assuming that this had been only
the first round. Given time, he had little doubt that she would
view the prospect more favorably, that she might even come
to see it as an exciting challenge, a new world for her to conquer and enchant. But he soon found that he was making no
headway. Eliane for a time refused to discuss the subject at
all, and when he finally forced her to hear him, she declared
her firm resolution never to cross the Atlantic except for what
she would have to be promised would be only a family visit.

At last he announced that he would go without her. This
brought on a fit of hysterics so violent that she had to be confined to a nursing home.

Her doctor warned Schuyler that she might be suicidal.
He suspected that this was an exaggeration, but did he dare
take the risk? When she came home from the institution, he
greeted her with the assurance that any idea of moving to
America should be indefinitely postponed.

Never had she been lovelier or gentler than when she put
her arms around his neck and gazed soulfully into his eyes.

"Oh, my love," she murmured, "you are too good. Maybe
I should think over America."

"We'll talk about that later. Much later. The thing for you
to do now is to get well."

He was lost.

Eliane could be a very pleasant person to live with when
she got her way. She knew that her husband had given up his
dream of a good life in order, as he pathetically believed, to

preserve her own health and life, but she never doubted that his illusion had been the best thing for him or that she had saved him from the folly of a sordid American political career. She applauded his purchase of a literary quarterly, which he ably edited, and she assisted him in the establishment of a significant cultural salon, nor did she object, so long as he bought her the many things she thought she needed, to his disbursal of large sums to American institutions in Paris, such as the library and hospital. The French years passed smoothly enough for Schuyler, but he never lost sight of what he had sacrificed for them. He was too fair-minded to place all the blame on his wife; he knew how large a role his own weakness had played in his surrender, and he was determined at least to make the dignified best of a life that he had fatally marred.

He would not, however, accept Eliane's rule for their only child. His adored Evalina must certainly become the mistress of her own life. No matter what his social engagements were, a part of every day was reserved for the child: he rode with her in the Bois; he read aloud to her from imaginatively chosen children's books; he tutored her in English, French, and Italian; he introduced her to American history and American legends. He took her on summer visits across the Atlantic to stay with her grandmother Lane and meet children of her own nationality. The brilliant and serious little girl bloomed under the care of this worshipped father; to her he was a god as well as a parent. Her mother, who was affectionate without being at all cloyingly maternal, was not in the least jealous of the situation; she regarded it as a quaint but harmless American obsession that took a lot of boring duties off her hands. She exacted, however, from time to time her full rights as a mother. Evalina had to learn the docile manners of a *jeune fille* of the old faubourg; she had to be strictly *comme il faut*. But Evalina was too wise and too well coached by Papa to give any trouble in this respect.

Did she love her mother? Yes and no. She was sometimes dazzled by her; she liked to watch her from the top of the stairs when Eliane, arrayed in *grand gala de soir,* received her distinguished guests. But she also knew that her mother could be dangerous. Her bark might be more lethal than her bite, but the bite was still sharp enough. And the child noted that though her father was inclined to be afraid of her, or at least to be cautious with her, the maternal relatives were not in the least of that mind. Evalina recalled a ladies' family lunch where the engagement of a Bourbon-Brassard cousin to a young man of respectable but little-known origin was discussed. Her mother let it be known that in her opinion the family was lowering itself.

Evalina's maternal grandmother, the old *comtesse,* who had been born a Mortemart, had coldly reproved her daughter. "That comment, *chère* Eliane, would have been silly enough coming from me. But coming from one whose family had to reach across the Atlantic to find her a spouse, it is simply ridiculous."

"But Mama, the Lanes are an ancient clan."

"No doubt, my dear. And of course we all love Schuyler."

Which gave to the table notice that the subject was closed. And Evalina noted that her mother had accepted the reproof meekly enough. There had been no such explosion as followed any criticism by her father.

By her fourteenth year, Evalina was still small and grave, with black hair and large brown eyes, but a keen observer could have seen that with a little more animation she might turn almost pretty. She had become aware that her wonderful father was at heart a deeply disappointed man and had guessed that his occasional low spirits had something to do with his expatriatism. She was also aware of her mother's distaste for any reference to his American origins — Eliane had not accompanied her husband and daughter on their visits to New York — but she certainly in no way shared it. Evalina got on perfectly well with both the American and the French girls at her fashionable private international school, but she always made it clear that she was more a Lane than a Bourbon-Brassard. And she had deeply loved her dear old grandmother Lane, whose silence on their New York visits with respect to her mother had been noted, if not commented on.

Evalina one day decided to plumb her father on a subject he seemed never to discuss.

"We *are* still American citizens, are we not, Papa?"

"Oh, yes, my darling, always."

"Then why don't we ever think of living there?"

"Because your mother, sweetheart, would hate it."

"Couldn't she learn to like it?"

"I don't really think so. Let's put it that the climate over there doesn't agree with her."

"But it's a huge country, Papa. Couldn't we find a state with air that would suit her? What about the West? Isn't the atmosphere there dry and clear? I've read about it in geography class."

"Oh, yes, I've had that in mind," her father replied, talking suddenly as if to himself. "I even thought of moving to New Mexico or Arizona. A magnificent ranch near Phoenix was once offered to me for almost nothing."

"Could you still get it?"

"Oh no. But of course there are others."

"Oh, Papa! Do let's go!"

Evalina was never in her life to forget the look her father now gave her. The eyes that met hers in that long loving stare were not those of a man to a little girl but those of one understanding adult to another. When he answered her at last, it was in a somewhat choked tone.

"Well, darling, we might. We just might."

"Oh, Papa, how wonderful!"

But nothing was to come of it. Their little chat was in the spring of 1914, and summer brought Armageddon. Schuyler, who had had some early military training at home in the National Guard, felt impelled to apply successfully for a commission in the French army and fight for the country in which he had lived for a decade and a half and whose benefits he had taken. He was soon sent to the front and was killed in the first battle of Champagne.

Perhaps it was a relief to him.

Eliane had been so keyed up by the excitement of the war, so almost hysterically patriotic, that she tended to regard her husband's death as a sacrifice on her own part that crowned her with a halo of glory. She converted a life of pleasure into one of rather frenzied service and volunteered for hospital work of the utmost drudgery, drawing on a rich supply of energy long hidden from herself as well as the world. Her poor little grieving daughter seemed irrelevant to a Paris in arms, and she decided to send the girl to the safety of her paternal grandmother in New York.

Evalina was glad enough to go. Crossing to England with her governess, she sailed on what was to be the next-to-last voyage of the ill-fated *Lusitania*. Sitting in a deck chair beside the apprehensive Mademoiselle, huddled in a blanket and gazing at the bleak, gray, restless ocean, she contemplated without fear the possibility of drowning in a submarine attack. Might it not unite her with her beloved father? But something like hope revived in her at the vision, bursting unexpected from under suddenly lifting clouds, of the towers of New York. It was an inspiring sight; it had been *his* birthplace and early home. And in another couple of hours she was being hugged and comforted in the warm embrace of her tear-stained lovely old grandmother. Evalina knew at once how tightly her grief was shared.

She was to stay with her grandmother for the remaining three years of the war. The time passed quietly and uneventfully in the old lady's serenely ordered brownstone existence. Fanny Lane was the breed of gentle and kindly dowager who mitigated the reputation of hauteur that social newcomers were apt to attribute to "Old New York." She made the rounds of the tenements owned by the Lane trustees and insisted on improvements, even at the expense of income, and she taught classes in poetry to stenographers attending night school. Yet she shared the discipline of many ladies of her class: her rooms were spotlessly neat, her maidservants silently efficient and trimly clad, her Rolls-Royce town car a brightly shining maroon. However humble her heart, her appearances were impeccable.

Evalina was enrolled in Miss Chapin's School for Girls, where she soon equaled her Paris record for high marks. She got on well enough with her classmates, though they were inclined to find her too serious and too averse to giggly confidences about boys and sex. She made one true friend, Ella Pratt, the daughter of a Presbyterian pastor, who hoped to become a poetess. Evalina remained a nominal Catholic, but she suspected that her father had been at heart an agnostic, and she supposed that she would be one as well. Her grandmother suspected this but said nothing about it, hoping that such a state of doubt might be the prelude to a return to the Protestant faith.

Mrs. Lane lived alone, her two married daughters having moved to their husbands' cities, and she and Evalina passed most of their evenings together in the big, dark, cool, leathery library, she at her needlepoint and the girl at her homework. Before retiring they would have a half-hour's chat. Evalina learned from her grandmother all the details of the family fortune.

"Ordinarily it would be the duty of your parents to explain these things, my darling child. But unhappily, you have no father to do it, and your mother is across the sea and besides, her lovely head was not made for business. So it is up to your poor old gran to prepare you for your future. As you know, neither of your aunts has been blessed with babes, and one day all the Lane trusts, for me and for both of them, will break and pour their contents into your little lap. That, in addition to what your father has already left you, will make you a remarkably rich young lady. Money, of course, can bring pleasure, but it can also bring problems. It will sometimes be difficult for you to distinguish between people who are genuinely your friends and those who merely want to stick their hands in your pocket. Unfortunately, the latter are often gifted with a deceiving charm. But it won't do to be always suspecting people. The great remedy is to distract yourself with the duty of disposing of the money for the ultimate benefit of your fellow men. You will find it no easy task. And you must not forget to benefit yourself as well as others. You must always look well and live well. I want you to be worthy of the Lane inheritance. That is what your father would have wanted. And I haven't a doubt but that you will be! Hug me, my child!"

Evalina threw her arms around the old lady's shoulders. "I shall do my best to be like you, Gran!" she exclaimed with an earnestness that she fully felt.

Nineteen-eighteen brought the armistice to Europe and graduation from school to Evalina. She was eighteen and ready now to return to her mother, whom she had not seen in three years and whose letters, brief and gushing, had given little information about life in Paris and shown little curiosity about life in New York. The New World, of course, had never really existed for Eliane. Evalina discussed her future with her friend Ella Pratt.

"Will you live in France now?" Ella wanted to know.

"Not permanently. My place is here. The family fortune was made here and will be spent here."

"Spent? Whoopee!"

Evalina frowned. "I mean used. Used for the betterment of all concerned. Gran has taught me that it's a kind of sacred trust."

"My father would certainly approve of that. But you make it sound so serious, Lina. Won't you kick up your heels a bit?"

"My father didn't kick up his heels, Ella."

"Didn't he ever? Just a little? How can you be so sure?"

"If he did, he made up for it at the end. He died a hero."

"Oh, Lina, you can't live on that!"

"Can't I?"

Before she sailed for France, Evalina received a grave warning from her grandmother about a matter she had not wanted to bring up before it should be absolutely necessary.

"My dear child, this is a painful subject, so sit down here beside me and just listen. You are going to be away from me, and anyway I haven't that much longer to live, so I must speak now, while I can. It's about your mother. Your mother, child, is an ill woman. Not so much physically, as she constantly supposes, as mentally. She cannot help her dark moods any more than she can moderate her high ones. That is in the nature of the disease. But God or Nature does not wholly neglect people stricken as she is. He endows them sometimes with the instinct to recognize and attach themselves to the particular humans who are adapted to support them. They are like certain natural parasites: vines that know what tree to entwine, small fish that ride on the backs of larger ones. Your mother found your father, who devoted his life to her. Don't let her do that to you!"

"But Gran," Evalina protested in distress, "if I can help her wouldn't Papa have wanted me to?"

"Up to a point, yes. I'm not saying you shouldn't love your mother. But you can help someone without becoming their slave. Your father was always worried about that happening to you. Don't doubt me. I *know*! You'll always have the means to keep yourself independent of anybody. Well, use them!"

Evalina arrived in France determined to have good relations with her mother. Eliane was still her legal guardian; Evalina would have to await her twenty-first birthday before she came into full possession of her property. She had learned a good bit about the family finances from her grandmother and been told to rely on the advice of Thaddeus Warwick, the reputedly brilliant young man at the Morgan Bank who was in charge of the Lane interests in France. She had also been warned that her mother had been making deep inroads into that part of the family capital that her father had unwisely bequeathed to her outright. But even if all of this portion of the fortune should be dissipated, a far vaster share was safely in the hands of trustees holding it for Evalina's sole benefit. She had been told that she had only to bide her time till the day when she should be utterly free.

She had little affection for this mother across the sea, and she blamed her for the waste of her father's life. Had he come home to America, he might have had a fine political career. Nor would he have been killed in the war, as by the time the United States entered the conflict he would have been above military age. But she was also aware that her father had deeply loved his difficult spouse and would certainly have expected his daughter to do her duty by her. Which indeed she would, though not without thorough and discreet observation of this Gallic parent.

She found a mother still beautiful and stylish, if faintly raddled, so to speak, about the edges, living superbly in the glorious old *hôtel* in the Rue de Grenelle and waited on by smartly uniformed footmen and maids. Eliane was one who had flung to the winds all the cares and worries of four years of carnage and resumed with a kind of ecstasy of relief the old life of pleasure, greeting the nineteen twenties as a golden age. She appeared to regard her commendable war work as the fulfillment of every duty she owed to her deity and a license to make up now for every hardship endured.

She greeted Evalina with more enthusiasm than the latter had expected, evidently regarding it as a high amusement to have an heiress daughter to launch in what was left of the best society.

"You are going to simply adore your new life here, *ma chère*. You will go with me everywhere and meet all my friends. They will adore you. But first we must get you a new wardrobe. I can see that your grandmother has had a hand in your outfitting. Oh, you needn't tell me. I have eyes! You will find yourself, as they say, in the desirable position of being naked with a checkbook. And you'll see what money well spent can accomplish. You don't have to be Helen of Troy, my sweet, for something to be made of you. You've really got quite a decent figure and complexion, and your eyes are fine—your best asset. And we'll get that Lane reserve out of your expression. We'll endow you with some of my family's *joie de vivre*!"

Evalina accepted this outpouring, as she did the many others that were to follow, with silent acquiescence. She submitted herself to the visits to dressmakers and milliners, conceding that the maternal taste in such matters was peerless and that Eliane would never buy anything that would clash with what she was keen enough to recognize as her daughter's unalterably subdued personality. A good workman, she accepted her basic material. But Evalina had more trouble with her mother when it came to her firm intent to take courses at the Sorbonne, which meant curtailing the social schedule to make time for reading and preparation. Her adroit argument, however, that her lessons in French literature would help her with some of the writers who attended her mother's salon brought the latter ultimately around.

"When I talk to your friend Monsieur Paul Bourget, Maman, it should help if I've read *Le Disciple*."

"There's something in that, I admit," her mother, who had not herself read the novel in question, conceded. "Society is becoming more and more mixed. Before the war, if you wanted intellectual chatter, you could go to Madame de Caillevet's and talk to Anatole France. Today you might meet him at the Noailles. But don't get the idea that the old values are gone. They lurk. Our faubourg used to be an ace of trumps. It isn't that anymore, but it's still a trump. You have to learn to play every card in your hand. I once asked Laure de Saxe which of the many handles to her name she was apt to use. 'It depends on the group I find myself in,' was her reply. And while I'm on the subject I should warn you that a *mésalliance* can still be just that. No matter how democratic we've become or how wide the doors are open. Your *dot*, my dear, is going to attract a lot of young men, some of whom, even the most charming, will be quite impossible matches. You must learn to discriminate."

Evalina wondered if her mother included Thaddeus Warwick, of the Morgan Bank, among the impossible matches. Certainly he was the most charming of all the men who came to her salon, and he reputedly had a brain on a par with his dark, dashing good looks. And he came to the house, moreover, less for her mother than for her whom he was supposed to educate in the financial responsibilities that would one day be hers. But he did his job with lightness and charm.

"I see you as a latter-day Isabel Archer," he told her one evening as they sat in a corner of her mother's crowded parlor, under the great green tapestry that depicted Louis XV at a hunt.

"In *The Portrait of a Lady?* Do you predict that I will fall victim to a shady fortune hunter?"

"Never! You'll be an Isabel Archer who has the sense to go home. You won't be taken in by wicked old Europe."

"You think yourself very perceptive, don't you, Mr. Warwick?"

"But anyone can see that in you. And call me Thad, please. And you'll be Lina. Or rather Evalina. It's a prettier name unabbreviated. Unlike mine."

"What about yourself, Thad? Will you be taken in by wicked old Europe? Or has it already happened?"

"Not on your life! This is only a tour of duty. Next year I'll be back in 14 Wall Street."

"And that will be it? Forever and ever?"

"Ah, don't rob my life of all interest. I've always played with the idea of one day doing something in politics."

Her heart gave a little jump. Like her father! "Oh, that *would* be interesting."

He was tall and well made, with a high broad brow, a fine prominent nose, a determined chin, thick raven-black hair, and yellow-gray smiling eyes. Or at least they seemed to be smiling, perhaps to mitigate some of his handsome straightness. She guessed that he could be quick, definite, incisive, but then, as if to warn the observer that he was not to be taken too seriously, that maybe nothing should really be taken too seriously, he would say something wonderfully witty. Evalina was put in mind of Talleyrand's *point de zèle, surtout point de zèle*. Did he not need someone to supply the zeal?

Her mental image of Thaddeus, adjusted to a vision of a silver-toned orator in the halls of Congress, became tinged with the faint pink hue of romance. And she was now more critically observant of his relations with her mother. He was halfway between Eliane's age and her own. Was Eliane the "older woman" in his life that she had read about in Henry James's *The Ambassadors*? But no, he was strictly her mother's *homme d'affaires*, and indeed the latter made no secret of finding his restrictions on her spending irksome. For the Lane properties in France—Magny, the Normandy chateau with its extensive farms and stables, the vineyard in Bordeaux, the villa in Cannes, the game park in Fontainebleau—were all under his direct supervision. Eliane took no interest in the business side of life, and Evalina, on the excuse of learning about her heritage, accompanied him on his tours of inspection. In Normandy they roamed together over the ancestral acres, visiting barns and dairies.

Thaddeus made learning the business side of wealth as easy and pleasant as novel reading—indeed, quite like it. He made her think of how Lord Melbourne made parliamentary debates amusing to the young Victoria, as described in Lytton Strachey's new biography of the queen, which everyone was reading. "But will your expertise in French agricultural problems do you much good when you're back in New York?" she wanted to know.

"Finance is pretty much the same the world over. The man who likes to get to the bottom of things rarely wastes his time. You'll find that most of what you've observed in France will stand you in good stead one day. Of course you have to apply the rule of *mutatis mutandis*. But something tells me you'll be able to do just that."

"How can you tell?"

"By the fact that you've remembered everything I've taught you. I haven't had to repeat anything."

"That's because you're such a good teacher."

"What good is a teacher, even the best, without an apt pupil? And you're the kind whose way a teacher has to get out of."

"I do try, it's true."

"Well, we're a pair."

Her heart swelled with pleasure. But her elation was diminished by her suspicion that she was a pupil to him and only that. Oh, yes, perhaps a bit of a pal as well, but never a girlfriend. No, she could tell. He was older, maybe thirty, and had been in the war. He would need a woman more mature, more sophisticated, one to dazzle the great world. And of course there were plenty of such. One was sure to grab him.

At length she felt sufficiently secure in their own special kind of intimacy to ask him a more personal question. What, at any, rate did she have to lose? "Why haven't you married? There must have been ladies who wouldn't have turned a deaf ear to such a proposition."

"Oh, that's a long story. It would bore you."

"Try me."

He told her, quite willingly and at some length, of his drawn-out and futile pursuit of a woman who was "simply the most beautiful creature God ever made." Obviously, he enjoyed airing something long in his innermost heart. Had he made a fetish of it? Her name was Pauline, and she had always professed to be his dear friend but nothing more. He had fallen in love with her at the age of sixteen, while a student at Groton School, at a Washington's Birthday dance to which she had been invited by his roommate, and he had adored her hopelessly until her marriage to that same roommate eight years later.

"I guess she was drawn to ugly men," he ended sadly. "Old Tom was always mortally plain."

"You mean it was a case of Beauty and the Beast?"

"Oh, hardly that. He's a good enough fellow. I hear they're happy as clams."

"Are clams so happy?"

"Maybe they don't know enough not to be."

It didn't occur to Eliane that her daughter could be much drawn to Thaddeus Warwick, because she wasn't herself. She preferred men who made a fuss over her, and the young banker had too skeptical an eye to do much of that. Her current beau was a fastidious, literary, and highly cultivated English bachelor and epicure, Peter Everett, who took at face value all her complaints and seeming ailments and enveloped her in a mist of uncritical devotion. For Evalina it soon became clear that her mother had greater matrimonial projects for her: she had in mind no less than a duke.

Raymond, duc d'Ivry, was a very gentle, very mild, very kindly, neat little man, possessed of a famous chateau and a glorious ancestry. He was also witty and companiable. He perfectly understood that it was essential for his family and himself that he should marry an heiress, and nobody could doubt that he would be a very proper and well-behaved husband.

Evalina liked him but was not romantically aroused. Besides, she had no intention of living in France. The time soon came when it behooved her to let the duke know he was wasting his time. This was when her mother informed her that she had invited him for a weekend at Magny.

"And I'm asking no one else but Peter Everett," Eliane added. "I thought we'd be just a cozy foursome for once." Here she gave Evalina one of her sidelong glances. "I'm sure Raymond will have no objection to that."

Evalina drew in her breath. The moment, the great moment that had always been to come, had come. She found herself thinking, with an odd inner smile, of her grand-mother Lane's favorite hymn: "Once to ev-e-ry man and na-tion comes the mo-ment to decide." Was courage so difficult, after all? Mightn't it even be fun?

"What are you thinking about, my dear?"

"I was just thinking, Maman, of how impossible it will be for me to spend a lovely idle weekend at Magny. I have a pile of reading to do for my philosophy class. I simply have to stay in town with my nose to the grindstone."

"But, my child, that's impossible! How can I offer an ex-cuse like that to Raymond? Why, it would be practically an insult."

"He needn't take it that way. But if he does, he does."

"You mean you don't care?"

"I don't care at all."

Eliane became grave. "What is behind all this, Evalina? There is something behind it, isn't there?"

"There is." Evalina straightened herself to deliver the blow. "If I go up to Magny with just you and Peter, it will look to Raymond as if I were not averse to something more serious."

Eliane's features hardened as she stared at her daughter. "Are you telling me that you *are* averse?"

"Certainly."

"It's nothing to you to be admired by the greatest catch in Paris?"

"Nothing at all."

"You don't wish to be a duchess?"

"I don't even wish to be the wife of a Frenchman. If I marry at all, I shall marry an American. As you did."

Eliane gasped. "But I wasn't an heiress! Look, child, let's not be rash. There's no need for resolutions at this time. Come to Magny and treat Raymond as you would any other guest. He will see at once that this is not the moment for anything further. He has perfect tact. Trust him. And trust your mother."

"I'm afraid I can't do that, Maman. If I continue to see Raymond on this basis, he will be justified in thinking that I am at least considering him as a husband. And a girl who considers it is generally taken as more than half won. If she backs out, she will be said to have led him on. The only way to make it crystal-clear to Raymond that I will never be his bride is to stop seeing him except on public occasions."

"That is nonsense, Evalina. You will be thought to be the kind of giddy girl who thinks that every man who so much as kisses her hand is about to propose. But I see there's no point arguing with you. You're too set in your ways. Very well. You force me to use my parental authority. For your own good, I insist that you accompany me to Magny this weekend."

"You *order* me?"

"If you want to put it that way."

"Then I must disobey you. You'll have to get a gendarme to get me there."

"Oh, Evalina!" Eliane's eyes filled with tears as she bowed her head and struck her fist on the table beside her. "How can you hurt me so? A mother who only wants what's best for her only child! It's not enough to have lost a beloved husband in the war and to be despised and scorned by his biased old mother! And to be railed at by her money man here for trying to keep up a half-decent appearance in the life her son wanted me to lead! And to be doomed with a weak heart that may go back on me any day! No, no, all that is not enough. I have to have a daughter who flings my love and devotion back in my teeth!"

Evalina gazed at her without flinching. "Don't you know, Mother, that all that won't work with me? Can't you tell?"

Eliane regained her control. The stare with which she fixed her daughter for several long moments glittered with something new. Was it hate?

"Yes, I *can* tell. You're a monster."

From this point on, Evalina's relationship with her mother underwent a drastic change. Eliane became cool and distant; she treated her daughter with the proud reserve she might have shown to a German officer in wartime occupying her chateau. But Evalina found this preferable to the exaggerated enthusiasm that had preceded it. She could attend her courses, visit museums, and spend her evenings reading, while her mother resumed, alone now, her frenetically active social life. Her twenty-first birthday was approaching, and then she would be free.

When Thaddeus tried to assure her that her mother's resentment was bound in time to thaw, she firmly shook her head.

"I don't think, Thad, that you fully comprehend what's wrong with her. My grandmother told me all about it. Mother knows, with a kind of instinct, just on whom her charm will work and just on whom it won't. She wasn't sure of me at first, because I was young and possibly unformed. But now she knows and hates me. I must face that."

"Oh, Evalina, you're taking it much too hard. Remember that she's a mother. A mother will always forgive."

"There's nothing to forgive."

"Well, forget then. She's basically too warm-hearted not to."

"You may be one on whom her charm will work. Most men are. Watch out!"

"Anyway, I have you to guard me," he retorted with a smile. "And of course you're quite right about Ivry. He's not the man for you at all."

"I'm glad you see that." She gave him an earnest look, but he continued in his humorous vein.

"No, you need a stalwart puritan, Evalina, as American as yourself. I wonder if Boston isn't the place for you to look."

"I'm not looking," she replied, endeavoring to hide the hurt she felt. "And now I want you to go over with me the steps I'm to take when I reach my majority next month."

"I've made a little memo, and I have it here. But let me first point out that although all the changes you're going to be making in your mother's way of life are essential to save her from ruin and although she will still be better off than all but a very few women in Paris, she is nonetheless going to scream that you are reducing her to pauperdom."

"You see it exactly," was Evalina's grim comment.

"So let me be the one to tell her. Let her wrath fall on my head. She will kick me out of the house and never see me again, but that's all right. I'm due to leave the Paris office anyway, and the bank knows and approves of the whole plan, so I have nothing to lose. You must stay away and let it appear that you had nothing to do with the matter."

"But she is entitled to know that she is not being just pushed around by a cold and indifferent bank. She is entitled to know that her daughter, representing her late husband, has given deep and conscientious consideration to every aspect of the reorganization of her financial life."

Thaddeus pursed his lips to emit a faint whistle. "Very well. But it's going to be quite a scene."

"Which you will witness. For I want you there."

The meeting turned out to be quite as bad as Thaddeus had predicted. They met, the three of them, on a cold, gray December morning in the parlor of the *hôtel* on the Rue de Grenelle. Eliane, who had some inkling of what was in store for her, listened in ominous silence while Thaddeus summarized the list of the Lane properties in France and gave their assessed valuations. Then Evalina delivered her carefully rehearsed speech.

"I am setting up a trust for your benefit, Maman, the trustees of which will be the Morgan Bank and the senior partner of the Lane family law firm in New York. It will be funded sufficiently to give you an income equal to what you had before you depleted the legacy that my father left you."

"Ah, you throw that in my face!"

"Only to assure you that you will be just as well-off as he intended you to be."

"But your father didn't subject me to the indignity of being controlled by trustees!"

"And you see what the result has been. I am not reproaching you, Maman. I am simply guaranteeing that it will not happen again."

"And what if I run into some emergency? What if the income is insufficient in the event of some disaster?"

"Your fiduciaries will have the power to invade principal in their discretion."

"So you've bound me hand and foot! What about Magny? Will I be able to keep it up?"

"I'm afraid not. Magny is, as you know, in my name. The high expense of maintaining the chateau and all the farms is out of all proportion to your use of it. Last year you were there for exactly three weekends. I feel compelled to sell it."

"The family chateau! You'll sell the family chateau! Which has been ours since the Dark Ages!"

"Actually, it was acquired by the Bourbon-Brassards only when they returned from emigration with Louis XVIII in 1816. But I shall endeavor to find a purchaser who will respect its historic value. If not, I may give it to the nation. The villa in Cannes where you now spend a good part of the winter, which is in our joint names, will be placed in yours alone."

"Very generous, I'm sure! And this house we're now in?"

"That is yours already. And I'm setting up a separate trust to maintain it. So your life should continue very much as it has been. And of course, if things should go really wrong, you will always have me to count on."

"Do you think I'd ever take a sou from you after the way you've treated me? Stripped me of my beloved chateau and tied me up to foreign trustees!"

"I shan't look to you as my judge, Maman. I must do as I think right."

"Oh, leave me, leave me alone, both of you! You say this house is mine. Then will you please go to some other part of it?"

"I thought you might be feeling that way, so I have already reserved a room at the Crillon."

Thaddeus at this intervened. "Please, Eliane, try to see things more reasonably. Evalina is only seeking to ensure your security. She —"

"And you too, Thaddeus Warwick!" Eliane almost screamed. "You've aided this crazy girl in every wicked scheme she's been plotting ever since I was naive enough to take her in. You and her mean old grandmother in New York."

In the front hall, while a footman placed Evalina's bags in the car that would take her to her new residence, she and Thaddeus exchanged a few half-whispered remarks.

"Was I all right, Thad?" she demanded, with a tremor in her tone. "Do you think I was really all right?"

"You were more than all right. You were Olympian!"

"You mean it? Honestly and truly?"

"My dear, you were like a heroine in a tragedy by Corneille!"

But that night, that sleepless night, in her splendid but lonely suite in the Crillon, Evalina was haunted by the memory of his eyes. Their aspect might have been admiring, even a bit awe-stricken, but it could never have been called anything like loving. A heroine of Corneille! Had she not read those plays? Had he and she not discussed them? Did she not know just what he thought of those so-called heroines? Sophonisbe, who loved her fatherland more than she loved either of her husbands; Rodelinde, who bade the usurper of her crown slay her infant son in order to mark him as a beast in the eyes of his new subjects; Pulchérie, who preserved her virginity even in marriage so that she might not share her sovereign power with a man. Who would want to marry such women? Were they not monsters all? Had her own mother not called her that?

She had several meetings with Thaddeus in the days that followed, for all her new arrangements had to be effected in legal documents and discussed with counsel, Thaddeus, of course, presiding at the conferences. But after the final signing of deeds and trust instruments, he invited her to celebrate the occasion at a lunch at the Tour d'Argent, and she took quick advantage of their isolation to show herself to him in a softer and kindlier light than that shed by the heroines of the seventeenth-century stage.

"I've been worried about Maman," she began. "She really needs someone to look after her. I wonder if Peter Everett isn't just the man. He adores her and finds her faultless. And he takes every symptom of her malaise with a reverent faith. What's more, he's always available. He can write those lovely laquered essays of his wherever she chooses to take him."

"You're thinking of him, of course, as a husband. But do you think she would ever agree? He's not precisely my idea of a great lover."

"Maman doesn't really need a lover. She loves to flirt, but I have an idea it's not apt to go much further. She likes the sound and flutter of romance. She likes to be fussed over. Peter suits her to perfection, and he's been around her for years. I think she might marry him if she had any real fear of losing him. The question is, would he marry her?"

"Why not, if he's such a lap dog? And then there's always the money."

"That's just it. That's what worries him. *Will* there always be the money? He's seen her blowing it. And to be left poor with Maman on his hands is not a fate any man would want."

"He doesn't know, then, about your arrangements?"

"How would he? You don't think she'd ever tell him, do you? Never! She's too ashamed of it. No, *you* must tell him, Thad."

"Me? Why me? Can't you do it?"

"Think of it! It would humiliate the poor man to take it from a mere girl."

He thought it over for a minute and then nodded. "Very well. I'll do it. And let me add that I think it's very good of you to give so much thought to your mother's welfare after the way she's treated you."

She could have clapped her hands. "Then you don't think I'm like one of those terrible Corneille heroines?"

"Dear me, is that what they are? But of course I don't think you're really like that. What an idea, Evalina! What do you take me for?"

"I don't know!" she almost cried out. "I don't know what I take you for." And then, in a kind of despair, she threw restraint away. "I only know what I *want* to take you for. I'm not like a Corneille heroine. I'm like one out of Racine. Like Hermione in *Andromaque*! Watch out, Thaddeus! I may kill you yet."

"Why, Evalina! I really haven't known you, have I?"

"You know me now."

He gave her a long, serious look before answering. "And I think I may like what I'm getting to know."

Immediately she picked up her menu. "Let's say nothing more for now. Let's order."

That evening she dined in her suite at the Crillon with Ella Pratt, who was visiting an aunt who lived in Paris. Evalina, very untypically, drank two strong cocktails.

"I think I'm going to marry Thaddeus Warwick," she announced.

"What!" Ella was agape. "The man at Morgan! I thought you told me he was in love with someone else."

"He was. It was the love of his life. The kind that doesn't come twice. But she's married now. I'll be perfectly safe with what he has left to offer. It'll be quite enough. For me, anyway."

"Heavens! And he's proposed?"

"Not yet. But something tells me he will."

"Lina, go slow. I mean it, dear. How can you marry a man if you don't even think you're his great love? How can you be sure he won't have another?"

"Because he won't have time."

"Does it take so much time?"

"More than he's going to have. Because I'm going to keep him very busy. I'm going to see that he becomes a great man. The man my father should have been."

Ella shook her head. "Mightn't it be better to make yourself a great woman?"

"The time hasn't come for that. We still have to marry greatness. It's the only sure way to achieve it."

Ella dubiously raised a glass. "Well, I'll drink to it, anyway. I can do that much."

⇥ 2 ⇤

The first dozen years of Evalina's married life brought her everything she had hoped they would bring. Thaddeus proved an agreeable, affectionate, and articulately admiring husband. If there was a mildly jesting tone in some of his compliments, if he joked a little too much among their friends about her "whim of iron" and referred to her as "the driving little angel of his conscience," she knew that *he* knew that she was just what he had always needed and that he loved the part of himself that she had striven to become. Had she not always known that his feelings for her were a good deal less intense than hers for him? Very well. She was certainly not going to be one of those silly women who try to console themselves with the illusion that marriage will create a deeper love than may have existed before it. She might deem herself lucky that the reverse had not occurred. And after all, she had been able to accomplish what she had set out to do: to dedicate her brain, willpower, and fortune to the goal of making him a great man.

Indeed, she seemed well on her way. After their return to New York he had continued his steady rise to the leadership of the Morgan Bank, interrupted only when he ran successfully on the Democratic ticket for a seat in the House of Representatives. After guaranteeing him financial independence from everyone, including herself, by establishing a large trust fund for his benefit, Evalina persuaded him to devote his full time to politics and writing on domestic and foreign affairs. "I want you to be free," she told him. "I don't want you to waste any of your talents earning a living." He had shaken his head, smiling. "Free? Don't you know, my dear girl, that you have shackled me to you by a hoop of gold? But don't worry. I think I'm going to like my shackles."

She was disappointed that she was able to give him only one child, a daughter, Wendy, but he adored the little girl to the point of not seeming to need any more. As a congressman he soon became well known for his outspoken and liberal views, and with the advent of the Roosevelt administration he came to play a significant role in the president's Brain Trust, drafting the legislation that was to be called the New Deal. The beautiful red brick Federal mansion that Evalina purchased in Georgetown became a principal political salon for the architects of a new economic future, and it was thrilling for her to feel a part of what was almost a social revolution. By 1937 she was beginning to wonder if there was any limit to what her husband might aspire to.

She had only to fear what to her were the potentially dangerous times when he relaxed into moods of cheerful but cynical self-deprecation. He was always too ready to mock himself and belittle what he and his fellow workers had accomplished.

"This whole business of economic reform is like making a clearing in the Brazilian rain forest. You trundle in cartloads of brilliant new ideas to act as bulldozers to tear up the trees and brambles, drag away the rocks, and level the hills. And at last there it is, your beautiful bare space, wide and flat and unencumbered, ready for all the great new things you will construct on it. But just wait. The jungle is patient. It knows in how brief a time it will creep back, like a remorseless glacier, and reoccupy all its stolen finery. And no one will know we've even been there."

Evalina at first had protested these predictions, but she had learned that it was wiser to smile, shrug, and appear to ignore them. At any rate, they always seemed to pass and not to interfere with his devotion to the Roosevelt programs. Some of his confreres seemed actually to believe that his underlying sense of the eternal comedy of things added to the charm of a personality that won him such a following among thinking people. But would that be true for the voters in a larger electoral area than the "silk stocking" district of New York City which had returned him? Didn't the great American public cling to gravity and windy oratory?

She found herself coming near to discussing this, at one of her larger cocktail parties, with Mary Appleton, who happened, most untypically, to be sitting alone in a corner. Mary was a fresh young thing, bright and sparkling, whom everyone cultivated because she worked at the White House.

"How gratifying to catch you alone, Mary. I rarely have a word with you."

"Oh, I'm just resting a moment. Thad said he was coming to join me. I suppose he wants to pump me."

"That doesn't sound like him."

"How do you mean?"

"Thad never pumps people. He says, Just wait. They'll tell you."

Mary laughed. "Well, I didn't think he was coming over for my *beaux yeux*. Everyone in Washington has a reason for anything he does. Even at a party. Or should I say, particularly at a party."

"Not Thad. Sometimes I wish he had a reason. Don't those who do get places?"

"Get where?"

"Oh, into the Senate, say. Or even the White House."

"Only that? But Thad will never be president. Or even a senator."

"Why not?" Evalina felt suddenly that she was facing an unexpected crisis. She didn't like it. "Why will he never be either of those things?"

"Because he doesn't believe in himself. And the public will always smell that out, even if they can't smell anything else. They want a man who's in love with himself. A man who thinks he's God."

"Does Mr. Roosevelt think that?"

"No, but he's the exception that proves the rule. Take my word for it, Evalina. A man with a sense of humor has two strikes against him in politics."

"What, then, should I do to make Thad conceal his?"

"Don't do anything. Leave him just as he is." There was

something now almost proprietary in the young woman's tone. "Thad's greatest contribution is always going to be made more or less behind the scene. That's where his wonderful brain and imagination can operate most successfully. Thad, I can assure you, Evalina, is appreciated on the highest level. And the highest level is not the dumb voter. Let Thad be what he wants to be."

"What else could I possibly want?" Evalina rose now to leave her interlocutor before she should forget herself and say something rude. Then she spied her husband crossing the room toward them. She turned briefly back to Mary. "Well, here he is now. Maybe he *is* coming for your *beaux yeux*, after all."

Going to the bar for the drink that she suddenly felt she needed, she encountered her old friend Ella Pratt, now Ella Simkins, who had married a very political Washington lawyer and knew much of what was going on in government circles.

"Come sit with me a moment," she urged her. "I want to ask you something."

She led Ella into the library, which was deserted, and they sat in two chairs.

"Thad always likes to talk of the novelist George Meredith's fondness for what he calls the imps of comedy," Evalina began. "They look down on us poor mortals and smirk. And when they spot a particularly pompous ass, they skip down to play tricks on him."

"And who is the ass you have in mind?"

"Evalina Lane Warwick."

"Well, I can think of words to describe you, my dear friend, but that is the last that would have occurred to me. Of what do you imagine your assaninity to consist?"

"In my perhaps willful failure to recognize that Thad is having an affair with Mary Appleton."

Ella's features congealed. That she uttered no immediate denial was sufficient evidence that she already knew. "What makes you think so?"

"Ella, you're my best friend. You wouldn't lie to me."

"But I don't have to say anything."

"But you might tell me what I should do about it."

"Nothing." Ella was very definite.

"I should simply look the other way?"

"It shouldn't matter where you look, so long as you don't *do* anything. Look, Lina. You and Thad have a great life. Don't wreck it."

"You mean I should continue to ask that woman to my house so she can make love to my faithless husband under my very eyes?"

"Thad is faithful to you, Lina. After his fashion, as the poet put it. This thing with Mary is only a fling. It won't last."

"How can I be sure of that?"

"Because the others haven't."

For several moments Evalina was speechless. The imps of comedy had not prepared her for that! In the tumbling whirl of her various reactions she felt plummeted into a new world, and a very strange one. When she spoke, it was in a muted tone. "There have been others, then?"

"I don't know how many, but I can think of two. Some men have to blow off steam every now and then. It's no big deal, Lina. It's as if he had masturbated without imagining he was making love to you."

"Ella! Is that really you talking?"

"Oh, it's me, all right. I'm trying to find some way to drum into your head that this isn't the end of the world."

"Would you feel that way if it was your Sam who was sleeping around?"

"No. Because if Sam ever had an affair, it would be a serious one. He and Thad have different temperaments. And anyway, Thad doesn't sleep around. He's too busy to give that slut Mary more than a late afternoon hour of his time."

"Ella, I appreciate your candor, but I think I've had about all I can take for now."

"Just remember, dearie. Don't upset the apple cart. You'll never get a better one."

Ella shook off the hand that tried to retain her for further colloquy and hurried upstairs to her room. After the party, she and Thad dined alone together. He had noted her leaving the parlor. He always noted everything. But he did not allude to it.

"Maman's having one of her seizures," she informed him. "Rather worse than usual. Peter writes that he would be glad if I came over."

"I thought your mother's seizures were largely imaginary. Is this one really so different, my dear?"

"As she ages they tend to become more real. I think I'd better go to her. Mademoiselle can take care of Wendy. I shan't be gone forever."

He didn't answer for a minute, and she remembered that he always sorted the mail to separate her letters from the many he received from his constituents. Of course, he knew that she had received no recent communication from her stepfather. But wasn't it better that way? It would be too ugly to have to articulate the real reason.

"I'm going to miss you badly."

"Oh, you'll survive."

After that he knew everything. It was not like her to make so cold a retort. But with his customary tact, he still offered no comment. Any discussion would have bordered on the vulgar. She was even grateful to him.

He assured her that his office would take care of all the travel arrangements.

Crossing the Atlantic on the *Normandie*, she slept little and read less. Sitting on her deck chair and watching the tumbling sea, she reviewed her life and wondered why it had been so shockingly sundered in two, leaving her with a stained past and a bleak future. Why, as Ella had put it, did she make so much of a common or garden species of adultery? Was she bitterly jealous? No. Was she passionately angry? No. Was what had happened not to have been expected of a man lured into what to him may have been a tepid marriage? Possibly, yet she had certainly not expected it. But there it was, and it seemed to have robbed her life of all its dignity.

What she at last seemed to make out was that she had been left on one side of an infinitely stretching fence with a limited number of fatuous and misguided idealists while the rest of humanity was on the other side. It was not that she wanted to leap that fence and join the fornicating, self-deluded advocates of the glory of sexual love, but that her cohorts on the minority side now struck her as shrill and futile. She wondered if she could fit in anywhere.

Eliane and Peter Everett greeted her warmly when she arrived at the beautiful Spanish pavilion in Cannes overlooking the wine dark sea. The former and Evalina had long since made up their early differences; Eliane was far too sensible to hold a grudge indefinitely against a daughter who was not only rich and fashionable but married to a man who might well become a famous statesman. Peter had proved just the husband Eliane had needed; he took all her ailments at her own valuation and fussed over her as much as any *malade imaginaire* could possibly have wished. Nor was it any loss on his part; their relationship was a case of symbiosis. He had no financial concerns, lived in grand style, and had ample time for the composition of his charming and increasingly popular belles-lettres.

Evalina got on easily and well with both her mother and her stepfather, and she found herself for the first time in her life submitting to a routine of idle drift. She played bridge with her mother and the local friends; she went out with Eliane and Peter to their elegant dinner parties; she read mysteries sitting on the beach in their cabana; she took walks with Peter.

It was on one of the latter that he asked her suddenly, "How long are you planning to stay with us, Evalina? I hope indefinitely, but it strikes me that we must not rob Thad of his adored spouse too long."

"Oh, Congress keeps him well occupied."

Peter paused to look at her harder. "Do you mind if I ask you an impertinent question?"

"Not in the least. Though I don't promise to answer it."

"If you decline to, that will be answer enough. Have you and Thad had a quarrel?"

"No. But we might have had. Had I not gone abroad."

"But will you? When you go back?"

"I'm not entirely sure I'm going back. I may just send for Wendy to join me here."

"Oh, Evalina!"

"Look, Peter." There was a bench near them, and she sat on it, patting the place beside her to indicate that he should join her, which he did. Her tone was very firm. "I don't intend to share my husband with another woman."

"But it's hardly sharing him if she takes only a tiny sliver."

She stared with something like curiosity into the blinking eyes of this wrinkled, brown-faced, lean, and oddly distinguished old man. "You sound like my friend Ella. What do you all know about my husband? What makes you so sure that he gives only a sliver, as you call it, to his mistress?"

"People from the States come to Cannes, you know, my dear. Rather too many of them, in fact. Including a gossiping aunt of Thad's."

"Matilda Gray? That old cat?"

"Exactly. But even she, under my cross-examination, admitted that Thad's little escapades seem brief enough."

"They may not last long for him," Evalina retorted grimly. "But they may last for a considerably longer time for me."

Peter's eyes quit blinking as they saddened. "Listen to me, dear girl. I'm not going to stand by and see you throw your life's work away. For that's what you'll be doing if you let this nonsense ruin your marriage. You've invested too much in Thad to toss it to the winds. And that's where it will go if you leave him. He'll never get ahead without you."

Evalina was shocked to feel that she was suddenly about to sob. "Oh, he'll do well enough without me."

"No, he won't, and you know he won't. You're his pilot, and left to himself, he may end up on a reef. You know your father threw his life away. First in peace, then in war. Don't be a copycat. It's not in your genes. You don't *have* to do it."

"Have to? How do you mean?"

"Well, my generation did, you know. England in 1914 was a kind of paradise on earth, at least for the privileged, and I was one of them. Oh, yes, our young men were brave and true and nobly spirited. Rupert Brooke. 'A body of England's, breathing English airs, washed by the rivers, blest by suns at home.' And they were all killed in the trenches. I would have been, too, had I not had the luck to be wounded. My friend Patrick Shaw-Stewart, who we had thought was safe on Mediterranean duty, was shifted at the last moment to Flanders. A poem was found in the copy of *A Shropshire Lad* that he had in his pocket when he was killed. Some of the stanzas show how grimly we all accepted what we were sure would be our doom."

Peter threw his head back and intoned:

> But other shells are waiting
> Across the Aegean sea,
> Shrapnel and high explosive,
> Shells and hells for me.
>
> O hell of ships and cities,
> Hell of men like me!
> Fatal second Helen,
> Why must I follow thee?
>
> I will go back this morning,
> From Imbros over the sea;
> Stand in the trench, Achilles,
> Flame-capped, and shout for me!

"You see, dear Evalina, we all knew that we had had everything and that we would lose everything, and that it was all for nothing, but at least we remembered our Greek."

She was temporarily distracted from herself. "But didn't Germany have to be stopped? Was it totally futile?"

"My dear girl, what do we have today? Hitler! He makes the Kaiser seem like a cherub! But why do I drag you through all this? To show you how *I* survived! When I picked myself up, so to speak, after the armistice, I gathered together my few assets and determined that, however shaky, I was still intact and was not going to waste another minute of my life. It takes guts not to give in to bitterness, melancholy, and false pride. But you have guts, Evalina! The guts not to give in to the temptation to wreck your life and Thad's and maybe even Wendy's!"

Evalina rose, and they walked back to the villa in silence. At the door she kissed him and murmured, "Stand in the trench, Achilles, flame-capped, and shout for me!"

That night before dinner she went to her mother's boudoir where Eliane was sitting before a triple mirror, applying the last touches of her makeup, and told her of her talk with Peter.

"I knew he was going to talk to you, darling," her mother told her, without turning from her task. "And I can only hope that you took it to heart."

Evalina, gazing at her thoughtfully and recalling how beautiful this parent had once been, heard herself asking suddenly, "Mother, before I came over to you, after the war, did you and Thad have an affair?"

Eliane whirled around and looked at her daughter in horror. "Whatever put such a dreadful idea in your sick, twisted mind?"

"Would it have been so dreadful? You were a lovely widow and he a charming and unattached young man. What could have been more natural? You had no reason to think he'd one day be your son-in-law."

"Evalina, you should have your mouth washed out with soap! Now get out of here, and get ready for dinner!"

Evalina went to her room with a lighter heart. It was not because she necessarily credited her mother's inferred denial. It was because she no longer felt obliged to believe or disbelieve it.

Ten days later, when the *Normandie* docked at her pier in New York Harbor, she spotted Thad in the crowd below. He had skipped a session of Congress to meet her.

"Darling, I've missed you so!" he cried, embracing her as she stepped off the gangplank.

Gently but decisively she released herself. "And what about Mary Appleton? Will you give her up?"

"I already have!" His smile was radiant. "And there won't be any others, I swear! Ever, ever!"

She too smiled as she sent him off to deal with her luggage and the customs. She no longer had to believe him, either.

The Grandeur
That Was Byzantium

IN THE EARLY SPRING of the year 330, by Christian tabulation, and such was the common use since the emperor Constantine had transferred the capital of the world to the city on the Bosporus named for himself, Caius Lentulus Desideratus, a still nobly handsome quinquagenarian, still a senator and still, despite all the modern changes, a lover of the old Roman ways and traditions, of the old Roman gods and poets, had returned to his long-abandoned city residence. He had left his family to enjoy the sea breezes in his Ostian villa and had come back to supervise the reopening of what he had once deemed his perfect little pink marble palace on the slopes of the Viminal Hill, overlooking the forum. And now, a day's work done, he was taking advantage of the mild evening air and the pleasant sight of the streets below, less clogged with daytime shoppers and sightseers, by stepping out onto the terrace, which commanded a distant view of the Arch of Titus and the looming gray wall of the Colosseum. With him was his old friend and cousin, Marcus Publius Varco, newly named one of the seven quaestors of the empire, soon to leave for his post in the new capital, and around them were some of the statues of Lentulus's collection, long in storage and now brought out for possible relocation in the refurbished mansion.

"You are certainly running against the tide, my dear Lentulus," the quaestor observed. "Half our friends are building sumptuous villas along the Bosporus and selling their old homes here for a song."

"Have you ever known me to swim *with* the tide?" his host inquired. "Let us sit down here and enjoy the sight of our city at its finest hour. You've always been one for dawns, my friend, and I for sunsets. Which is why I've decided to resume this old residence."

"Does a sunset get the preference even if it's political as well as celestial?"

"Much more so! Rome, even in its greatest days, would have been too noisy and crowded for my tastes. Without the gilded trappings of the imperial court, which I fled a decade ago, we shall be more restful. I shall sit here quietly in the evenings with my Horace and think of you listening to the ravings of the hairy priests of the Jesus god over the Arian controversy."

"You know I won't be doing anything like that. I don't even know what your Arian controversy is."

"Please don't call it *mine*. But I have indeed made a survey of this new cult that Caesar has seen fit or politic to join. And I advise you to do the same. You may find it handy in the days to come."

"Isn't it just another religion that we've agreed to tolerate? As we have done all the others? Hasn't that always been our policy? To respect the gods of the people we conquer? What's new about it?"

"Two things. First and foremost, Caesar has adopted it.

Secondly, they, the Christ lovers, do not admit the existence of any god but their Jehovah. Now that was always true of the Jews, of course, and Titus finally had to lay waste to their capital and their temple. Unhappily, he didn't kill them all. And now they've spawned this new sect. Granted, the new sect hates them, for they slew the new sect's god, or god's son, whichever it was. And so they're busy killing each other. But when they've tired of that, they'll look for other prey. For they're peculiarly ferocious. They like both being martyrs and making martyrs."

"Lentulus, you're a bit of a stuck whistle on that subject. Let's have a look at some of this art you've brought out. Is it all Greek?"

"A good deal of it. What else? But you know, it's funny. Some of this stuff is so bad I can hardly imagine what I originally saw in it. Look at that old matron taken from a tomb in Thrace. I must have thought she was a masterpiece of Greek realism. But she's nothing but a hideous old crone, and she's going back to the cellar. I'm not so sure one's eye improves as one ages. Perhaps we begin to dote on what we like to think is our rare percipience. But now there's a beauty! Bought when I was near the age of the subject!" He pointed to the glorious marble effigy of a nude youth.

"Antinous?"

"Of course it's Antinous. And one of the finest of a thousand versions. I could almost forgive Hadrian his silly idolatry of the Bythinian lad if the lad were really as beautiful as that. Of course, the sculptor probably never saw him. It was only after the poor youth had drowned himself as some kind of weird eastern sacrifice to his beloved master that Hadrian ordered his image put up throughout the empire. Think of it!"

"But Hadrian was a very great emperor, Lentulus."

"Have I denied it? One of the greatest. But even with the best of them, there's always something one has to put up with. We don't care on whom they discharge the seed of their natural lust, but for Hadrian to spread nude statues of the boy he buggered throughout the marketplaces of the empire was going a bit far, you must admit. Still, he was the least vulgar of the imperial lot. Compare him with a brute like Diocletian. But let's not. Let's have some wine."

The two were silent for some moments, gazing out over the forum as a Greek slave boy, silent and immaculate in white, brought them wine in round golden cups, pleasant to hold in the palm of the hand. Publius reverted to the subject most on his mind.

"Wouldn't you and Cornelia consider at least a visit to Constantinople? You could stay with us and see whether it wouldn't do for perhaps a part-time residence."

"Are you serious? That I should take that ghastly trip twice a year? And for what, pray?"

"To be in the city of the future! It's going to be more splendid than Rome. You should see the building plans. And, of course, everyone of any importance will be there. Not that you care about politics and power. I know that." He held up a hand to foreclose the anticipated rebuttals of his host. "But it will also be the world center of arts and letters. The most eminent poets and philosophers will flock to your friendly salon."

"Not to mention the smelly and unwashed rabbis of Constantine's new faith."

Publius's frown was now impatient. "Lentulus, you know as well as I do that the adoption of Christianity was only a political move. It was the wise and practical thing to do. Matters were getting out of hand. Rome has always known how to deal with alien gods. Augustus would have done the same thing. So would Hadrian. The time had come. It's like our tolerating the gore of the public games and gladiatorial combats. You and I don't go to them, but they keep the mob happy and out of trouble. This new sect isn't going to make any difference in our lives. We needn't have anything to do with Christians. The old gods will be undisturbed."

"Well, that's good to hear, anyway. If it indeed be so. But it's not only the Christians I object to. It's the new court. One hears it's to be swamped in the stiffest kind of eastern ceremonial, with jeweled crowns and incense and prostration before the throne. Is that true?"

"There'll be some concessions, yes, to what is expected in that part of the world. But you know how people exaggerate. The basic Roman things will be preserved."

"Just tell me one thing, Publius. One thing. And please be honest with your old cousin."

"Very well. What is it?"

"Does Constantine dye his hair green?" As Publius twisted his shoulders irritably without answering, Lentulus continued, "They won't throw you off the Tarpeian rock if you tell me, will they? If he dyes his hair, he must expect it to be seen by the multitude, mustn't he? Perhaps they take it as the natural color of a god's tresses."

"Actually, it's a wig," Publius snapped. "And he doesn't wear it all the time."

"Only on special occasions? Perhaps on Christian holidays?"

"It's not an aspect of our imperial master's personality that

I care to stress," Publius retorted. "Constantine has enough virtues to be forgiven a minor weakness."

"But so visible a one! Must we paint his statues accordingly? I wonder really, cousin, if you should not drop a hint in the imperial ear that he's going a bit far. As a quaestor, are you not one of the seven greatest powers in the land?"

"Lentulus, you're too astute an observer not to know that the title is nothing. It's the proximity to Caesar's ear alone that counts."

"But I thought you were indeed close to that august organ."

"Constantine listens to me at times. But he listens to others more often. He is not a man to be led by anyone."

"Not even by the high priests of his new faith?"

"There you go again, Lentulus. Can't you stay off that subject for one afternoon?"

"No! Not, anyway, until I've explained something to you. Something that I feel very strongly a quaestor should know. And that is this: Where this sect differs from others and where it is dangerous is that its priests aim not merely to control the conduct and the creed of its faithful; they aim to rule the state. And if the faithful are converted, and if the faithful become a working majority in the empire, to which end Constantine may have unknowingly contributed, they may raise their ferocious priesthood to the seats of power it claims."

"Lentulus, you go too far. Much too far. I don't know much about the sect, but everyone knows it was founded by a lowly Jewish thaumaturgist who promised an afterlife of bliss to the lowly and never offered the least threat to the empire. He even allowed himself to be crucified by the Jews, who took him from our procurator, who found nothing wrong with him but who, like all wise governors, knew when to throw an occasional tidbit to the mob."

"I know all that, of course. It's even in their creed. But here's the rub, my friend. The man Jesus was harmless enough, I concede. He believed that the end of the world was imminent and that it behooved him to preach preparedness for some kind of final judgment that would decide whether you would be transmitted to a state of bliss or cast into outer darkness. Obviously, with such a fate around the corner, there was no point worrying about your business or your family ties or your government. Just get ready, that was all you had to do, and the ticket to a happy afterlife was faith. That was what his god wanted: laudation and plenty of it. None of this was of any concern to Rome. Why should it have been? It seemed a harmless delusion. But when time passed and it became evident that the end of the world was not coming, it was necessary for the now established priests of the sect to fabricate a revised religion to hold on to the converts they had already acquired. And this they have done in one of their councils at Nicaea. And where does the revised religion put the priests? One guess! Right! At the very top of the ecclesiastical and political ladder!"

"All of which is highly speculative."

"All of which is verifiably true."

"In any event, it will take a long time. I think we can count on living out our lives under the old regime."

"Don't be too sure of that!" Lentulus rose with his guest, who was preparing to depart. "In the meantime, I can enjoy a Rome more peaceful and benign without the glitter of your eastern court. And highways uninterrupted by the blare of some general's alleged triumph."

"A Rome shorn of its old glory!"

"A Rome that may have found its soul."

"Let us hope so, anyway." Publius strode to the doorway and turned back. "I'll see you before I go. We'll have a banquet or something. And Lentulus, one word of caution. Say what you like to me and men you trust about the Christians, but don't air your views in public. After all, our emperor has adopted their creed. And you know that Constantine can be vindictive."

"I know that he killed his wife and son."

Publius raised a finger to his lips. "Hush about Fausta. That's not acknowledged. Crispus, of course, is."

Lentulus chuckled. "Ah, I'm right then. You *are* afraid of him. And of the Christians. Shall we be baptised, you and I?"

Publius shrugged as he departed. "You make a joke out of everything, cousin."

"Perhaps it keeps me alive. Or will it do just the opposite?"

Pa's Darling

PA'S DEATH, in the cold winter of 1960, at the age of eighty-seven, was a crucial event in the lives of his two daughters, but particularly for myself, the supposedly most loved, the adored Kate, the oldest. As I sit in my multichambered apartment, the last of my many wasted efforts to impress him, looking out on the strangely white and oddly dreary expanse of Central Park, with the newspaper clippings of his laudatory obituaries in my lap, it seems a timely if unsettling opportunity to review my own life, no longer, I can only hope, in the shadow of his, unless it will be even more so. For people, I know, always think of me not as the widow of the brilliant young attorney Sumner Shepard, gallantly dead in the 1940 fall of France, nor even as the present wife of Dicky Phelps, senior partner of his distinguished Wall Street law firm, but as the daughter of Lionel Hemenway, the great judge of the New York Court of Appeals, renowned sage and philosopher, author of provocative books on law and literature, and the witty deity of the Patroons Club. God rest his soul if it be capable of resting.

I have decided to write up this assessment of my past to make a probably vain attempt to get it off my chest. Whether I shall ever show it, or to whom, I do not know as yet. I am sure, however, it will not be to my husband, fond of him as I am. Perhaps to my daughter. Or to a grandson, if I ever have one. But that needn't concern me now.

As I have already suggested, I was always supposed to be Pa's favorite daughter. He made a good deal of me, particularly before company; he liked to show me off—he was proud of my good looks, of what he called my "pale-faced, raven-haired beauty." But he was like a financial magnate showing off a master painting he has just acquired, inwardly confident that the owner of the picture is superior to both the work and its artist. There was always a distinct vein of sarcasm in his ebullient mirth. Did he really value me very much? Did he even value women very much? Oh, he had to make a fuss over them, of course; he had to be the gallant gentleman who elevated the fair sex to the skies and left them there, but when it came to a question of real work, the real thing . . . no, give him a man.

But I have now just learned that all of this may have been the cover-up of doubts as to his own masculinity. This exploded before me last night, at a family gathering in this apartment. It erupted from what Uncle Jack Sherman, brother of my other, also now deceased parent, told me when he and I, after dinner, were sitting apart from the others in a corner of my living room, discussing who among Pa's surviving friends and disciples might be the best qualified to write his biography.

After considering and discarding several names, Uncle Jack paused and glanced cautiously about the room, as if to be sure that none of the others were within earshot. This, I knew, was his usual prelude to some particularly odoriferous piece of gossip. He was a tall, thin, rather emaciated old man, a lifetime bachelor, who wanted to bring down any man who had done more in life than he, which was almost everyone. He liked to pretend that he and I were the only truly sophisticated members of the family.

"The first job of your father's biographer," he told me emphatically, "will be to explain why he lived for so many years on such intimate terms with his wife's lover."

"Oh, Uncle Jack! That old canard! Surely you don't believe it. Of your own sister?"

"My dear, I had it from Sam Pemberton himself. One night when he was in his cups."

"The filthy braggart! And you credited him?"

"I did not. At first. But when I warned your mother about what he was saying, she explained the whole matter to me in her own cool, measured way. Your father, it appeared, had become impotent while only in his forties. He had agreed to her finding an outlet for her very natural desires in this unconventional but by no means unique fashion. She assured me grimly that she would see to it that Sam Pemberton should hold his tongue in the future. And indeed he did, to the very day he died. He even became a teetotaler! And your mother pledged me to silence in your father's lifetime."

Some cousins at this point crossed the room to bid me good night. The party was over, and Uncle Jack departed, leaving me to my troubled thoughts.

Perhaps the strangest thing about Uncle Jack's revelation was that it gave me a nasty kind of exhilaration. Of course, I knew perfectly well that a certain number of family friends and relations believed that there had always been something more between Mother and Sam Pemberton than an *amitié amoureuse*. But my sister and I had both firmly repudiated the idea. That Mother, so tall and straight, so grave, so unbending, so somehow chastely beautiful, with her prematurely snow-white hair, her lineless face, high cheekbones, and noble brow, could ever have shared her couch with a man as unimpressive as Sam was unthinkable. Sam, however grinning and good-natured, however accommodating, was still a balding, rotund little bachelor who taught French at a fashionable private girls' day school. We thought Mother liked him because he read Gallic plays and poems aloud with her and that Father put up with him because he listened, seemingly impressed, to Pa's monologues. It was true that he was a household fixture, but such a harmless one!

And why should all this now titillate me when all three participants are dead? I suppose it is possible that I felt in Pa's humble acceptance of the eternal triangle some settling of an old score between him and me. He, who had been so superior, despite any effort he may have exerted to condescend, whose towering masculinity had seemed to relegate his daughters to a kind of mock respect and reverence, had in reality allowed a silly little man to be his pal, his constant houseguest, and the lover of his wife!

How the past now unreeled itself through my mind, like a film played backwards! I saw Mother passing serenely through the years, calmly going about her domestic tasks, efficiently organizing the social gatherings that Pa required for an audience, attending to the myriad problems of complaining daughters, always in control of everything, yet always placidly aware of the respite that awaited her in the arms of her lively if diminutive bedmate. Mother was never unreasonable in her requirements; she rarely raised her voice, because she rarely had to: there was something ineluctable in her tone and demeanor. Her daughters knew—and Pa knew—that she revered the rule of reason, and that if ever reason was ousted by emotion in her house, she would simply walk out and never return.

I can remember a party that Dicky and I gave for a visiting English economist who expounded after dinner on the subject of a novel theory of taxation. Pa took extreme objection to some of his points and even heckled him, to the poor man's obvious embarrassment. Mother at last spoke up in her fine, clear tone that everyone heard: "Lionel, if you make another objection, we're going home." That was the way she would do it, without a trace of anger or even criticism in her voice. And when Pa *did* make another crack, she simply rose, went over to him, and told him, "We're leaving now," and he followed her out of the room like a dog with its tail between its legs.

It was probably in the same fashion that she had put to him her proposed solution for their more intimate marital problem. I am sure that she never reproached him for his bullying manners at parties or for his sexual inadequacy; she simply took the steps she deemed appropriate for the situation at hand. She was always a realist, but one doesn't always relish so much realism in a wife or in a mother. Pa, of course, must have blamed himself for his impotence, if that was what it was. I don't think many men could have helped that, no matter how fiercely they told themselves it was not their fault. And I don't blame them. I even think I might have admired Pa more had he smothered Mother with a pillow, like Othello. What I suppose I resented was that, however small he may have come to think himself, he still thought he was bigger than I.

It was like him to overdo his role of *mari complaisant*. There was always something of the ham actor in him. Was it his way of recapturing the lead from his wife? Surely otherwise he wouldn't have made such a pal of Sam Pemberton. He wouldn't have invited him for long visits to our summer camp in Maine, or made him a member of his elite men's discussion group, the "round table," at the Patroons Club. Was it even his way of taking Sam from Mother? What she thought of her lover and her husband being such friends I cannot imagine. Perhaps it amused her. She would have been capable of that.

Sumner Shepard, my first husband, and the only real love of my life—which reminds me, I must hide this manuscript from Dicky, who is utterly amoral about reading things not addressed to him—was one of Pa's golden boys. He had been first in his class at Harvard Law and editor in chief of the review and on graduation could have gone to any of the great Wall Street firms (which, of course, he eventually did), but he chose instead to go first to Albany and clerk for a year for Pa. This was not, in 1927, considered the bright choice it is today, but Sumner was in love (there's no word more fitting) with the luminous prose of Pa's judicial opinions and yearned to sit at the great man's feet. And it was no surprise to anyone that Pa rejoiced in an esteem so flattering and reveled in a brilliant and handsome young assistant who saw, as he did, the law as great literature.

Pa stayed in Albany only while his court was sitting; the rest of the time, except for our Maine summers, he was in Manhattan in our East Side brownstone. In order to have Sumner available for discussions, particularly in the evening, he arranged for him to occupy a spare bedroom on the top floor whenever they worked late, as a result of which he was frequently present at our family board. I was attracted to him at once, for he was not only bright but beautiful. But at first my sister, Edith, and I were cast in the role of rather dumb listeners while he and Pa argued about law, and Mother and Sam Pemberton, another constant guest, discussed French literature. Of course, my ears were open only to Sumner. To me the law was mere nitpicking, something men adored and women had little use for. But I noted that Pa and Sumner seemed to be looking for beauty, even when they worked on the draft of one of Pa's opinions; you might have thought they were carving a statue out of marble. I couldn't for the life of me see why it was such a big deal to dress up a dry legal opinion in purple prose. Who but other lawyers were going to read it, anyway?

I should make it clear that I was no philistine. If I cared too much for dancing parties and smart clothes, if I spent too many weekends visiting rich friends in chic resorts like the Hamptons, if I had a bit of a yen for gambling and casinos, I was still up on the latest novels and plays and served three afternoons a week as a docent at the Metropolitan Museum of Art. It was not from a lack of appreciation of the finer things in life that I found Pa and Sumner's ecstasy over some silly little phrase excessive.

Of course I had the ancient weapon of sex, and I decided it was time to wield it. I began to ease myself into their discussions. One night, when they were making rather heavy weather over how best and concisely they could phrase the excuse of a defendant who had severely damaged a plaintiff while pulling him out of a burning house through the jagged glass of a shattered window, not having noted that the same room had an open door to the outside, I had a bright idea.

"Peril blunts caution!" I suggested in one of my rare flashes. I had always been clever at parlor games.

"Peril blunts caution," Sumner repeated slowly and thoughtfully. He turned to Pa. "It's perfect! Just three words. Let's start the opinion with them."

"Out of the mouths of babes and sucklings!" Pa murmured approvingly, and he pulled out his notebook and jotted down my suggestion.

I didn't have to say another word, and I had the sense not to. I had gained Sumner's full attention, and that was all I needed. He looked at me; he really saw me, for perhaps the first time, and Pa thereafter got only his second glances. I won't say that I caught Sumner with three words, but they gave me a start. To keep up his image of the bright and thoughtful woman he had idealized for himself I had only to let him develop his own conception. I wouldn't have to do a thing until we were married. Then, of course, I could relax. Hasn't that been the story of millions of women?

❧❧❧

We were married right after the completion of Sumner's year's clerkship with Pa and enjoyed a glorious honeymoon in Hawaii before he started work in the great law firm of Harris & Eyer, of which he and his friend and ultimate successor to my hand, Dicky Phelps, were to become partners. Pa had wanted to keep him as his clerk for another year, and Sumner had wanted this too, but I had pointed out that we might as well get started on a career that would bring him eventually the income we were both going to need. It was the first time that I had to take a firm position in my share of the direction of our joint lives, and it was not by any means to be the last. Sumner always had a tendency to espouse the ideal as opposed to the practical, but he was at the same time generous and malleable, particularly with a woman he loved. And he certainly started by loving me. By loving me almost to distraction.

Yes, I'm getting to it. Getting to the point. Sumner in time discovered that he had attributed qualities to me that I did not have. He had assumed that I was much more my father's daughter than I really was, and I had certainly, at least until our marriage, done my best to sustain that illusion. I daresay he agreed that it was all very well, to some extent anyway, for a woman of the earth to be earthy, but he had expected this to be counterbalanced by something more ethereal, and there was very little of the sky in my nature, except the suspicion that those who claimed it bordered on the hypocritical. Yet I have to admit that he never breathed a word about this; he was always the perfect gentleman, and, yes, the perfect husband. I could nonetheless feel his concealed disillusionment at finding that I did not share my father's tastes and appreciations and that our life together was not going to be a joint search for all that was glorious and inspiring in the universe. However, he put the best possible face on it.

We never quarreled about it; we did not even talk about it. We had many friends, and we went out and about socially, at least on weekends, for he worked too hard to do so on weekdays, and we both loved and fussed over our only child, Gwendolyn. We were considered a well-matched, happy, and attractive couple, and to some extent we were. But now I think I can see that the reason he worked so hard was not only that he loved the practice of law, which he did, but that he wished to bring me the worldly success he knew I wanted.

At least, he may have generously thought, he could do that much for me.

And he did. He became a partner in the firm at twenty-nine, and it was evident to all that he was destined to be one of the leading lights of the New York bar and no doubt, when his fortune was made, a judge on a high court.

Oh no, I had nothing to complain about, but that never stops one from complaining. I fretted constantly at the notion that I was not the woman he had dreamed of, and tended more and more to resent the fact that he had presumed to have such a dream. I offer this memory of the kind of thing that used to exasperate me. It was on a night when Pa and Mother were dining at our place—just the four of us—and Sumner and Pa were discussing John Gielgud's performance as Hamlet, over which they were both lyrically enthusiastic. Mother had preferred John Barrymore's earlier interpretation of the vengeful Dane, but they had almost violently disagreed with her.

"Nobody," Pa murmured in his most velvet tone, "has a voice as musical as Gielgud's. The poet Alfred de Musset is supposed to have fainted dead away when he heard the divine Sarah utter that exquisite line in *Phèdre* with the two *accents circonflexes*: *"Ariane, ma sœur, de quel amour blessée / Vous mourûtes aux bords où vous fûtes laissée."* I felt almost that way in the final scene, where the dying Hamlet addresses the staring onlookers: 'You that look pale and tremble at this chance / That are but mutes or audience to this act.'"

"Yes, what glorious lines those are!" Sumner exclaimed. "It is as if Hamlet is suddenly breaking out of the play and addressing not only the gaping Danish court but the audience at the Globe Theatre. We have been sitting on the edge of our chairs for two hours, and now, at last, at the end, we are with him!"

That was one of the times that I spoke up. "How can you both go on so about a simple sentence? One that anyone might have written. 'You that look pale.' What's so great about that? 'And tremble at this chance.' Oh, come off it, Sumner! And you too, Pa! It's really too silly to make so much of that."

Sumner said nothing, but Pa turned on me. "Aren't you exposing something of a tin ear, Kate? Though perhaps your reaction would have been shared by some of the great ladies of the Tudor court. I seem to see you as one of Holbein's pale, grave beauties playing the deadly game of power because it's the only game to play, even if you end with your head on the block. Isn't Lady Macbeth one of them? Resolute, realistic, eager to shake her husband out of his inhibitions and fantasies? Of course, my sweet, I don't accuse you of murder."

"Lady Macbeth had no imagination," Mother commented. Mother would. "She could not foresee what guilt would do to either of them."

Of course, it was a crack at me. But Mother was wrong. I had quite enough imagination to see the flaw in my marriage.

The great grief of my life—at least as I have always tried to see it and make others see it—was Sumner's death as an officer in the British army in the evacuation of Dunkirk, in that grim spring of 1940. But what I can now privately inscribe is that the blow to my pride was as heavy as that to my heart when I learned that Sumner had confided to my father but not to me all the tumult and agony of his decision to leave his wife and child and country to enlist in what was still a foreign war. To his "beloved Kate" he had presented only the "kinder and quicker" last-minute announcement of a fait accompli. Quicker it certainly was; kinder it was not.

Of course I had known that Sumner was following with the most intense interest every item of European news, from the Munich Pact to the invasion of Poland, and that he passionately believed that we should have been in the war from its start. And of course I was aware of his keenness for military training; he belonged not only to the Seventh Regiment but to the National Guard. But it never crossed my mind that he would do anything so rash as to desert his family and the great firm of which he was so valued a young partner to rush abroad and join a fight in which his nation was still neutral. He simply came home from the office one night, grim and tense, poured each of us a stiff drink, and told me he was leaving for Montreal on the morrow. He had already assigned all his work in the office to Dicky Phelps.

"I knew, dearest," he told me in a thick voice, "how violently you would have opposed me. I just couldn't face the argument. I can't now. For God's sake, try to accept this. Tell yourself that you married a madman and let it go at that."

Well, for some time I *did* take it that way. After the first shock of his departure had worn off, I even began to take pride in what he had done. I was unique among my friends in actually having a soldier in the war. In the riotous discussions that soon broke out between the interventionists and the sponsors of America First, I noisily joined the former and found myself seated proudly on the dais at pro-war rallies. Like Teddy Roosevelt, I took "my stand at Armageddon to do battle for the Lord."

The elation so evoked helped me to endure the bleak news of Sumner's death from a strafing plane on a beach in northern France. I even gained a wide reputation for nobly accepting grief from a letter that I wrote to the *Times*: "In a day when many young men on this still unassaulted side of the Atlantic are asking why they should be concerned with ancient European animosities, it may be illuminating to cite the example of one who, without a word of reproach to those who felt otherwise, silently shouldered a gun and joined an alien army to fight for the patch of civilization we have left on the globe." Oh, yes, as the widow of one of the great war's first American victims, I had a fine role to play.

What changed all this for me was an article that Pa wrote for *The Atlantic Monthly* as a memorial tribute to Sumner. That it was a beautiful piece, nobly expressed, can be taken for granted. But the article revealed something that had, no doubt, been deliberately concealed from me: the long heart-to-heart talks that Pa had had with Sumner before he had given his blessing to his son-in-law's proposed enlistment in the British army.

Could anything have told me more clearly that I was not of the intellectual or spiritual stature to share those Olympian conferences?

I had not been a widow for long before Dicky Phelps began to show me a marked attention. Dicky was not only Sumner's partner; he had been a law school classmate and a deeply admiring friend. Yet I had always been aware that, however loyal a pal Sumner was of Dicky — and Dicky's openly demonstrative nature inspired affection — he did not return Dicky's admiration to anything like the same degree. The circumstances of Dicky's divorce from his dull little first wife were probably responsible for this. Dicky had explained to Sumner, at the time both had been made partners at Harris

& Eyer, that the improvement of his legal position called for a corresponding improvement in his social one, and that his wife had failed to understand this. She had clung stubbornly to the old bunch from which he now sought to detach them, which had led ultimately to their separation and a bitter divorce.

It is certainly at times embarrassingly true that Dicky has always been absolutely shameless in admitting his social ambitions and the steps he is willing to take to effectuate them. But he honestly believes that they are shared by everyone and that it is perfectly proper to make no bones about them. And it's quite possible that he may be more often right than wrong in this assumption, but it nonetheless startles and sometimes shocks people. Pa used to say that Dicky was like a character in O'Neill's *Strange Interlude* who uttered the thoughts on his mind when he stood motionless on the stage and the thoughts that were socially acceptable when he moved.

Some people, like Dicky's first wife, deeply resented this trait in him, but more found it amusing. It seemed so natural from this big, stalwart, black-haired, bushy-eyebrowed, impressive male who embraced all the world with the same hearty candor. And, of course, Dicky, to boot, was a great corporation lawyer whose astute handling of the most complicated mergers and reorganizations was to carry him to leadership at the bar and the presidency of the New York State Bar Association.

Dicky virtually took charge of my widowhood. He telephoned me several times a week; he took me to plays and concerts; he sent me flowers and the newest books; he insisted that Sumner would have wanted me to enjoy a full and entertaining life. He showered with expensive gifts my eleven-year-old daughter, whose dislike of him he blandly ignored, and worshipfully cultivated the favor of my father, who made ribald fun of him. When he proposed that we should become lovers, and I at length agreed, it was as if he were paying the ultimate tribute to Sumner. But he proved himself as good a lover as he was a lawyer, and what could I better do than marry him? Which of course I did.

Mother, who was already ailing with the breast cancer that was to kill her, dealt me her final blow in her cheerful recognition that Dicky was just the man for me. Pa had his doubts, but he was fascinated by this new son-in-law. When Dicky told him frankly that he was postponing the wedding for two weeks so that his richest client, who was abroad, would be back in town to attend the small reception (small because of my widowhood), Pa said to me, "Imagine his telling *me* that reason! When he could have invented a dozen more innocuous ones! But that's Dicky all over; he puts things just as they are. Your man's unique, Kate. We should keep him in a jar!"

Yet Dicky seemed sublimely unconscious of the fact that Pa was laughing at him. When he heard Pa at a dinner party hilariously describe his first visit to the newly decorated offices of Harris & Eyer, Dicky laughed as hard as the others. Yet Pa had said, "As I stepped into the reception hall where my son-in-law's handsome likeness hung in all its painted glory, I tottered and gasped. I had sunk knee-deep in carpet!"

But in the years that followed my marriage, Pa and Dicky's joshing relationship began to develop into something like a real friendship. Pa must have found some kind of consolation for the doubts that his frequent melancholy cast over even his fame in the fulsome compliments of this big, bluff son-in-law, who professed to deem his own accomplishments and wealth as only trivial in contrast to the golden law opinions of this great but meagerly salaried judge. Indeed, Dicky appeared to regard his greatest claim to notice his connection with my sire. And Pa, who was beginning to show his age and to repeat himself, who was, if the truth be told, already something of a garrulous bore at dinner parties, was depending more and more on the uncritical and vociferous support that he received from my spouse.

But did Dicky ever aspire to emulate or even comprehend Pa's never-ending search for beauty in words, in art, in music, in history, in philosophy? Never. He wished to be crowned by the muses without imbibing their products. He wanted success, but success in *all* its manifestations. The world might admire power and money, but it also esteemed the arts. By associating himself with Pa, might he not borrow a few rays of Pa's aura? To Dicky, appearance and reality were the same. If he looked as if he had everything, why, then, he had everything. It was why he was perfectly happy. I had again been married for my father.

Dicky irritated me by taking on over Pa's death as if he had lost his own father. He wore a long face for weeks and insisted on sporting the black tie and black armband that had gone out of fashion years before. I was just able to refrain from sarcastic comment until he stipulated that we should turn down an invitation to what promised to be a stimulating dinner party and to which I had particularly looked forward.

"Really, Dicky, aren't you carrying things a bit far? It isn't as if we were being asked to a dance or some sort of jubilee. It's just a small circle of interesting friends sharing a few drinks and a meal. We'll be called hypocrites if we stay home on the excuse of mourning."

"Kate, I don't think you realize how broad a shadow your father's demise has cast over his family. Our friends, even our closest friends, tend to see us in relation to him. Therefore more in the way of mourning is expected of us."

"Do you think I don't know about that shadow? Haven't I spent my life in it?"

"Then you should know how to act."

"Acting is just the word for what you want me to do! Well, I'm going to that dinner party! With you or without you!"

"It may be acting for you, my dear. But it won't be for me. I feel as if some of the light had gone out of my life with your father's passing."

"Don't be more of an ass than God made you!"

Dicky at this rose from the breakfast table without a word and departed for his office. He will think things over, as he always does, and when he comes home tonight he will utter no word on the subject. He has always been a great one at putting unpleasant things behind him. But I shall have a job to do in learning to live with his absurd faith that he enjoyed a unique accord with a father-in-law who actually found him an amiable fool. He is the second husband that my greedy parent has taken from me. Pa has done me two evil turns: he has made me feel unworthy of Sumner and worthy of Dicky. Why did he have to take out on me his bitterness over Mother's infidelity? Just because he was mortally afraid of her and I was the nearest available vulnerable woman?

Due Process

I CAN LAUGH at myself at eighty but not too hard. One's own conceit can be a kind of fortress; take care how one batters down the walls. I even have to remind myself that I am no longer eighty; today, Labor Day, appropriately named, is my birthday. The day was not so denominated in 1874, before the triumph of unions over individuals, when I first saw the light in Blue Hill, Virginia, in the westernmost part of that great state, an area that tempered the high civility of the old planters with some of the roughness and vigor of the American frontier. To be eighty is a kind of victory; to be eighty-one is simply senescent. Like Akela, the aging leader of the wolf pack in *The Jungle Book*, I have to snarl at my cautiously circling partners. But I am still the chief, more so anyway than any other senior of the great downtown law firms of Manhattan. Everyone on Wall or Broad Street in this year, 1955, knows that Rives, Bank and Tobin is essentially Langdon Rives. But how much longer that will last, no one can fathom. It will not, however, end tomorrow. Or even the day after. I still have some time, and I hope only death will terminate it.

The double doors to my large office remain firmly closed. No one opens them until my faithful old hound of a secretary, the big, blocky Mrs. Turnbull, has buzzed me from her outer chamber to seek my approval. I am content to be alone with my bleak dark prints of old English judges, my framed newspaper accounts of Confederate victories, my father's copy of a portrait of General Lee, and the black, now deemed ugly, mahogany chairs and settees taken from the family mansion in Blue Hill, currently on loan to a great-nephew I have to support. The image I have of myself fits into this rather awesome chamber, which is, somewhat contradictorily, flooded with light from the french windows on three sides opening onto a terrace, for my firm occupies the penthouse of an edifice beetling over New York Harbor. I say that my image fits it, for though in my youth I favored my mother's plain, bland features, with age I have come to share my father's craggy and stalwart grayness, together with his thick hair, high brow, and prominent nose. Oh, yes, I can look the part all right of the grand old lawyer, the despot whom the clerks try to see as benevolent, and sometimes almost succeed.

For there is a hammy side of my nature; I have to face it. I could have been an actor in a repertory company, playing Othello one night and Iago the next. But there's a difference. When I play the kindly old boss who will fill his old green Minerva limo with young associates if he spies them walking to the subway after work, or the tolerant leader who with a smile and the rapid scribbling of his pen can turn the bumbling brief of a junior partner into a work of art, I am acting a part—and with some relish, too—but when I shout at a stupid clerk to grab his hat and go home to his mother (knowing that he will be stopped by the experienced receptionist at the door and told to wait till my fit has passed), I am being genuine. If my benevolence is put on like stage makeup, my wrath is true.

Which is why I have picked up my pen to indite this memo. I am disgusted with the young professor at New York University Law School who has undertaken—with the financial backing, I have no doubt, of my partners—to write up the story of my litigating career. These silly coworkers of mine, who know nothing of books or their authors outside of law reports and whodunits, have the naiveté to suppose that a biography by a reputedly serious scholar cannot help but add to my glory and the firm's, no matter how fiercely the author may repudiate my political views. And it is true that the draft of the chapter that this indurated liberal has submitted to me on my constitutional battle in the 1930s with the New Deal legislation is not too unfair. But now that he has come to the desegregation case, he has dropped all pretense of neutrality. Indeed, he and I have had a near shouting match, and I have sent him packing. Lord knows what he will write now, even if he has to give back the sums my misguided juniors have given him!

Why, he wanted to know, did I have to drag into the pool of defendants in *Brown* v. *Board of Education* my old school district in Virginia? What need was there to add my brief to the already quite adequate one of John W. Davis? What had induced me, by entering a case where my point of view was already perfectly represented, to tarnish my own reputation and that of the firm I had created by backing a cruel discrimination against a much wronged race?

To answer these questions I have to go back, way back, to the unspoiled rusticity of western Virginia. Blue Hill in 1874, only nine years after Appomattox—the small shabby town, the rather tumbledown farms, the barren fields—was still desolate in defeat and near despair. There wasn't much to see or to live on, but what there was belonged largely to my father. Not that that made us rich. Far from it. We lived in a now shabby red-brick cube of a "mansion," whose inevitable portico of chipped white columns seemed grimly intent on maintaining its once lofty eminence over the neighboring village, and were waited on by two old Negroes who had once been family slaves but who had elected to remain with us for little more than their board and keep. Yet we sat down for dinner at night, dressed in what faded finery we could find, at a table bearing the old silver which had been buried in the garden during the war, just as if we were still waited on by a dozen in help. It was all Father's doing. I revered him, but as a boy I sometimes hated him.

He had been, of course, a hero in the war. He had served under Lee, whom he had idolized and with whom he remained in correspondence until the latter's death. He had lost an arm in the Battle of the Wilderness just before the surrender. And he hated the Yankees with an animosity that never ebbed with the passing years.

Yes, he was a great man, a big one anyway, a frog that couldn't even immerse itself in its exiguous puddle. He ran everything there was to run in Blue Hill: he was mayor, state senator, head of the local bar association, and the principal farmer of the countryside. He was determined to save his home area, to bind up its wounds, to make it prosper, and to the very mild extent that it did that, it was owed to him. He was equally resolute to train his only son and heir to carry on his good work. And as he evidently believed that I would have a hard time in accomplishing this, he made sure that I should be as hard as he could make me.

If Father had ever voiced his deep and undying resentment

of our northern victors, it might have helped me. Growing up, and particularly after I had matriculated at the University of Virginia, I might have critically assessed it against the increasing sense among my contemporaries that the past was past and that it behooved us to get on with the present. But Father's worship of General Lee motivated him to follow his leader's principle of silence about old wrongs. And so I was always conscious at Blue Hill, in the formidable and stalwart presence of my unloquacious sire at the head of the table, of a will to discourage all idle chatter or gossip and a tolerance only for subdued comment on the weather and the performance of daily tasks. The great unsaid was any reference to the churning of a fierce and constant inner protest against the source of all our sorrows: that northern nation which had so crushed us that we could barely afford to repair the leaking roof over our heads. Could such a man as Father be wrong? Particularly when he uttered nothing for me to rebut? I came to accept his rigid discipline and his hatred of our conquerors as a marine in boot camp might accept the rigors of his initiation as the necessary preparation for inevitable battle.

My earliest sense of injustice arose from my perception of the difference with which my sister and I were treated. Father indulged Dora in her every whim; to her he showed the respectful and at times the incongruously playful gallantry of the southern gentleman for his lady folk. I did not then see that this was the mask of a serenely assumed sense of complete masculine superiority over the supposedly weaker and gentler sex, and I wondered at moments if it was really so good a thing to be born male. But this was always tempered with angry fantasies of dominating Father by growing even fiercer and stronger than he. Of course, I yearned for his approval, even for his love. If he had any to give. But didn't he? I can remember moments when his eye seemed to soften when he gazed at me, and I distinctly recall my thrill at a rare moment when he cast his arm over my shoulder. Oh, how we might have understood each other! Or am I being nostalgically sentimental? Mightn't a Freudian today say that deep in Father's psyche he resented the fact that I was growing up hale and hearty, exempt from the bloodshed of a losing war, possessed of two arms and unburdened by the weight of an undying hatred for a conquering foe?

At any rate, all chance for an ultimate partnership between father and son exploded when my inexorable parent chose to see the humiliating and final defeat of his glorious plans for me in an unfortunate episode that occurred while I was studying law at the university. On the beautiful multicolumned lawn of Mr. Jefferson's masterpiece, I had encountered new friends from the old families of the Richmond area, who were considerably more liberated than the sons of the Calvinistic clans of Blue Hill. I was introduced to gin and whiskey and went to parties where I met and made love to women whom my mother and sister would have crossed the street to avoid. Indeed, I ran a bit wild—not surprising, I suppose, considering the repressions of my boyhood. All this might have been forgiven, even by Father, who, after all, had been to the university himself, had it not been for an incident that was not in keeping with his code of gentlemanly conduct.

Among my new friends there was a particularly rowdy small group, and not, I may add, from the better families, who made a fetish of preserving the resentments of the old South and glorying in violent racism. Some were simply showoffs; a few were grimly in earnest. I made the mistake of identifying their creed with the one that my father never articulated, and it seemed to me that I was simply proving myself a chip off the old block in joining them. Most of their activities reduced themselves to silly toasts at drinking parties, but at last they planned an overt act that obliterated the smile and shrug with which the university had so far viewed them.

A visiting law professor from Harvard, invited to Virginia to give two lectures, ventured to criticize the South's voting restrictions and expressed the hope that lynching would soon be a thing of the past. My little group took strong exception to such sentiments, and breaking into his assigned study on the Lawn late one night, we covered his desk with every kind of filth. We were witnessed, exposed, and expelled from the university.

Father, when I came home, was cold, distant, and unforgiving. "You have associated with trash and become trash. The man whose desk you violated was the guest of the university and entitled to believe that he would receive the hospitality of gentlemen. He will return to Harvard to say, with every justification, that our proudest seat of learning has become the haven for brutes. I can only conclude that some of the bad blood that came into the family with my grandmother's McClintock connections may have found its way into your veins."

The terrible thing about Father's obsession with genealogy was that it barred one from redemption. If you were cursed with bad genes, you were doomed. It might not be your fault, but you were still a kind of pariah. Father allowed me to come into his law firm and to take the bar exam, which did not then require a law degree, but, though he no longer supervised me with a meticulous care, his new coldness was worse than his old ire. Yet I worked hard and well, and I was even beginning to hope I could see a chink in the armor of his sustained disapproval when my life was changed by the passion that erupted between myself and my cousin Clara Caldwell.

Clara was my mother's niece, and it is time that I should say something about my mother. In many ways she was the perfect mate for Father: a tall, handsome woman, if a bit put-offing by the severity of her dress and manner, a wonderfully efficient housekeeper, and a much respected, even venerated leader of the local society. She was a woman of few words, but her words were very much to the point. She deferred to my father in almost all of his views and decisions, but on the rare occasions when she disagreed, she could be as firm and as stern as she had been at the end of the war, when she stood off a band of drunken ex-slaves who had threatened to take over the mansion. Mother had had to concede to her husband the apparently inalienable right of a father to train his son for the succession, but she had also seen that it was necessary to supply the driven lad with a minimum of sympathy, and she had allowed me as much of that as her undemonstrative nature permitted. Of course, I loved her.

Clara, her niece, small, dark, as witty as she was pretty, and as cheerful as she was frail, suffered from tuberculosis and spent most of her days in the house next to ours, the home of my uncle, Mother's brother, and his numerous brood. It was the second-best house in the village, and the Caldwells were the second-best family, and there was nothing to prevent a marriage between me and Clara but our kinship, easily over-come in the South of that day, and her illness. But this last obstacle, never mentioned, was silently accepted as a reason that poor Clara could never wed. She was not expected, as the brutal phrase was, to make old bones. Yet her buoyancy, her gaiety, the lovely ripple of her laughter, the shrewdness of her comments, the generosity of her attitudes seemed to defy the dismal if unuttered prognostications. To me she was the one shining light of Blue Hill.

Only with her could I discuss my troubles with Father. She was quick to put her hand on the essence of my problem.

"It sounds terrible to say it, but it has to be said," she told me. "You'd be better off, Lanny dear, if you could accept your resentment of Uncle James as something he deserves. Your hang-up is your reverence for his war record. Deep down—maybe even without being aware of it yourself—you think that such a hero can't be wrong. But he can, Lanny! He can be very wrong and still a hero, still a great man, if you like. To you he takes up all the room in Blue Hill. How can there be two such men in so small a place? So there you are! There's no room for you here!"

"And what can I do about that?"

"Isn't it obvious? Go elsewhere."

"Where?"

"Well, what about New York? That's where Roger Pryor went. You remember who he was?"

"Wasn't he the young firebrand in Charleston who waved his handkerchief to excite a mob of secessionists? And didn't he shout, 'Fire on Fort Sumter, and with this handkerchief I'll wipe up all the blood that's spilt!'"

"Exactly. He must have had a cloudy crystal ball. But he fought gallantly through the war and then went north to become an important judge in New York. Go thou and do likewise."

"Father would simply die if I did that."

"No such thing. He's much tougher than you think. And he's too tough for you. That doesn't mean that you're weak or in any way deficient, Lanny. It's simply that fathers have an unfair advantage. It's not cowardice to flee them. It's only common sense. Anyone else you can beat. Or at least you have a fair chance."

This was the first time we discussed my breaking away from Blue Hill, but thereafter it was the constant theme of our discourse. I began to be excited by the new image of myself as a man in charge of his own life, for better or—what did it matter?—even for very much the worse. I suddenly saw that I might become what the French writer Sartre today calls an existentialist. And out of this grew my awareness that my feelings for Clara had nothing to do with our kinship and that she was going to be an essential partner in any new life on which I embarked.

She had no shyness or reluctance in admitting that she fully returned the love that I at last found the courage to offer her, but she insisted, with a firmness that showed that she had anticipated our crisis, that we had to confine ourselves to friendship, as marriage was out of the question.

"Oh, dearest Lanny, you want to see yourself as an ardent Robert Browning breathing a new life into poor me, but I'm not Elizabeth Barrett. I'm neither a poet nor a *malade imaginaire*, as she probably was. I know what I am and what I'm in for, and I have the will to accept it. So let well enough alone, my love. *Help* me!"

But I couldn't accept this. I insisted that without her I was bound to lose my way. I finally induced her to take her doctor into her confidence and ask him if marriage was feasible for her, and she reluctantly did so, receiving the dubious answer that a recovery of health in her case was not an absolute impossibility. I clung to this; I built on it; I argued that it was all we needed. I worked myself into the full belief that I was indeed a Robert Browning and that love would work miracles with her lungs. In fact, I even persuaded myself that Clara would probably die if she *didn't* marry me.

At this point, both families awakened to what was going on. You might have thought that they were oddly late in doing so, but the notoriety of Clara's illness and the fact that as cousins and next-door neighbors she and I had always been close allowed them to attribute my visits to sympathy over her condition. Now, of course, such visits were strictly prohibited. Clara, however, was twenty-one, and her parents could hardly stop her from walking with me in their garden. They appealed to my father to use his influence, and he took a high stand with me.

"Do you want to be the death of your unfortunate cousin, sir?" he demanded. "Playing on the poor girl's emotions may be fatal to her. I forbid you to see her except at family gatherings, and I doubt if we shall have many of those until this sorry business has died down."

"I am not playing with her emotions, sir! It is my intention to marry her and take her to New York!"

That same day I moved out of the family mansion into a room in the one poor inn our village boasted. Father owned even that. He did not, however, throw me out. I resigned from his law firm and waited to hear from Clara. I had a few savings that would keep me for some weeks. After that I was on my own.

After three days of silence from both families, I received this note from Clara:

It seems you have crossed the Rubicon, my love. I fear that Uncle James may never forgive you. I do not see how I can desert you now. I have warned you, and you are resolved to ignore my warning. Very well. A girl can resist so long and no more. Let me know your plans, and I will join you. I have a little money. I enclose a bank statement showing how much. Consider it your own.

The person who brought me the note was my mother! She sat beside me, grimly silent, in the shabby little empty bar of the inn while I read it. Then she spoke.

"I don't suppose either of you has enough to live on if you marry and move north. You may know that I had a small legacy from an aunt who married in Boston. I have never spent it, as your father called it abolitionists' gold. It should keep you for a year. I am placing it in your account. It is not that I approve of what you and Clara are planning. But it's your lives, not mine."

"But, Mother dearest, what will Father say?"

"He will be much vexed. But I can handle him. Now I must go. Bless you, child."

Clara and I took a train to Richmond, where we were married and spent a week's honeymoon. Her parents pursued us, but what could they do? At length they gave in and even sent us a check on condition that in New York I should take her to a well-heated building. I of course agreed.

I got a job, after much treading of unfamiliar streets, with a wily old shyster, a near genius with juries, who scandalously underpaid the three slave clerks who prepared his trumped-up damage claims, and who gave me just what I needed: a broad experience trying cases in the lower courts of Manhattan and Brooklyn. It was there that I learned the arts of a litigator and how to deal with a multitude of humans with backgrounds as different as possible from my own. It was also there that I learned that there need be no limit to what an able and determined man can make of himself.

Clara was a constant aid, a steady light in my toil. I can see now, only too well, that in my egotism and in the distraction of my long hours of work, I did not sufficiently note what the harsh New York winter was doing to her condition. I did once offer to send her back to her parents, who would have been glad to receive her, until the advent of warmer weather, but she adamantly refused to go. And then she became pregnant, which offered me a pleasanter excuse for her increasing frailty.

"Whatever happens," she told me once, "I want you always to remember that the happiness we have had was well worth it to me."

I attributed this to her old habit of taking the dark view of her ailment and maintained my resolute optimism. I had no real notion of the danger of her state until my little world blew into pieces with her death in childbirth.

Our son, Philip, survived. He has always, I suspect, harbored the secret suspicion that I resented him for causing his mother's death. He is wrong. I have always known that I caused it.

I never returned to my office, even to finish up my work there. Mother and Clara's parents came up from Virginia, and it was agreed between them that the baby should be taken to Mother's in Blue Hill; obviously I was in no state, emotionally or financially, to care for an infant. I could only acquiesce. Besides, the war with Spain had started, and I made the sudden decision to enlist. It was one solution, anyway, and I hardly cared whether or not it might prove a final one.

Life, however, never tires of playing tricks on us. Instead of death in Cuba, I found new life. My very recklessness seemed to insure my immunity. In the famous charge up San Juan Hill, I actually heard Colonel Roosevelt's sharp rebuke to a soldier crouching in the rear: "Are you afraid to stand up when I am on horseback?" There was a man to follow! And I was a man, too. Indeed, I received a medal for being one.

On my way back to New York, where I had decided to resume the practice of law, I of course stopped for a visit to Blue Hill to see my son and mother. And my father as well. I no longer resented him. We were equals now. And he even seemed ready to acknowledge it.

He looked older and grayer; he was having the periodic heart attacks that were soon to end his life. Almost timidly—if one could associate such an adverb with him—he placed a hand on my shoulder.

"I'm proud of you, my boy."

If I had been capable of tears, that might have been the moment for them. "Oh, well, wars, you know," I replied instead with a shrug. "It's all in the cards. The cowering man on San Juan Hill I heard Colonel Roosevelt order to stand up, stood up and was shot down. If he'd stayed a coward he'd be alive."

Father did not smile. "He has nothing to do with you, Langdon. And I hope you've come home to stay. Your office is ready for you. Or rather, mine is. You'll be the senior now."

"Oh, Father, really!" I exclaimed in a sudden burst of something curiously like love for this sick old parent. But then I checked myself. I was a new man now. Could I say it? Yes, I could say it! I was even glad to. "But I'm afraid, Father, that I've decided to try my luck again in Yankeeland. Clara thought I should get away from home. From Blue Hill. Even from all of you. She married me, as the only way she could accomplish that, even at the cost of her life. I can't let her down after that, can I?"

Father shook his head sadly, and I saw Mother actually smile. "No, I guess you can't," he murmured.

"And when you're settled up there," Mother intervened, with a decisive cheerfulness, "we'll bring little Philip up to you."

⤞ 2 ⤝

I started building my career around the law firm that at first existed only in my resolute imagination, by the unlikely stratagem of returning to the wily old shyster whom I had so abruptly abandoned when Clara died. He was glad enough to have me back, for with age his forensic abilities had begun to tatter, and I propped up his failing practice until his sudden and dramatic demise in the midst of an impassioned oration to a jury. The publicity of this collapse helped to cover up some of the ineptitude of his final phase, and control of a too-long-cowered firm passed easily into my awaiting hands. I made a junior partner of the ablest of his clerks and discharged the rest. From this point on, I saw to it that every new member of the firm was a man on whose personal loyalty to me I could count.

Of course it was my rapidly growing fame as a litigator that drew them to the firm. When I agreed to represent a client, I was concerned, perfectly properly, with only two factors: was his case either winnable or capable of a good settlement, and could he pay my high fee? It was said of me, I know, that I could have got Judas off with a suspended sentence, but I took it as a compliment. I have always been aware that true justice was not invariably promoted by my victories in court, but let those who wail about this devise a better system. If I was never much concerned with what some sentimentalists call the "spirit" of the law, it is also true that I never broke one. A trial to me is a game to be played, and why play a game in any way but to win?

It may have been true, in the early years of my practice, that my indifference to the heavy cost to defendants of what my critics called the grossly inflated damage awards that I obtained from juries sprang from my feeling that such defendants, after all, were northerners who had ravaged my homeland. Yes, that is possible, but it certainly didn't last, and later I achieved some significant victories over corporations in the South. I do not think today, despite my stand on desegregation, that I can be rightfully accused of any regional bias. And one thing I have assuredly observed is that fame, even fame as a tricky lawyer, brings not only a half-reluctant popularity but actual esteem.

In building my firm from a handful of lawyers to its present size of fifteen partners and thirty associates, I have not followed the procedure of many of the major downtown firms in selecting partners, sometimes exclusively, from the ranks of clerks hired directly out of law school, with the hope of creating a homogeneous organization of dedicated members. No, I have never hesitated to grab a promising outsider and take him in as a partner even ahead of those who have toiled longer in the vineyard. Anyone who objects can go elsewhere. Nor have I ever stooped to the fashionable anti-Semitism or anti-Irishness of some Wall Streeters. I have not only brought in many Jewish lawyers, I have even used the language of flagrant racism to make them acceptable to prejudiced clients: "What you need, you see, is just what you don't like: a rough, tough kike of a lawyer who won't look under every bed for a scruple." Nor have I succumbed to the craven preference of so many firms for the elegantly trained products of Harvard and Yale law schools; I have always regarded my firm as the real law academy from which my clerks must graduate. Not that I spurn Harvard, but Fordham does me just as well, sometimes better. I would have taken Negroes, but their time had not yet come, and I have never been a pioneer.

Which brings me to how I have been able to maintain absolute and still undisputed control of my firm. Needless to say, it has not been an unconscious process. Let us suppose that I had been retained by the president of a large company to represent it in a particular litigation in whose field my trial talents happened to outweigh those of its general counsel. I would alert my partners to the need of cultivating the corporate officers of the new client and somehow conveying to them the knowledge that we had skill in corporate affairs as well as jury trials. In the flush of my subsequent court victory there was sometimes the occasion for a grateful company president to move all his business to my firm. But in assigning a junior partner to this new account — for I couldn't do all the work — I never, as did so many managers, allowed him to take over the client. Busy as I was, I was always kept abreast of the client's problems, and attended the more important conferences, and occasionally lunched or dined with its chief officers. This was usually enough to maintain the illusion in the client that I was always primarily in charge of its matters. Sometimes it didn't work, and there were occasions when I had to expel a too greedy partner from the firm. But I usually made a great point of being all genial smiles, acting as a kindly uncle to the younger men who came into the firm, asking them to my country house for a weekend and even loaning them money for their struggling families. I think they even took a certain pride in my reputation downtown as a benevolent despot. It is something to be well known, even at that price.

I knew the story that was circulated about me. It was said—and widely believed—that a daring partner had once come to me to suggest a more even split of the net profits among the members of the firm. "Good, good," I am supposed to have blandly replied. "Divvy them up in any way that seems fair and square to you. So long as I get my fifty percent, I don't care what you do with the balance." Well, of course no such discussion ever took place, nor do I take anything like such a lion's share of our earnings. But there is some truth in the fable.

What really keeps me in power is that the firm as a whole recognizes that it owes its health and prosperity basically to my efforts and reputation. Otherwise the authority that I exercise would not be tolerated. Now we are approaching the time when my grip is bound to be loosened. But the legend of old Langdon Rives, mellowing with age and still a formidable figure at the bar, has swollen to the point where even my most envious juniors are more anxious to use it and promote it than to blow it away. If you become a landmark, you become a permanent part of the landscape. It might take an earthquake to tumble you.

I should turn now from the firm to my domestic life. Yes, I

married again, but I'm coming to that. First was the business of raising my son, Philip, who shared with me the increasingly grander residences that I acquired as my income waxed: the Beaux Arts mansion that reared its overornamented but only forty-foot-wide facade on East Seventieth Street and the inevitable red-brick Georgian manor house in Westbury, Long Island. I have never been one to hide my light under a bushel. Philip had everything a lad could desire: a swimming pool, a tennis court, a horse to ride, membership in any club he cared to join, and a father willing to entertain house parties of his friends. And no, he did not turn out to be a disappointment to me, as you might have expected from the above.

Indeed, he proved in many ways the ideal son and heir. At least he would have been to any parent with less unreasonable requirements. He was very handsome, favoring his mother, with thick black hair and large, dark, brooding eyes, pale skin, a trim muscular figure, a bit on the slight side, and a charming courtesy of manner, more like that of a French or Italian youth of good birth than an American. To watch him enter a room and join a group was to watch an act of gracefulness. An able student, a competent athlete, at ease with both his own generation and mine, he fitted smoothly into the routine of my busy life. Why wasn't he perfect? Maybe that was just the trouble. He was.

The fault, of course, was mine. It seems it always is. I wanted more than he had to give. I wanted his love. I wasn't loved by my partners, and I had given too much of myself to the law to have more than casual friends. My parents were long dead, and Clara's family had never forgiven me for taking her north. What my second marriage gave me I shall come to, but it wasn't love. For that I turned to Philip.

Mind you, I could never fault him. He treated me with every show of respect and friendliness. He showed an intelligent interest in my cases; he was a pleasant companion on our vacation trips; when his pals came to visit, he always included me in their jokes and discussions. Away at boarding school and later at Yale, he wrote me newsy and informative letters.

What was wrong was that for all his charm and goodness, for all his wonderfully controlled patience and temper, the boy could not find it in his heart to give me what he was too sensitive not to feel that I craved. He would have simulated love if he could have, but he was far too honest to do so. He would have cut his tongue out rather than admit that he was ashamed of me. But that was it. To him I was a shyster.

This had to come out when he went to law school. Indeed, I was surprised that he chose law at all, though now I rather wryly see it as not unlike Benjamin Cardozo's joining the bar as a chance to redeem the family name from his father's corrupt use of his judgeship. Did Philip choose a legal career to atone for mine? Crazy as it sounds, I'm afraid so.

He became an editor of the *Yale Law Journal*, but he never submitted the "notes" or "decisions" that he contributed to that distinguished periodical in draft to me. When I read them, I saw why. They were entirely concerned with the role of law in the development of a more egalitarian society, with the problems of remedial legislation, with misconducted trials and hoodwinked juries, and his principal piece dealt with the danger of excessive jury damage awards.

It was not, therefore, any surprise to me when, on his graduation, Philip instructed me that he was declining the job that I offered him in my firm and was joining Legal Aid instead. The time had come at last for some plain speaking between us, and despite my natural irritation, I felt a small throb of pride that Philip was so evidently up to it.

"I might as well put it to you frankly, Dad."

"What better way?"

"Well, in my possibly too prim opinion, your firm doesn't make any significant contribution to society as a whole."

"You mean that my devising of a perfect legal tool is no use to society? What did society want but a system of justice where every wrong could be righted? My firm is finely constructed to achieve just that purpose. If I were a Praxiteles, it would be deemed my masterpiece!"

"But it overcompensates, Dad. And not all your clients' wrongs are really wrongs."

"Then it's up to the bar to strengthen the opposition! It should be the best against the best, my boy. That's how the best is accomplished—at least in America."

"But in the meanwhile, those who are not the best get trampled on."

"They are not my affair, Philip."

"But they may be mine. Which is why I'm going where I'm going."

At last I gave in to my temper, even knowing it was a mistake. "Supplementing your miserable salary with the money that I've settled on you, earned, of course, by my trampling on the weak."

"Money is just money, Dad. It's only the use it's put to that counts. You've told me that often enough. You gave me that money to spend as I chose. If you want, I'll give it back."

Quickly now, I beat a retreat. "No, no, no, dear boy. It's yours to keep, and there'll be more, no matter where you practice law. But it's not, you know, that I haven't contributed substantially to Legal Aid myself. Why, I think they even gave me a plaque. It must be somewhere around here."

"I know that, Dad. But you never offered them legal services, either your own or those of any lawyer in the firm."

"Damn right I didn't! They were welcome to my money but not to my genius. That I keep for the real tests. And honestly, Phil, I think you might show a little more appreciation of a father who has always cared for you and provided you with everything you could want or need."

"Dad, you know that I appreciate all that! But now I'm treating you as a man who's entitled to the truth from his son. And nothing but the truth. Isn't that how you treated your own father?"

"What do you know about how I treated my father?"

"All that Granny once told me. You saw him dooming you to live in what you considered a wasteland, and you broke away."

"Are you implying that my firm is a wasteland?"

"Of course not, Dad."

I should have known better than to go to my wife for comfort. Irina had a bleak Russian way of assuming that facts couldn't hurt.

"I suppose he meant that your firm was a kind of moral wasteland," she commented mildly, as if she were describing a variety of soup.

"Irina! Surely you don't think anything like that of my firm, do you?"

"Oh, no, dear. But Philip is so strict, so moral. My aunt Olga was the same way. And the poor dear czarina was like that. Maybe she got it from her grandmother, Queen Victoria."

"And look what happened to her," I muttered.

Philip and his stepmother had formed a kind of alliance, not in any way against me but not including me. She liked his utter honesty as she liked mine, but I call it a "kind" of alliance because Irina had left too much of her heart in czarist Russia to view her American chapter as much more than a restful and not too disagreeable finale. She was beautiful, serene, charmingly kind, and vaguely sympathetic, but always detached. She had lost her husband and son in the war with Germany and had escaped the Reds by fleeing her vast Ukrainian estates on a British freighter across the Black Sea. She had joined some fellow White Russians, all penniless, in New York, where she had found work as a French teacher in a fashionable girls' school.

I had met her at a dinner party given by one of the school's trustees. The latter might not have invited a lowly instructress, but New York society was well aware that Princess Irina Sobieski had been the landlady of a hundred thousand former serfs and an intimate of the imperial family. Society was also aware that she reached a constant hand toward their pockets for indigent kin, but after all, one could always say no. I didn't, which was one of the reasons, perhaps even the principal one, that she married me. But I was shrewd enough to know that she was exactly what I needed, and so it proved.

I had no need of a housekeeper; I already had a most efficient one, whom my indolent Irina was glad enough to retain. I didn't need a mother for Philip, who was already in boarding school when Irina and I were married. Nor had I ever really loved a woman since Clara; socially I had moved easily in many circles as a contented widower under no compulsion to alter his status. But the idea of having a beautiful and aristocratic lady to preside over my establishments without unduly interfering with my settled ways had intrigued me. And Irina gave me just what I wanted.

She was at all times the perfect lady. She never had the crudity to articulate a definition of our relationship, which we both understood to be a classic case of symbiosis. She viewed the passing scene of my law practice, my partners, my court victories, as she might have viewed a mildly diverting comedy, and she acted with a charming grace on the rare occasions when I had some real need of her social skills. She was properly grateful for my generosity to her relatives and never overdid her demands. And I think she liked me well enough, when she thought of me, though I never shared the importance to her of the shades of her first husband and son. But then, did she ever share the importance to me of the shade of Clara? I was fair about it. We both were. It was our bond.

I offer this example of both her essential indifference to the New York scene and her ability on occasion to take advantage of it. She was nobody's fool. When I asked her once what she thought of one of my most brilliant younger partners, who, dining with us, had obviously been intrigued by his lovely hostess, she replied, "He reminds me of a very good coffee blender. It makes excellent coffee. But only coffee. Your partner makes very good law, I have no doubt. But that's all he makes."

Did she think that of me? At any rate, she never said so. And she had an eye on my young partner, for she later succeeded in marrying him to one of her indigent nieces. And it was a happy marriage, too.

With Philip, however, she showed something like a real warmth. Perhaps he reminded her of her slain son, one of the lost army of noble youths who, in her fantasy, might have saved Russia from the Red tide. Philip listened sympathetically to her tales of former glory, and she liked him to tell her about some of the more pathetic of his Legal Aid cases. Neither of them spoke of such matters to me, perhaps in the fear of boring me, yet I experienced something like jealousy over it.

"I don't quite see what you and Irina have so much in common," I couldn't help observing to my son one day. He had his own apartment, but he had made it a habit to come to Sunday lunch at my house. "I should have thought your political views were about as far apart as views can be."

"Irina doesn't really have political views, Dad."

"What about all those serfs? What about sending liberals to the Siberian mines? That's where the Sobieskis would have sent you, my lad."

"That was another world. It doesn't exist for her now."

"I sometimes wonder how much ours does."

Philip was silent, as he often was now when he felt we were approaching a gulf. Had he given me up?

The Great Depression did not catch me unprepared; I had liquidated many of my stocks while the market was high, and litigation survives every disaster. But the huge numbers of unemployed revived some of Irina's nightmares of the Russian Revolution, and she actually showed some slight interest in our situation.

"Have you monies, Langdon, invested outside this country?"

"Very insignificantly. Why do you ask?"

"Because it has come to seem strange to me that none of my family had the foresight to set up a bank account in London or Paris. I suppose they had too blind a faith in the stability of the czar. So when the storm hit us and we lucky ones got out—if we *were* the lucky ones—it was only with a few jewels sewn in our coats. My brother would still be driving a taxicab if you, my dear, hadn't come to our rescue."

"And you think I'd better look to my laurels now? With a bank account abroad? Where?"

"Well, isn't Argentina pretty sound? Helena Adamowski seems to think so."

I had to chuckle at this further evidence that, despite a lifetime of experiencing the disastrous folly of her clan, she would still take the word of a crazy old Slavic dowager over that of her brilliant spouse.

"So you see the guillotine being erected in Times Square for the likes of us?"

"Well, I suppose it would be better than being thrown down a mineshaft like the poor dear Grand Duchess Elizabeth. I'm not thinking only of myself, Langdon. I've been through all that. I'm thinking of *you.*"

"And I appreciate it, my dear. But if there should be a revolution, I doubt they'd want our lives. Our money should satisfy them. Though it won't do them much good after it's been spread around, as your former countrymen have already discovered. And you and I can go down to Virginia and hole up in what's left of the family mansion. Actually, it's not in too bad shape. I've kept it up. As a matter of fact we might both rather like it. In my end is my beginning."

"Oh, Langdon, do you think we really could do that?" Irina's voice took on a note of enthusiasm that was new to me. "It might be like the Ukraine! Why don't we go now? Do we have to wait for a revolution?"

I had a sudden picture of Irina in the wide field behind the back of the old house, gazing at the distant blue hills. She would belong there!

⇥ 3 ⇤

Well, we didn't have a revolution. We had the New Deal instead. And in lieu of losing my money, I made a pot of gold out of it. I became in the early nineteen thirties one of the principal proponents, in the federal courts, especially the supreme, of the unconstitutionality of FDR's social legislation. I saw myself as the champion of the individual against the government. Of course, my opponents maintained that I was the champion of the giant corporation against the government, which brought our conflict into sharp focus, for indeed I tended, and still tend, to identify the corporation with the individual. What is it, legally and even morally, but a person? And why should it not be entitled to the same rights and privileges? The child has grown into a man and should not be forever subject to a hovering nurse.

In this respect I should mention an experience that happened in the year 1907 which very much accentuated my early faith in the individual citizen as opposed to his democratically elected representative. It was the year of the panic, and one of my clients, a banker, took me with him to the library of the great J. P. Morgan, where we waited patiently, even reverently, for our turn to pass into the vast, high-ceilinged office hung with Renaissance masterpieces and gleaming with silver and gold, and submit our proposal of how to deal with the financial crisis. Never can I forget the sight of the silent tycoon, with his great glaring eyes and misshapen

nose, bending over the game of solitaire that, listening without comment to my client's proposition. He did not cease to
play, simply dismissing us with a grunt when we had finished.
He did not adopt my client's plan, but he did adopt another
one suggested on that same day, and chaos was averted. President Teddy Roosevelt complained that Morgan treated him
as an equal. TR was wrong! Morgan, quite correctly, treated
him as his inferior.

By the nineteen thirties, however, the pendulum had
swung in the other direction. The great Teddy's distant
cousin was now distinctly in the driver's seat. But for a time,
a blessed time, five of the nine justices on our highest court
shared my constitutional philosophy, and in some exhilarating battles with Uncle Sam's menials we threw out socialist
law after socialist law. These were the great days of my legal
career. I was fighting for the rights of free men to make their
own contracts, fix their own wages and hours of labor in their
own businesses, to hire non-union workers if they chose — in
short, to manage their own affairs. I believed that the men
who had made America a world power could be counted on
to keep it one, as opposed to ward politicians with their dirty
hands in the public trough. I wanted to be the white knight
who kept the commerce clause from becoming a despot's
tool and due process from turning into the noose that would
strangle the liberty of the individual.

There were plenty of big men behind me, too, men who
saw in my struggle a modern crusade. Some of them helped
to swell my already impressive list of corporate clients, for
they would be so inflamed by my briefs that they would feel
it was almost unpatriotic to limit their retainer of my firm to
constitutional problems.

Well, of course, it all ended when FDR was at last able to stack his court. It had never occurred to me that he would have a third term, let alone a fourth. I had even had reason to suppose that Wendell Willkie, if elected, might appoint me to the supreme bench. I am sure that my son, Philip, though he never says so, attributes what he calls my bitterness against the New Deal to my disappointment over this. And I suppose there might be some truth in his supposition, though I think my animosity to the sweeping socialization of the times would have survived any appointment.

Philip and I had worked out a kind of modus vivendi that worked moderately well, even after he accepted a job in the Justice Department and actually argued a case against me. He married a dear girl, and I was unable to resist her efforts to keep the peace between her husband and me. She prevailed in her insistence that politics not be discussed at family meetings. Irina, who detested political discussion in any case, helped in this.

And so time slid by, as did the Second World War, in which Philip, thank God, was too old and his children too young to engage. And finally it could be said of myself, as Anatole France said of his protagonist in *The Procurator of Judea*, "It was in the midst of such works and in meditating the principles of Epicurus that, with a faint surprise and a mild chagrin, he met the advent of old age."

But at eighty I was still in active charge of my firm. I had become a legend in downtown Manhattan. Philip had left the government to become a partner in a well-known Washington firm specializing in civil liberties. He was kind and dutiful as ever and came up regularly to see me, but I always felt that he regarded me as the respected relic of a past that had been largely and happily superseded. I might have been a Holbein portrait of Thomas Cromwell in a gallery of modern art.

Irina had aged, but, as one might have suspected, serenely. She had memory lapses, and she made increasing references to persons of her Russian past of whom I had never even heard her speak. But she seemed content to stay on in the Long Island house, even in the winter months when I had moved to town, and take little walks in the woodland paths and across the fields. She seemed to have found a kind of peace there. A Russian peace, no doubt.

Such was my situation in 1954, when the great desegregation case arose. Of course at first I had no connection with it. Jimmy Byrnes, the South Carolina governor, for whom I had not only friendship but the profoundest respect, had, very appropriately enlisted the aid of John W. Davis to carry the banner for those who wished to uphold the old and tried ways. I had no notion that Davis was inadequate for the case, but I thought it might be helpful to rally as many school districts as we could behind him and file as many briefs as should be allowed. To me it was a question of showing a united front to a nation divided by radicals.

When Philip had notice of what I was doing, he made a special trip to New York to plead with me. He angered me by talking to some of my partners without my permission, and it hardly improved my temper to have him tell me that almost all of them had thoroughly agreed with him and deplored my taking so unpopular a public position and what it might do to the firm.

"Dad," he insisted, "even you must admit that the separate but equal doctrine for the treatment of black students and white is not practical. Black schools in the South are never going to be on a par with white."

"I admit they are not at present," I had to concede. "But that's no reason they can't be. The money's there for it, or could be furnished by Uncle Sam, who, God knows, seems willing enough to pay for things. I'd go even further. Averse as you know me to be to federal interference with state matters, I would endorse a program to compel the southern states to provide equal treatment. Anything rather than force poor white parents to controvert their passionate belief that the races should not be obliged to mingle!"

"Dad, you're fighting the future. Don't you know you're bound to lose?"

"No, I do not. And if I am, the nation loses."

I had no particular feeling about Negroes. Northerners know very little about the subject. They worship Thomas Jefferson, for example, who not only chased after his escaped slaves but had them soundly whipped when caught. He may even have slept with female slaves, though that interests me less. Who knows? The women may have liked it. But I certainly don't believe that I would ever have beaten a slave, and I am convinced that my father never did. Had the North not been intoxicated by abolitionists and shown a little patience, slavery, already doomed abroad, might have died a natural death. Certainly the blacks in the Reconstruction years were not much better off than they had been.

Justice Holmes put it well when he defined freedom of speech as the right of a fool to drool. We are fast approaching the point where only the fool will be allowed to drool, where the thinking sort will have to hold their tongues for fear of offending some screeching minority. Why should I care? I won't live to see it.

Irina, at any rate, has the odd virtue of always having the last word. This is often true of people who don't give a damn. When she saw how dejected I was by the unanimous ruling of the court that condemned desegregation in public schools, she evidently thought it incumbent upon a wife to offer some brand of consolation. Here is what she brought: "Isn't it possible, my poor Langdon, that this tribunal you so excoriate has been saving us from just the sort of dreadful uprising that swept away my family and its whole generation?"

I knew there was no point getting into an argument with Irina on *that* subject. But I shall still die unreconstructed.